THE PROMISE OF DREAMS

Hearts of Valor Book 2

Liminal Books

Liminal Books is an imprint of Between the Lines Publishing. The Liminal Books name and logo are trademarks of Between the Lines Publishing.

Between the Lines Publishing
9 North River Road, Ste 248
Auburn ME 04210
btwnthelines.com

First Published: November 2024

ISBN: (Paperback) 978-1-965059-12-8

ISBN: (Ebook) 978-1-965059-13-5

Library of Congress Control Number: 2024945497

THE PROMISE OF DREAMS

Hearts of Valor Book 2

K.T. Munson

For Evelyn, the sassiest person I know. You can't read this until you're eighteen.

To my family, friends, and fans, thank you for all the support. It makes a world of difference.

For everyone else—dream big.

Chapter 1

Dream

Annabel felt the guard's fingers dig into her arm as she was escorted from the cell. She felt sick to her stomach as he marched her from the bowels of the castle up to the throne room. They didn't think she was a threat from the lack of shackles, and for the first time she wished she was. Instead, she was useless as she walked the hallways of her childhood, sandwiched between two guards.

"Queen Annabel," a man said stepping down from the throne.

He was handsome to be sure with his blond hair and blue eyes touched with gold. He was dressed in the royal colors, a noble crown upon his head. If it wasn't for her knowledge of what a monster he was, his striking features would have made him a perfect knight in shining armor or charming prince. Now all she felt was hatred at his glittering exterior that hid the devil within.

"Lawrence." Her voice was purposely flat.

"Is that any way to address your king?" He asked, his eyes were hard but glinted with amusement.

"You will never be *my* king," she replied, keeping her gaze steady.

He laughed out loud. "Unfortunately for you, I am the King. It has been ratified and so it shall be."

"The Kingdom of Mavrid will never go to war. I warned them," she informed him, trying to keep the hatred she felt from her voice.

He pulled a piece of paper from his belt. "You mean this letter."

Annabel felt lightheaded. "And the man carrying the letter?"

"Oh, he's quite dead." Lawrence replied with a chuckle.

Her knees shook as she felt her entire world crumble. *Not him,* she thought, her heart breaking, *not him.*

"He thought of you until the last moment. I was told your name was on his lips as he died," Lawrence said, bending over to send a triumphant grin in her direction. "You shall join him soon, but before then, I must have the symbol of Valor."

"You shall never have it," Annabel replied. Each kingdom on the continent of Valor had a symbol of royalty and she had the one for their kingdom. Her brother had passed it to her when he'd been on his deathbed.

"I thought you might say that." Lawrence said with a barking laugh. "It does not matter, with no living family and no children, you are the only thing that could stop me from carrying out my plans."

He had killed everyone, carefully, so that they all seemed like accidents or natural deaths. It had started with her uncle and ended with her brother. All along, Lawrence was a goblin in sheep's clothing as he courted her. If only she'd seen through his act, her family might be alive today.

"I am the only thing that legitimizes you," Annabel reminded him. "My death will do nothing to benefit you."

"Ah," Lawrence said as he wagged his finger at her. "That is where you are wrong." He walked around her, the last tendrils of light streaming in through the windows at the top of the vaulted ceilings. "You will have your part to play to ensure this war."

"I'll never support it." She was steadfast.

"I don't need you to." Lawrence touched her cheek, and she jerked away. "Your death at the hands of a Mavridian is enough for me to spark the conflict."

2

"You can't," she gasped trying to pull free from the unwavering grip of the guards keeping her in place.

"Thanks to you I'm king," he laughed, his eyes sharp as he drew his sword from the sheath on his hip. "I can do whatever I want now." He lifted the sword high above his head, admiring it. "Don't worry dear wife, I'll make sure you are properly avenged."

The sharpened steel of the sword shone from the setting sun a moment before he swung it across her neck.

Present

Princess Annabel woke with a start, her hand at her throat. Her skin slick with a cold sweat as her stomach twisted into knots. Stumbling from the bed she walked on wobbly knees to the vanity where a cold basin of water sat. Splashing it on her face she tried to calm her racing heart. Never in her nineteen years of life had she ever had a dream like that.

It felt like she'd actually been there, standing before that man—Lawrence. Whoever he was. Shaken, she went to the window and threw back the heavy curtains. Dawn was breaking and a few birds were announcing it as she tried to shake off the disturbing dream by wrapping her arms around herself.

There was a knock on the door. "Come in," she called out.

Heddie, her lady's maid, walked in with a bewildered expression. "Princess, you're awake?"

"Too excited," Annabel lied, unwilling to share the terrible nightmare.

"You don't even wake up early on your birthday, but *this* gets you excited?" Heddie teased, going to tie up the curtains as Annabel strode to the center of the room.

"It isn't often we get visitors from the isles," Annabel explained. "Plus, I'll have a new lady-in-waiting before the day is out."

"They are exotic," Heddie agreed as she began to dress Annabel. "Are you excited to have your last lady-in-waiting before your debutante ball?"

"It is only a week away." Having recently turned nineteen meant she was set to put herself on the market for an eligible husband. It reminded her of the dream, strange that she should remember so much of it. Though nightmares had a tenancy to linger longer, even they faded with the rising sun.

"Is something wrong?" Heddie asked, her lady's maid eyed her closely.

"Lost in thought," Annabel replied. "Is Mayven awake?"

Heddie finished securing Annabel skirts before moving on to her corset. "The prince is likely at the practice field."

Of course, Annabel knew that, but she was so distracted she'd temporarily forgotten. These days Mayven, her closest brother, seemed to spend all his time practicing. Ever since he'd been named the crown prince over their half-brothers, half-sisters, and cousins, he'd been working with different weapons to become proficient. Her always dedicated brother, who was her complete opposite, wanted to be prepared for anything and everything. He would make a fine king.

By contrast, as the seventh and youngest royal child, Princess Annabel was far from the lady she should be. Her father, the king, indulged her every whim and she knew it. Which is why the entire debut into society was a silly endeavor—she had no intention of marrying. As a princess there was no need to, her position was secure either way and her three older sisters meant there were more than enough royal marriages to secure whatever alliance was needed. Which is why her dream held no water—it couldn't possibly be real.

Once her overly fancy dress with its empire waist, gold thread, and woven pearls was secured, Annabel wished it was any other day so she might go horseback riding or hide in an alcove in the library. Perhaps spend time with her younger cousins or play pranks on the knights. Despite her earlier bravado, Annabel was not a fan of royal events. Particularly ones that would make her the center of attention. Fortunately, in three months it would all be behind her, and she could go back to declining invitations from misguided nobility and doing as she wished.

"Thank you, Heddie. Let my mother know I'll join her for breakfast in the gardens before the audience and presentation of my last lady-in-waiting," Annabel said before heading towards the training grounds.

Instead of going through the main entrance, Annabel went the long way around and up onto the barrack's outer wall. She was able to watch her brother train without interrupting him. He was practicing with a long spear. His movements were tight and sharp—deadly to the exercise dummy with which he sparred.

She leaned forward to rest her elbows on the battlement and watched Mayven, not ready to interrupt. His wheat-colored hair was a hallmark of the royal family, her sisters all had it, but she'd been gifted pale blond locks from her mother's family.

Dalus, the oldest prince, walked in with the Commander of the Guard. Annabel watched Dalus approach Mayven. She couldn't hear them, but she could see he was giving pointers. Mayven may have been the crown prince, but their older half-brother was the hero. He'd taken down every kind of monster and won every hunting tournament. He also was blunt, crass, and had the diplomatic nature of a toddler—which is to say, he had none.

Annabel loved him dearly.

Their eyes met and Annabel straightened. Dalus pointed at her and called out, "Don't even think of hiding here. Father will have my hide."

Annabel stuck out her tongue in childish spite. "I promised father I would attend this last one dutifully."

Mayven said something to Dalus who nodded. Likely explaining that they were going to be having breakfast with mother—the whole reason she was there. He handed the spear off and trotted over to the stairs. He picked up his jacket and quickly secured it before taking the steps two at a time.

"You're early," Mayven said, falling in beside her as they walked along the battlement.

"Even I wake up early sometimes," Annabel countered.

"Once every decade perhaps," Mayven replied, bumping his shoulder against hers.

She gave him a sideways glare. It didn't take them long to arrive at the gardens. Her mother was already there, but breakfast was not. Their mother set down her teacup and looked up in surprise.

"Heddie said you'd be joining us soon, but I didn't believe it," her mother said with a kind smile. "You look lovely today."

Annabel bent and kissed her mother's cheek. "As do you, mum."

"Have the delegates arrived?" Her mother asked.

"Last night," Mayven confirmed.

Her mother smiled broadly. "I'd heard the warriors of the isles are very dashing."

Annabel rolled her eyes. Ever since her second eldest sister became engaged and her eldest sister had given birth to her second child, her mother had been relentlessly trying to push her in that direction. Each time with less and less subtlety. Her brother found it all quite amusing—even now hiding a laugh behind his hand—perhaps it was time she taught him a lesson.

"Perhaps our future queen shall come from the isles." Annabel smiled coyly at Mayven.

Her brother was no longer smiling as her mother's eyes shone with delight. The only thing Mayven showed little interest in was women. The ladies of the court seem to be in two fields of thought—that he was an absolute heartthrob or that his overly severe nature made him boring. Since becoming crown prince, both sides had decided to redouble their efforts but as of yet her affable, yet serious brother had shown zero interest in forming an attachment.

"Mayven, have you seen any of their delegation?" The same playful tone Annabel was known to use came from her mother. The apple didn't fall far from *that* tree. A fact Annabel was proud of.

"Do not start, mother," Mayven shook his head, his eyes drilling holes into Annabel but to little effect.

"Oh, look breakfast," Annabel said, reaching for one of the scones. That ended the discussion of marriage as they exchanged pleasantries and discussed Annabel's upcoming debutante ball. Anything was better than discussing the marriage mart.

Chapter 2

Annabel was in a decent mood when she headed for the throne room. She only hoped her father was appreciative of her efforts to arrive early and allow her the outing she'd requested. When she reached the entryway her three ladies-in-waiting were there: Lady Ariah, Lady Pheobe, and Lady Zerwin.

Lady Phoebe of the Western Isles spotted her first. "Princess Annabel, you're early."

Apparently, Annabel would be surprising everyone this morning with her punctuality. The thought caused her to sigh; she in no way wanted any of them to believe this was more than a one-time fluke. She was very aware they all viewed her as a spoiled baby. A reputation she'd worked very hard to create. It allowed her the maximum freedom that she desired.

"I am excited to meet the last of our lively group," Annabel replied with a curt smile. "Let's get this over with."

Lady Phoebe laughed. "I've heard they are very exotic."

Annabel wished she could have picked her ladies-in-waiting. If she had been in charge of the arrangement Lady Phoebe would have been dismissed after day one. She had the attention span of a ticking clock and the tact of a raging bull.

"Try to show some decorum," Lady Zerwin from Mavrid's capital city said. At least she took her duties seriously—overly much at times.

As was the norm, Lady Ariah, who was also from Mavrid, said nothing. Her eyes were appraising but she kept her own council. She spoke only when spoken to, and honestly was rather unnerving with her sharp green eyes. The three of them had been there only a few weeks and Annabel had done everything to avoid them. By the end of the season, they would all be gone anyway.

The doors opened as they were admitted into the throne room. Their names were announced as Annabel took her place by her father's side. Mayven looked like their mother but was built like their father. Annabel was slim like her mother and had her pale locks, but everything else was from her father. He was a towering figure that commanded a room with his very presence, nary a word need be spoken, and others were hurrying to fulfill his every order.

As was customary Annabel turned to the delegation as she and her entourage's final introductions were being completed by the attendant. At the front of the party was a dark-skinned girl with beautiful ebony curls. Her manner of dress may be similar to Mavrid's, but the colors were bright and the beadwork exquisite. Standing next to the woman was a man who could very well have been her twin. His hair was short, clothing darker but equally as fine, and his face as pleasing.

Despite all of that, it was their eyes that she took the greatest notice of. While hers were lively, his were cold and guarded. It was as though they were perfect contrasts of each other. What could cause such a chasm between their two personalities?

"May I present Lady Cierra and her brother, Lord Cain, of the Van Brandt's of the Southern Isles," the delegation's announcer declared.

Lady Cierra curtsied as she was presented, and Annabel nodded her acceptance. Out of all her ladies-in-waiting, Annabel found herself most interested in Lady Cierra. Something about her was unexpectedly appealing.

"Welcome to King's Spire, heart of Itreia," Annabel said holding out a hand as was customary on the Southern Isles. "May your stay be pleasant."

Lady Cierra's eyes lit up as she pressed the back of her gloved hand against Annabel's. "Thank you for your kind words, Princess Annabel. We are thankful for your hospitality."

"You are most welcome," Annabel's father, the king, said. "Tonight, shall be a banquet in your honor." The members of the delegation smiled and bowed politely in gratitude.

"We shall show you to your room," Annabel told Lady Cierra.

"Thank you kindly," Lady Cierra curtsied one final time to the king before joining her group.

She spared a glance back and Annabel followed her gaze. Lord Cain nodded to his sister before briefly glancing at Annabel. A visible frown appeared, and Annabel resumed facing forward as annoyance pricked her brow. As appealing as Lady Cierra was, she found her brother to be equally unappealing. Hopefully, they would have little contact before he departed with the delegation.

"It is lovely," Lady Cierra said, as she swept through the room.

"Please take the next hour or so to settle in. Then I would suggest you rest, for I am sure the banquet shall go late into the night," Annabel said with a smile.

To her surprise Lady Cierra took her hands. "You are most generous!" Her open and warm manner put Annabel at ease instantly.

"I am very happy that you have come," Annabel said and meant it. For the first time Annabel felt she might find a friend amongst her ladies-in-waiting. "I shall take my leave but will return around dinner time." She left the room as servants carried in Lady Cierra's trunks.

"You are all dismissed to rest. I shall see you all before dinner," Annabel said, continuing down the hall without seeing if her other lady-in-waiting's obeyed.

The delegation may have been a distraction but now that she needed to wait, her earlier contemplation returned. The dream had bothered her more than she cared to admit, but her intuition forced her to accept the possibility that she may now be a Mystic.

Some years ago, her family had been assessed for powers after her older brother presented an uncanny ability to hit his mark. Once an assessor was called and he was declared a future Mystic, the lowest of the classes of magic users, they were all looked at. She was the only one they said had the spark—that she would one day awaken. That was right before...the incident.

Habit, or perhaps, melancholy drove her to the Hall of Ancestors—a long gallery filled with portraits and busts of her forefathers. The gallery ended at a junction where another hall ran perpendicular to it. This was where she found the portrait of the reigning king—her father. Continuing down the hall to the right, she took stock of the images of all of her father's wives.

She paused in front of the portrait of her father with his first wife, one of the most beautiful women Annabel had ever seen. She had four of the seven children, which included two elder sisters and two elder brothers. The next painting was of his second wife, a frail woman with wide eyes, who died giving birth to Lenora. The last picture was of her mother when she was much younger; before the carriage accident left her partially crippled. She felt the claw of guilt wrap itself around her heart at the thought. She grappled with the feeling, shaking herself free as she always did, before she continued on her way.

It was too early to tell—after all, she'd only had the one dream—but she supposed it was possible that she was finally manifesting her ability as a Mystic. Yet the ability to see the future seemed far too powerful for the beginner magic user. Perhaps her Mystic ability was so subtle she wasn't aware of it and was already a Mage. Although, how could that be when her power just now revealed itself? Besides, she found it very unlikely she could leap to the level of Magician unnoticed, and with an untapped power.

One thing was for certain. She didn't intend to tell anyone about her ability until she knew more. To others, the ability to tell the future would seem to be a gift, but Annabel knew about gifts being burdens. Her grandmother had the ability to tell when people were lying, and it had led to her eventual death.

For now, she would be the only one to know of this potentially prophetic dream. Others may find her cheerful and foolhardy, but that was intentional, the part of herself she shared with others. But the part that was from her father—the shrewd strategist—was always right at her fingertips.

Chapter 3

The hall was lively with music when they arrived. Lady Cierra had been dressed in an impossibly bright pink dress with silver beading. Lady Phoebe had been practically green with envy, which put Annabel in a surprisingly cheerful mood. It was well known that Lady Phoebe prided herself on her beauty and having the flashiest dress at every event, no matter the occasion. It seems she would likely be facing a stylish competitor.

"Everyone is dressed so beautifully," Lady Cierra said, her voice filled with wonder.

"Wait until next week," Annabel replied, enjoying her enthusiasm. "This is but the small dance hall, we shall be in the grand hall next week where it will be filled to capacity."

Annabel would hate it, but perhaps she would dislike it less if Lady Cierra continued to show such joy over the splendor.

"Do you not have such events where you are from?" Lady Phoebe asked, her eyes cunning.

"On our great island of Nemion, you can see the churning sea under your feet in the ballrooms as you dance, and the grand music halls are cut from the cliffs," Lady Cierra replied, completely missing Lady Phoebe's quiet jab at the islands not being as refined.

"That sounds far more charming than what you described the Western Isles as having to offer," Annabel added, her gaze sharp at Lady Phoebe who bowed her head. There were few instances that brought out Annabel's serious side, but bullying was one of them. As the youngest she'd been subject to ridicule from time to time and would not stand for it if she had the means to prevent it. "Though I imagine it takes a stout heart to walk with the sea beneath one's feet."

Lady Cierra's head bobbed excitedly. "Many have fainted!"

Annabel laughed. "Unfortunately, here we are tried with other tests of mettle."

Lady Cierra appeared stricken at her words. "Such as what?"

Annabel offered her hand to which Lady Cierra placed hers on top as they turned towards the row of men. "Dancing."

Her brother Mayven bowed to them. He held out his hand. "Lady Cierra, would you do me the honor?"

Her brother was excellent at playing the charming diplomate. Even though he disliked dancing and would not repeat the act. Lady Cierra's dark cheeks had the barest of blushes as Annabel helped her new lady-in-waiting along by depositing her hand into her brother's waiting one.

"Gladly," Lady Cierra replied, bashfully following him to the dance floor.

That was when her cousin, Varen, appeared practically out of thin air. He bowed to Lady Zerwin, and almost before she accepted his invitation, he led her towards the assemblage of dancers. It wasn't long until a young lord approached Lady Phoebe. One by one, her ladies-in-waiting had been whisked away, until only Lady Ariah and she remained.

Just as the music started, her eldest brother, Dalus, sidled up beside her and offered his hand. "Would you do me the honor?"

Annabel glanced around the room, looking for the one person she should be dancing with. It was customary for her to dance with the most prominent member of the delegation. However, as of yet, none had arrived, which left her free to gleefully accept her brother's offer.

"The honor is mine," Annabel said, taking his hand.

They joined the dancing, coming in on the back end of the line. Everyone was clapping their hands as each couple danced up the path. She ended up next to Lady Cierra when they reached the front of the line and went to each side—divided by gender.

"Enjoying yourself?" Annabel asked, her voice raised over the excitement and music.

"Most assuredly!" Lady Cierra replied, her face beaming. "I wish my brother would be joining us."

That caught Annabel's attention. "Will he not be?"

"I know it is customary, but he is feeling poorly," Lady Cierra explained. "I do hope you can forgive him."

"I am not one to hold such things against a man. I hope he recovers quickly." Annabel smiled to reassure her.

Lady Cierra nodded with a grin as it became her and Mayven's turn to lead the group in the next part of the dance. Annabel gladly took Dalus' hand, in part relieved to be alleviated from her courtly duties. Feeling genuinely happy, Annabel decided she would enjoy the night. There was plenty of time to deal with the delegation's departure on the morrow, and reluctantly face her own societal obligations for the remainder of the summer.

"Can you say that again, father?" Annabel said slowly as she sat beside him at breakfast.

Once a week the royal family made time to sit as a family—though few of them were present to do so. Her oldest sister was married with children of her own—such a pity they lived so far away. Her other two sisters, Yenni and Lenora, were with her other half-brother, Baltus, touring the west, but were not scheduled to return for two more days. She missed her siblings terribly, now more than ever.

"Lord Cain has petitioned to stay behind and study in the royal library," King Alin repeated before taking a sip of tea.

"Have you decided if you shall grant it?" Annabel asked.

Her father was busy reading but paused. "Do you have an interest in the man?"

"I like his sister," Annabel replied. "I am just curious if they are similar."

Her father's gaze watched her closely before he flicked his eyes towards her brother. "What do you think, Mayven?" King Alin asked.

"He is reserved and serious. If he is requesting to study, I would wager a guess that is exactly what he'll do," Mayven said, stirring his tea.

Annabel hadn't taken him for the bookish type but looks could be deceiving. "Do you know what he is studying?"

"He mentioned something about medicinal properties of plants." King Alin said, pinning her to her seat with his stare. "This could be very beneficial to strengthen our relationship with the Southern Isles. So, know when I ask you to look into the matter I do not do so lightly."

Annabel groaned internally. This is what her curiosity had gotten her—a task. She should have known better than to draw attention to herself. Her father would normally leave her be but with most of the household away, it was harder to stay out of his scrupulous gaze.

"I shall meet with him posthaste," Annabel said before burying her nose into her breakfast, quite determined not to accidentally get herself an additional duty.

Mayven elbowed her. "Have fun dear sister."

"When you have reached a decision, let Mayven know so he can see to the details," King Alin added, amusement in his eyes. "What are your plans today, my dear?" He reached for his wife's hand, in a show of affection.

Annabel turned her head far enough that it would be difficult for her father to see before sticking out her tongue. Her brother chuckled before buttering a roll. Annabel would be lying if she said she wasn't interested. He was handsome to be sure, but there was something about him that felt almost haunting. It stirred something within her that was both unnerving and exhilarating. She only hoped her first assessment of him was off the mark and their exchange uneventful.

Chapter 4

As fate would have it, she found the Van Brandt siblings in the eastern garden. They were quietly conversing when Annabel approached. When they took notice of her making her way towards them, they both stood and greeted her with a curtsy and a bow, respectively.

"Good morning, your highness," Lady Cierra said, her face beaming. "Did you need me?"

"Actually, I am here to speak with your brother," Annabel replied and took note of the surprised expression on both of their faces.

"What about?" Lord Cain asked, his voice smooth despite his short tone.

Annabel hadn't expected such a curt response. "My father, that is *the King*, asked me to speak with you about your request. I have some questions."

"What do you need to know?" His expression never changed.

For some reason his flat responses were unnerving, and his blatant lack of courtesy was making her lose her temper. "Why do you want access to the library?" Her own tone bordering on disrespectful, Annabel could be equally as direct.

16

"The royal library has some of the most extensive collections of books on the continent. There is much I can learn," Lord Cain replied. Did he just tighten his jaw, or had she imagined it?

"I meant specifically."

"Plants!" Lady Cierra blurted out; her eyes wide as she glanced between them. "My brother wants to research their application for medicinal use."

"What kind of medicine?" Annabel asked, her question directed at Lady Cierra.

"Do you need to know that to grant me access?" Lord Cain rudely cutting in.

Annabel felt her toe start to tap in frustration. She'd never met a more infuriating man in her life. "As a matter of fact, yes."

Despite his emotionless expression, he was starting to sound annoyed. "Why?"

"Why? I have the discretion to grant or deny your request. That is why. Consider it my barrier to entry," Annabel replied, stubbornly as she gritted her teeth.

"It is a private matter," Lord Cain replied, tipping his chin up.

Lady Cierra touched Annabel's arm. "Please consider it a personal favor to our family. We would be greatly indebted to you."

"Are you a man of your word, Lord Cain? Do you pay all of your debts?" Annabel asked, her gaze fixed on him.

"Without fail." The words a rumble of poorly concealed anger, and she glanced down to see his fist was clenched.

"We shall see," Annabel replied, intentionally raising one brow before turning to Lady Cierra. "I shall tell my father to grant your request."

"You are most generous!" Lady Cierra said, taking hold of her brother's arm in enthusiasm. "This is wonderful news!"

Then Lord Cain did something Annabel would never have expected. He smiled at his sister. It changed his entire face and demeanor. She inhaled sharply at the complete transformation that overcame his features. Before, he had been broodingly handsome, but now—he was stunning. For a moment her brain simply wouldn't respond. She excused herself as she stiffly walked away, still reeling from how different he appeared. It was amazing how love could alter a face—be it familial or romantic.

She found Mayven in his personal study. The attendant didn't dare stop her even though he appeared conflicted over her arrival. That was fair, she had played a few minor tricks on her dear brother from time to time. No doubt he was on the lookout for the possibility of another of her schemes.

Her brother's desk had paperwork in small piles on top of it. His pen scratching the only sound in the room as she slipped through the door. He glanced up at her, but continued writing after he saw who it was. Annabel plopped down into one of his comfortable chairs, cradling her chin in her right hand.

She could understand sibling affection; she loved all of them dearly. Yet complete devotion to them was a foreign concept. Was it because she was the youngest? Since she had no responsibility to anyone but herself? Despite her brother being the youngest son, he had taken on responsibility when Dalus joined the knighthood and Baltus joined the temple. Perhaps that is what made him such a perfect crown prince. He was always letting everyone live their dreams, while he fulfilled the responsibility thrust upon him.

Mayven set the pen down before taking the wax and pouring it onto the folded letter to seal it. He pressed the emblem of their royal house, a crown with a sword through it, into the cooling wax. Once he set it aside, he turned his full attention to her.

"I will not renew the discussion of you leaving the day before your debutante ball," Mayven said, steepling his fingers. "No matter how well behaved you are."

Annabel pursed her lips on purpose. "Killjoy."

His gaze narrowed. "That isn't why you came."

"No," Annabel replied with a coy grin. "Though thank you for reminding me that I must write to the poor orphans that I will be unable to visit until I have sufficiently filled my dance card."

Mayven sighed. "You'll visit them next week."

"But who will deliver the bread?" Annabel asked, exaggerating her exasperation. "It is too cruel." Truth be told she'd arranged the day before the delegation arrived to have the bread delivered along with a few cakes. They might as well celebrate in her absence.

Mayven shook his head. "Why have you come?"

"Lord Cain's request," Annabel said, purposely not making eye contact as she slouched in the chair. "I belabored over it—it really was quite diverting—but have at last come to conclusion his request should be granted."

Her brother glanced at the clock on his desk, an eyebrow raised. "It's been an hour."

"Took even longer than I thought." Annabel let out a sigh as she met her brother's amused gaze. "Now, that my duty is done I really must get on with my very busy day."

"Where are you going to hide now? The library?" Mayven asked with a sigh as he leaned back in his chair.

Annabel stood and tipped her chin up on purpose. "If I told you, then it wouldn't be a very good hiding spot." She held her head high as she sauntered from the room, Mayven's laughter trailing behind her.

Chapter 5

Annabel stood anxiously as she stretched her neck out to try and spot the carriage that was already an hour late. Her half-siblings were set to return, and she'd been anxiously waiting for their arrival. Everyone else had left, but she remained. What else did she have to do? Not to mention she wanted to be the first one to greet them.

The row of trees on each side of the driveway were in full bloom, the pale, cloud-like blossoms had become entangled in the leaves. A gentle breeze rustled against her lacy skirts as she slipped some loose hair behind her ear. Eventually she would have to relent, but she would be heartbroken if she was not there when they arrived.

"Princess," Lady Cierra called coming down the steps.

"How are you this fine day?" Annabel said with a smile, thankful for the momentary distraction.

"I am well." She came down the steps to stand beside her. "How long have you been waiting?"

Annabel sighed. "Well over an hour."

"When I asked where you were, I was surprised to learn that you were outside watching for you siblings' return." Lady Cierra grinned widely. "You must value your family as much I do mine."

"That is true. I have missed them. Especially Lenora." Just thinking of her closest sister made her yearn for her company. While Annabel was known for her wild, non-conforming nature, her sister was exceedingly kind. She was the one who first convinced Annabel to spend time at the orphanage—which had become her favorite days of the week.

"It must be lovely having a sister." Lady Cierra's eyes shone bright: her statement genuine. "I always wished I had one."

"You have two brothers if memory serves," Annabel said, trying to recall the Van Brandt household.

"Yes, though I am quite fond of them, they were not very fun to play with growing up," Lady Cierra said with a resigned sigh. "Quite often Charli would pick on me and Cain was too busy with the burdens of being the oldest to have much time to play."

"Cain is the oldest? I thought your brother Lord Charli inherited the Dukedom because *he* was the eldest." In that moment Annabel wished she paid a little more attention to the nobility of the Southern Isles.

Lady Cierra shook her head. "My brother, Cain, abdicated the dukedom to Charli."

Before Annabel could inquire further, she heard the whinny of a horse and spotted the carriage with its armed escorts coming up the lane. Excited, Annabel could hardly stand still as they rounded the circle.

"I shall depart," Lady Cierra said with a curtsy.

"Thank you for the company," Annabel managed. "I shall find you later."

Barely were the words out of her mouth when the carriage stopped with a crunch of gravel. She quickly moved to the bottom step, her excitement rising. To her surprise Lenora was not the first out of the carriage. Their brother Baltus stepped out first. He wore the robes of the temple with a sash that dictated his rank. He was a great scholar for the temple, well versed in their scriptures and a powerful administrator at the main temple despite his young age. She would expect him to never leave if their father had not requested the temple allow

21

him to escort his sisters on their pilgrimage to visit their newly born niece. Had Annabel debuted any other time she would have joined them, but those darling babies would have to wait for her unfortunate obligations.

Yenni stepped out first, she had a big smile that almost matched her equally large nose. After Baltus helped her out of the carriage, she wrapped her arms around Annabel. A sense of kinship washed over her.

"Been staying out of trouble?" Yenni asked cheerfully.

"Have I ever?" Annabel shot back. "How was Yvette?"

"Tired," Yenni replied with a giggle. "But well. She misses us all. Just as I have missed you all."

That was when Lenora stepped out of the carriage. Just four months earlier her awkward sister had been covered in blemishes and her hair frizzed out like an old broom. Yet this girl had flawless skin and her hair was in perfect order. In fact, she appeared positively refined.

"Len?" Annabel said, taken aback by her complete change. "Is that you?"

Len smiled and her old sister was back. "Of course, it is silly."

They embraced and Annabel felt tears threaten. It was as though she'd missed a caterpillar turning into a butterfly. How had she changed so much in mere months? Granted she was only a few years older than Annabel, but to have such an extreme change was shocking. Not to mention much of her round cheeks were gone, making her appear even older.

"You haven't changed at all!" Lenora laughed.

"I cannot say the same for you," Annabel said sweeping back to indicate Lenora's change. "I barely recognize you."

"Much has happened." Lenora gripped her hand. "I shall tell you all about as I settle in."

Kissing Yenni's cheek as she passed, Annabel was pulled along by Lenora. "I shall see you later."

"I cannot wait. I have gifts!" Yenni called.

Baltus was already halfway up the stairs but accepted a kiss on his cheek as well. "Where is Mayven?"

"I missed you as well." Annabel laughed. "The study no doubt."

"Congratulations, sister." Baltus said, awkwardly patting her shoulder before Lenora pulled her along.

"Len, wait!" Annabel called with a gleeful chuckle.

Despite her half-hearted protest, they were soon in Lenora's room. It had been cleaned and the soft scent of soap filled the room as sunshine glinted off the glass table. They collapsed hand in hand onto her love seat, scattering a few of the embroidered pillows that added elegance to the room.

"I have missed you!" Annabel exclaimed, tightening her grip. "Tell me everything that happened."

"There is so much to tell!" Len replied gleefully. "Yenni's fiancé came and took us on a tour all around the northern territories. We even were set on by monsters. I danced and dined all across the north. Now that you are set to enter society, we must all go together so I can show you all of the wonderful places."

"That sounds terrifying!" Annabel couldn't help but laugh, knowing that it addressed multiple statements.

"You would love it, Bel," Lenora replied, her eyes shining. "There were grand halls like I've never seen. Unlike here in the south their buildings are much newer. They are modernized and breathtaking. There was even a city in the mountains to the northwest by the sea. It was the oldest place we saw and even predated much of the capital. The history, there was nothing like it."

Annabel listened to her sister ramble on for an hour. Listing the places they'd gone, the gentlemen she'd danced with, and even the type of food. Then she spoke of their sister and her children, how darling they were.

"Have you changed your mind about your debut?" Lenora finally asked as they leaned into the fluffy couch.

"I've promised mother I'd be on my best behavior." Annabel knew nothing more would need to be said.

"She's the only person you listen to," Lenora said with a chuckle.

"You seem...more mature," Annabel asked, eyeing her closely. "What happened?"

Lenora touched her hands against her cheeks and shook her head. Her cheeks were a soft pink as she looked away. Annabel leaned forward at her reaction and giggled freely. Her reaction could only mean one thing.

"Who is he?"

"A young noble," Lenora replied, her expression soft. "I think I was more interested in him then he was of me."

"Where did you meet?" Annabel asked, picking up a pillow to hug it.

"He was part of the group that helped us when we were attacked." Lenora shook her head. "He may be at the hunting tournament. Only then will I know if he is interested in me, and it was not all imagined."

"What house is he from?" Annabel asked.

Lenora shook her head. "Oh no you don't." She raised her hand like she could stave off Annabel's plans. "When Yenni was being courted you looked into Lord Euros. We all remember how much you dogged his every step over his business. It was worse with Yvette and the Marquis."

"I don't know what you're implying," Annabel said trying to feign innocence.

"You had someone spy on him for a few months. It nearly caused a full scandal because the Marquis thought it was at the order of the king, only to find out it was you meddling." Lenora sounded like she was trying to scold her while also sounding impressed.

Stifling a smile, Annabel patted her sister's hand. "I've learned my lesson." She said, while mentally adding, *to hire better staff*. Now it was just a matter of finding out who. If Lenora wouldn't relent, perhaps Yenni could be persuaded, or Baltus may know something—she had options.

Lenora's eyes narrowed. "You haven't changed at all, Bel."

"Oh?"

"Therefore, you won't get a word out of me on the subject," Lenora declared. "Is your dress ready for the ball tomorrow?"

"Yes," Annabel said glancing at the clock on the mantle. "I shall show you after lunch. I'm sure everyone will want to see you as well. I have four ladies-in-waiting that I'm sure will be overjoyed to meet you."

Lenora nodded. "I had heard they'd all arrived. Let's make haste before I decide that a nap sounds more appealing than food."

Chapter 6

The room was filled to the brim with all manner of people. From rich commoners to poor nobles, everyone who was anyone was in attendance. It should have been flattering that so many had turned up for the debutante ball of the youngest princess, but Annabel felt only burdened by their expectations. If her mother were not in attendance, she might have wormed out of some obligations, but tonight she must act like the proper princess she rarely was.

"Are you well?" Lady Cierra asked, with a note of concern in her voice and a friendly touch on Annabel's arm.

Her newest friend appeared concerned as they hid behind the curtain. Her other lady's-in-waiting appeared equally as worried. From the tightness of Lady Zerwin lips, she looked ready to lecture her if Annabel tried anything. All but Lady Cierra, who had yet to suffer from any consequences of her occasional antics, seemed more anxious about what she would do, rather than how she felt.

"I'll be better when this is over," Annabel replied, and watched with satisfaction as Lady Zerwin's frown deepened.

There was a trumpeting to their right as she heard two doors swing open. It had begun and she tried to console herself that it was but one evening. She would do everything to make sure the night went smoothly. It wasn't often her mother had the energy to attend.

"His imperial majesty, King Alin and her grace, Queen Marriot," the announcer declared as a hush came over the crowd. A moment later, the herald called out, "The Crown Prince Mayven." Annabel sighed before forcing a smile on her face. It was her turn. "And presenting, for the first time, Princess Annabel and her ladies-in-waiting."

The curtain raised and Annabel stepped out. There was clapping and many clamored how lovely she looked. Forcing a wide smile onto her face she joined her family. She bent forward to receive a kiss on her forehead from her mother before her father waved an attendant over. Opening the ornate box, Annabel caught the flash of something blue before he moved to pick it up.

Turning around he held up a tiara. She bent her head forward as the blue gems glistened. The gold would complement the silvery gold of her dress that melded with the gray. She had considered bright red but discarded it for a nice empire waist, decorated sash, and a silver ombre skirt that grew to a dark gray closer to the ground.

"I recognize you now as an adult of the court, free to join hands with a man of good standing," King Alin said, his voice carrying over the hushed crowd. "May you uphold the principles of my court and carry the lessons of our ancestors to guide you as you navigate the world. Know always that my hand is held out, you need but take it."

Annabel took her father's offered hand and curtsied over their joined hands. "I shall do all that I can to bring honor and grace to our noble family."

After she stood, he placed the tiara atop her head. Everyone clapped and Annabel felt exhausted despite the evening having just begun. She turned to face the crowd and gave a royal wave; showing the back of her hand, turning it halfway, then back again. She did this several times as a way to accept their congratulations without having to say a word. Soft music punctuated the applause, signaling those who may wish to ask for a dance to step forward.

As was the tradition, all eligible men were now required to greet her, in hopes that they might win the right to her first dance. Unlike other events where she could use her brother as a human shield from such attention, here it was expected. In fact, it was required of her.

"Lord Havik of the northern providences." An attendant read a card as a tall thin man bowed to her.

"Princess Annabel," he took her hand and bowed over it. "You are truly enchanting this evening."

"How generous."

And so, it went. Man after man, introduction after introduction, with names spinning around her head like a carousel. Each of them seemed eager to dance with her, a few uncomfortably so. She should have felt flattered, she knew, yet it was burdensome because none of it felt genuine.

"Lord Cain of the Southern Isles." The attendant announced.

She'd been so overwhelmed that his presence had gone unnoticed. He stiffly took her hand when offered, his own gloved, reminding her that she should be wearing hers.

"May your evening be enjoyable," his words were bland and for the first time Annabel felt a spark of hope. Here was the one man who was not at all interested in her status or plying her with pleasantries.

"Tell me, Lord Cain, do you find dancing enjoyable?" Annabel watched him closely, the men still in line to meet her leaned around him to see what was happening.

He seemed almost uncomfortable with her question. "I believe many find it enjoyable."

"But you do not?" Annabel pressed, glancing at Lady Cierra whose eyes were wide as they swung back and forth between them.

His expression darkened. "No."

"You do know how though?"

"To dance?" He asked, clearly wishing to leave from the way his feet were already turned away from her. "When forced."

"Then it seems I must force you since you shall be my first dance," Annabel said, lifting her head high as she heard hushed murmurs of disappointment. The first dance was a distinction, it signaled who had caught her eye.

He blinked at her, and she saw him struggling. Likely looking at any reason to deny her but must have come to the conclusion that he was trapped. There was no feasible reason why he could deny a royal request and she knew it. No doubt the attendant had indicated to the musicians that she had selected her first partner, as the music signaling the first dance filled the hall.

"Your gloves," Lady Cierra said, hastily shoving them towards her.

Annabel couldn't remember the last time she'd worn them. She was about to turn them down when she saw the desperate look on Lady Cierra's face. Not wishing to disappoint her thoughtful gesture she took them and quickly dawned them.

Lord Cain stiffly offered his hand. If one had seen them without context, certainly they would surmise he was going to his doom and not to dance. Finding his reaction amusing, she struggled to keep her lips in check. Perhaps he disliked such events as much as she did—thus they had common ground on which to fix their rocky start.

They stood before the middle set of glass doors leading to the outside, where the stone dance floor was framed by lilac trees and a decorative rock garden. The servants opened all the doors with a flourish. The blossoms, already falling, created a sweet-smelling snow as the dancers moved into place.

Lord Cain led her into position as the first strings of her favorite song began to play. They moved around each other like they were propelled by some outside force. He moved well, gracefully, and Annabel wondered why he disliked dancing when he excelled at it. Yet his gaze seemed to indicate there was something on his mind.

"It seems like you have something you wish to ask," Annabel said as their gloved hands touched.

He hesitated a moment as they turned. Annabel's dress swept around her as Lord Cain turned her in a circle. "Why ask me?"

"To dance?" Annabel asked, surprised. She'd thought he would ask about the request she'd granted. He nodded as they switched hands and turned the other way. "Because you were the only person who seemed reluctant to do so."

28

Was that a blush on his dark cheeks? His manners suggested that she had embarrassed him, but he didn't look away. They parted for the next steps of the dance before joining hands again in a few controlled turns.

"I do not mean to offend, Princess Annabel." Lord Cain sounded surprisingly repentant.

"You misunderstand, Lord Van Brandt." Annabel used his full formal name and title for the full effect as they switched directions. "You are the only person who would not ask something of me or say useless sweet words purely for my position."

He met her gaze in surprise, likely due to her honesty. Life at court did not often allow for such open communication, but Annabel was never one to follow the rules. Particularly when they didn't suit her.

Their hands touched above their heads as the music came to an end. "It seems we may find common ground after all," Annabel stated, hoping that they could start again.

He nodded to her, a long bow of the head that indicated he agreed. They left the courtyard's dance floor and returned to Lady Cierra whose eyes were sparkling. Annabel removed her gloves and handed them to her lady-in-waiting. They felt so restricting—she was recalling why she never wore them.

"You danced beautifully," her voice was full of awe as she held the gloves to her chest. "I have never seen you dance so well, brother."

"Her highness is a skillful dancer," he said turning his head away as though surveying the crowd.

That's when she saw a petal from the lilac trees in his hair. "Oh," Annabel said reaching for it. "You have—"

Before she could finish Lord Cain jerked away from her and yelled, "Do not touch me!"

The room quieted immediately. Her hand was still hovering in the air as all eyes turned to her. Her shock quickly turned to mortification as her cheeks burned. Lord Cain appeared more distressed than her as he eyed her in anguish. Did he find her so repulsive that even the thought of her touching him made him react so violently?

Her stomach twisted in knots as everyone stared at her. Her debut into society and already she had made a spectacle of herself. Her gaze locked with her mother across the room. Tears threatened as she stiffly left the room, her mother's concerned expression haunting her as she fled. For the first time in her life, she wished she wasn't so flippant, no doubt her mother thought she'd been the cause of such an outburst. Likely that she deserved it.

"Princess!" Lady Cierra's voice cut into her thoughts.

She stopped and glanced back, expecting Lord Cain to join them. Perhaps to apologize for his behavior, but instead it was only his sister who came. She was stunned at his complete lack of propriety.

"He meant no offense," Lady Cierra insisted once she caught up to Annabel.

"Whatever his intention, offense was taken," Annabel replied, the sting of his reaction still too fresh as she began walking again with no destination in mind.

"Please, forgive him," Lady Cierra begged which caused Annabel to stop in her tracks.

"I admire the way you defend your brother, but you cannot take back what happened." Annabel gestured behind her, where she'd last seen Cain in the ballroom. "His actions would indicate he is nothing more than an unlicked cub."

For the first time Lady Cierra's optimism faded and in its place was a somber air. "He was not always that way."

There was such sadness in her voice that Annabel was temporarily caught off-guard. "If you are worried that I'll expel you from your post, do not fret on that account."

Lady Cierra shook her head. "You are not that kind of person. I know my brother behaved poorly. I only wish to try to...mend what has happened."

Much of Annabel's anger left her at Lady Cierra's compliment. She sighed heavily as she glanced back at the busy hall. Music was wafting through the doors, reminding her that she'd have to return eventually.

"In two days, I'll be visiting an orphanage. Accompany me and bring a donation on behalf of your brother, only then will all be forgiven," Annabel said, at least her suffering would result in some good.

"I shall!" Lady Cierra hugged her and then seemed to remember herself. "Forgive me. I shall return and let my brother know how he can return to your good graces."

Before Annabel could correct her, she was hurrying up the hall and back to the party. Rubbing her neck, she took the opportunity to sneak out the side door and into one of the many gardens. This one had a plumeria tree, its blooms vibrant and sweet. She basked in the moonlight, listening to the birds sing in the treetops.

"Hiding?" Mayven said, as he stood in the doorway.

"If I was, you wouldn't have found me so easily," Annabel replied, forcing a smile.

"Should I revoke his stay?" Mayven's voice was tight.

Annabel shook her head. "I should not have acted so familiar with him." Though it was innocent enough what she had done, it was childish of her to have nearly touched him. Even if his reaction was extreme.

"You are too generous," Mayven replied, it had been a long time since she'd seen him angry.

"Perhaps," Annabel replied. "Or perhaps anything I do will only make me appear worse and him perfectly justified."

Mayven's face darkened. "Should I handle it?"

Annabel walked up to him and patted his arm. "I love you for saying that, but no. My pride is wounded more than anything. I would rather forget the whole event then risk a diplomatic incident."

"Shall we return and show how unaltered you are?" He lifted his arm, elbow out.

"Gladly," Annabel replied taking his offered arm. "Will you fill most of my dance card for the evening?"

Mayven kissed her temple. "Gladly."

Chapter 7

The carriage rattled down the road. Annabel sighed again at being trapped inside as she gazed longingly out of the window. The sun made the day almost unbearably warm within the contraption. If only she could ride on horseback.

Lenora and Lady Cierra sat across from her as they admired a handful of decorative ribbons they'd each embroidered. It was no surprise that with Lenora's kind nature and Lady Cierra's sweetness, the two had become quick friends. It now made sense to Annabel why she'd liked the young Miss Van Brandt so much—she was much like her beloved sister.

"How did you give this bloom such definition?" Lenora asked, lifting the ribbon.

Lady Cierra's dark cheeks appeared to warm at the compliment. "It is a stitching technique my grandmother taught me. Would you like me to teach you?"

"I would be most grateful if you did," Lenora replied with an excited grin.

"Really, Len," Annabel said her chin resting on her hand. "You should offer her something in return. For all you know it may be a family secret."

32

Lenora's eyes widened. "How thoughtless of me. Is there something I can teach you?"

Lady Cierra was shaking her head and waving her hands. "I really couldn't ask that of you, your highness."

"I must insist," Lenora replied.

After a moment of hesitation, Lady Cierra pointed at one of Lenora's ribbons. "How do you do this part?"

"A feather stitch?" Lenora replied. When Lady Cierra nodded, Lenora seemed excited. "It would be my pleasure."

Annabel tried to keep her lips in check though they fought to tilt upwards into a smile. As the repurposed manor came into view, Annabel leaned out the window and waved. The children who saw her waved back, calling for her.

Lenora grabbed onto her skirts and tugged. "Really, Bel, you mustn't make a spectacle of yourself!"

Her laughter started in her belly and burst out of her throat as she plopped back into the seat. "It has been two weeks since I saw them last. I was just excited."

Lady Cierra hid a smile behind her hand as her sister laughed as well. "You really haven't changed at all, Bel."

"Debuting doesn't change who I am. Though traveling seems to have turned you into a stick in the mud," Annabel replied as the carriage slowed. Barely had it settled before she burst out of it.

The children gathered around her, hugging and pulling at her skirts as she excitedly listened to them. Most were telling her what she had missed, a few thanked her for the food, but most were just yelling her name, trying to get a moment of her attention.

Their two guards jumped down which caused the children to stop their antics and take a few steps back. Annabel rolled her eyes as she kept her hands firmly on two children's backs as they clung to her skirts. "Really, Sir Harl. All of your years of training and you use it to intimidate children who are of no danger to anyone."

"I have my orders," Sir Harl replied stiffly.

"Do try to relax." Annabel fixed him with one of her sharp gazes—the one she rarely used. "Having an arrow up your posterior cannot be good for one's health."

"Annabel!" Lenora said, shocked.

Pleased at Sir Harl's stunned expression she ordered the baskets of food be brought in as she followed the children inside. It took nearly zero prompting to get the darlings chatting again. Apparently one of the boys had fallen from a tree and a girl had been taken on as a ward in a prominent family. Her favorite story being the one of the toads they'd tried to smuggle in before the headmistress had caught them.

Lenora mostly spent time instructing the older girls in their letters and giving pointers on their sewing. They were used to her more reserved kindness but did not know what to make of Lady Cierra. Annabel kept an eye on the young lady-in-waiting. She seemed overwhelmed by everyone wishing to talk to her. Many of the children had no qualms about asking why her skin was so much darker or how her hair was so finely curled. Despite her obvious discomfort, she tried to answer their inquiries, once more proving why Annabel found her such a wonderful companion.

They stayed through lunch but as the dinner hour approached, they finally had to call it a day. Closing the book she'd been reading to them, Annabel looked at the sky. It truly had been the perfect day. The warm sun, the innocent children who cared for her, and those she cared for with her. It was such a balm to her soul.

"Princess?" Lady Cierra said, blocking out the sun as she stood in front of her. "Did you hear me?"

"We must go?" Annabel asked as the children all groaned in disappointment.

Lady Cierra nodded. "Princess Lenora says it is time."

"Come," Annabel said opening her arms. The children piled around, each taking turns hugging her or kissing her on the cheek before returning inside. When it was done, she dusted off her skirts and stood.

"You seem very happy." Lady Cierra smiled softly at her.

34

"I am." Annabel linked her arm with her lady-in-waiting. "I am very happy you agreed to come."

"I hope to come again," Lady Cierra replied. "We do not have such beautiful orphanages in the isles. Most are taken in by family or considered charity cases by the nobles." She had such awe in her voice. "These children are all so healthy and happy."

"Children are our future. It is our duty to see they are cared for. Why should they suffer because their parents are gone?" Annabel replied. This was one of the few topics she was serious about, since what they did was necessary. No one would ever convince her otherwise.

"Just when I think I understand you, you surprise me once more," Lady Cierra said, trying, unsuccessfully, to hide a wide smile behind her hand.

Lenora was waiting by the doorway and reached out her hand to Annabel. "It should not surprise you to know that the only thing that matters more is family." She took Lenora's hand and knew that no matter what changed with her debut, she would never let that fact faulter.

Chapter 8

Dream

The music played as Annabel watched her cousin, Varen, hold hands with his new bride. Lady Zerwin had never looked so radiant—her unencumbered laughter made her appear positively altered. Her heart warmed as the happy couple kissed.

"I am surprised at their quick marriage," Lady Phoebe said, seeming almost put out.

"She seems happier for it," Lady Ariah said with a smile. It was one of the few times Annabel had seen any expression on her face.

"To think they were only engaged a month." Lady Cierra sighed contently. "So romantic."

"I should thank them. They have taken all attention away from me once they became betrothed a mere week after my debut." Annabel truly was happy for her cousin. Even if she thought her too serious, Lady Zerwin was an excellent choice for a wife, and her demeanor would serve her cousin well in the long term.

Lenora laughed and leaned forward. "It was as though you were happier about their engagement than they were. You even insisted upon having the wedding before the Masquerade Ball."

Annabel felt uneasy but didn't say anything. Her gaze seemed to sweep around the room as though looking for someone, but finding no relief when they weren't there.

"It was the least I could do," Annabel finally replied. "They gave my mother something else to focus on. It was a nice reprieve that will likely now come to an end."

"Has she still been asking about your interest in my brother?" Lady Cierra said. She appeared concerned as though it was somehow her fault.

Annabel felt a strange tug in her chest. "Right up until I announced his intention to leave within a fortnight and that he was more like another Mayven to me."

"He does miss our home," Lady Cierra said, relaxing back into her chair. "Though I shall miss him."

"So will I," Annabel said and meant it.

Present

Annabel's eyes opened slowly as her most recent dream came to her in flashes. If the timeline was correct her cousin would propose in just a day or two. The imperial picnic in two days was the most likely event that he would take such an action. Part of her knew it would happen, knew that the first dream was as real as the second.

As to whatever had happened with Lord Cain, that remained to be seen. She had no idea what could change in a month, but obviously they'd overcome their difference to the point that she considered him like a friend or even a brother. A disconcerting thought to be sure considering how their last encounter went.

With a groan she rolled over and buried her head into the pillow. Perhaps if she could return to sleep it would be that much longer before she had to accept these weren't just dreams, they were premonitions. Had Dalus felt this way when his own ability emerged?

She knew she should see the palace Mage to confirm that she was a budding Mystic. When she'd reached her thirteenth year, like all her siblings, she'd been tested. The test wasn't completely accurate, but if the orb took on a glow it meant there was a possibility of an ability developing.

Nearly a decade before her, Dalus had undergone the same test and it had confirmed he had developed an ability. He was a Mage with increased strength and an eye for accuracy. It is what made him such a powerful hero—he could take on some monsters barehanded and win. Her brother was truly a force of nature.

The rest of her siblings had no affinity for magic, she could still remember the day the orb had glowed softly for her though. Promising that at some point in her life something would happen. She'd nearly given up hope, thinking it would never come, and then this. Of all the abilities this was the last one she would want for herself. Annabel preferred to live in the now—yet her new ability was forcing her look to the future.

Draping an arm over her face she let out a heavy sigh. "Stupid blood."

When there was a soft rap on the door and Heddie entered a moment later, Annabel resigned herself to the fact she could not hide in bed all day. No matter how tempting it was, she had much to prepare for. After the imperial picnic, they would be sent southeast to the Black Forest for the Annual Hunting Tournament.

It was an event she was responsible for the execution of. Well, partially responsible. She was to schedule the events and present the awards. Whoever won the tournament would gain her favor and a promise for the first dance at the Huntsman's Ball. Not to mention the jousting she'd added to make the whole event more interesting.

"It is time to wake up, princess," Heddie said opening the curtains.

"I'm awake," Annabel said sitting up, albeit reluctantly.

Heddie stopped and blinked at her. "Twice in one week? My goodness, your grace, are you ill?"

"I'm perfectly healthy," Annabel replied, tipping her head to the side and smirking. "Are either of my sisters awake?"

"They both are." Heddie was pulling out a dress and preparing accessories. "They are preparing for the Imperial Walk."

It was something they did in the capital once a month. The entire royal family went in different directions throughout the city to greet the common folks. They were paired up and sent off in a direction, to offer support, food, and see to the needs of their people. It was developed by their ancestor, a usurper, to remind them of those they served. They had overthrown a king who had forgotten that the people came first. He'd lost his head on the steps of his dais—an event her ancestors had wished to prevent from reoccurring.

"Please pick something simpler," Annabel insisted when she saw the dress Heddie had selected.

"You have debuted, princess, you should be wearing your finest gowns," Heddie replied, holding up the opulent gown with its beaded skirts and gold threading.

"That is hardly proper attire for the walk." Annabel swung her legs off the bed and stood. She regarded the clothes in her closet before pointing at one. "This will do."

Annabel strolled beside her brother, Dalus. They randomly split off into groups to walk the city. Since Lenora, Yenni, and Baltus returned, they would be able to split off into groups of one sister with one brother and then her parents could gather in the main square. While her siblings had been away, her, Dalus, and Mayven had been exhausted at the end of the day because they'd had to cover so much more of the city.

Despite it being summer, the day was cool, and Annabel was happy she'd opted for a high collar and long sleeves. It was much more practical attire than the elaborate dress Heddie had tried to put her in.

She eyed her brother as they weaved through the streets—wondering how she might ask him about his ability without raising suspicion. Many greeted them as they passed, their servants passing out bread to those who approached and asked. They were on their way to the builders, to see if there were any major needs in the city. Mayven had handled this visit the previous month, so he'd taken the trade guild instead. That left the Healer's Hall, a massive hospital in the heart of the capital, to Yenni and Baltus.

"Should I beat him?" Dalus finally said.

"Who?" Annabel asked, glancing up at her much taller brother in confusion.

He appeared uncomfortable; despite his strength and intimidating size, their brother was not very comfortable around women or emotions. In fact, he wasn't very comfortable with a lot of things if it didn't involve a weapon or strength. Which is why he refused to attend a ball or diplomatic events unless it was mandatory. Everyone knew he didn't like them and was better suited for the barracks.

"Lord Cain," Dalus finally said, watching her closely.

In light of her dream, she'd temporarily forgotten that embarrassing event just two days earlier. Her cheeks warmed as she shook her head. "Though I appreciate the offer, I have a feeling the matter will resolve itself."

"Wish I'd been there to whoop him." Dalus frowned deeply, causing a few citizens to shy away from him.

"Please don't be afraid," Annabel called to them, waving them towards the bread baskets. "Really, Dalus, you're glaring again." She smiled at him warmly as she teased him. "You look about ready to trounce the next person we encounter."

Dalus's expression relaxed. "Sorry. It just makes me angry."

"It made me angry, too." There were other choice words Annabel would like to use to describe how it made her feel, but refrained from doing so. "It was an unfortunate event I'd rather put behind me."

"Did he really smack your hand away?" Dalus asked, his voice gruff.

Annabel blinked. "No. Not at all, he just asked me not to touch him. It was more embarrassing then hurtful." Annabel touched a hand to his arm. "I promise it was not so terrible."

"I'm glad you weren't hurt," Dalus replied as they reached the builder's establishment.

"Princess," a woman called, carrying a baby. "Will you bless my daughter?"

Annabel reached for the child without hesitation. The baby had a tuff of hair on her head and sleepy blue eyes that blinked slowly. The mother preened eagerly, not even glancing at Dalus as he peeked down at the baby in Annabel's arms.

"May your beauty be matched by your wit," Annabel said softly before kissing the child's forehead. The baby squirmed slightly before settling back into the comfort of her wrap, cooing softly. She handed the child back to her mother. "May you both be blessed. Please take this as a token of her blessing."

Annabel took a ribbon from one of the servants and held it out. They were supposed to be embroidered by the princesses, but no one should have to suffer her inept stitches. Instead, she'd liberated a few of Lenora's for her use. They were both princesses so the blessing should still apply.

"Thank you, your highness," the woman said beaming as she took the ribbon and stepped aside.

Dalus and Annabel continued on as the woman was handed bread behind them. Annabel glanced over her shoulder. "Give her two."

"Bless you," the woman called as she was given a second loaf.

"By his grace," Annabel replied. She glanced up at Dalus once they were out of earshot she asked, "Did you want to hold her?"

Her brother's head bobbed. "Though she was too small and fragile."

"You were afraid to? Because of your...extra strength?" Annabel asked, implying it was about his ability.

"That, and I scare them." Dalus said pointing forward. "Let's go."

Annabel contemplated his words before asking, "Do you wish you didn't have it?"

"Wishing for such things is not worthwhile," Dalus replied as though her question was ridiculous. "It is as much a part of me as my hand."

Annabel felt a sudden rush of comfort at his words. She was still Annabel despite her blooming ability. It didn't matter what it was, it didn't change who she was. Dalus, for all his claims of being slow witted, have proven once more to be insightful. This is why she loved her brother, everyone saw his size and assumed how he would be, but few recognized his levelheaded approach to life. It made her appreciate him more.

"I'm glad you're my brother," Annabel told him as they waited to cross the street.

A big grin spread across his face as he wrapped an arm around her shoulders. "Me too."

Chapter 9

The day was beautiful, the sun was shining brightly, and the air sweet as she opened her parasol. She'd chosen a white lace dress with pale blue floral embellishments and cap sleeves. It was one of her favorite dresses because it had once belonged to her mother. Although the style was old, one benefit of being a princess, no one would say a thing to her—debut or no debut.

To her surprise the only lady-in-waiting that was out on the lawn was Lady Ariah. She seemed about as interested in the coming event as Annabel. She was watching the gentry milling around with apparent indifference.

"I'm surprised you are waiting for me," Annabel said as she paused next to her.

"Lady Phoebe insisted they get a very specific blanket by one of the trees," Lady Ariah responded plainly. "I said I'd wait for you."

"Am I the last to arrive?" Annabel asked, glazing behind her.

Lady Ariah nodded. "Everyone else arrived early to get everything prepared."

Annabel glanced around to see if she could spot her cousin, Varen. If her dream was what she suspected it to be, today was the most likely day that he'd make his move. At first Annabel had thought to find him and lend a hand, but decided it was best to prove this was meant to happen organically. Any interference might make the event occur or not occur, just because of her possible premonition.

"That was thoughtful," Annabel replied, absentmindedly.

"Shall we join them?" Lady Ariah asked, eyeing her with interest.

"Is Lady Zerwin there?" Annabel asked, trying not to buzz with excitement. How did anyone who could see the future stay calm?

"All of them are." Lady Ariah turned to lead her to their spot.

Annabel followed her without question. She kept a keen eye open for Varen, but only saw her brothers milling around. Dalus and Baltus were speaking to each other while Mayven was across the lawn with their mother. Annabel waved at them but continued to follow Lady Ariah. Her father was unlikely to attend until later when he had to make the proper announcements that were required of him.

"Princess," Lady Cierra called waving to them.

"What a lovely arrangement," Annabel managed as she approached, still glancing around for her cousin. She knelt and popped a raspberry into her mouth as she scanned the manicured lawn and decorative pathways.

"Lady Zerwin saw to all the arrangements," Lady Ariah said as she joined them.

"Lord Varen was generous enough to relinquish this spot," Lady Zerwin said, a soft smile on her lips.

Annabel inhaled at her cousin's name and then began to cough. Her eyes were watering as the raspberry piece wreaked havoc on the back of her throat. Multiple pairs of hands patted her back as she tried to gain control again.

"My goodness," Lady Pheobe exclaimed.

"Here. Some water," Lady Zerwin said as she helped bring the cup to Annabel's mouth.

Despite struggling with it, she was able to get a few swallows as coughs wracked her body. Her ladies-in-waiting gathered around her, patting her back and trying to help.

44

"I'm well," she finally managed between inhales. She tried to clear her throat before taking another swallow of the water.

"You gave us quite a scare. Nearly stopped my heart," Lady Cierra said, placing her hand upon her chest.

"Is everything well?" Mayven's voice cut into her attempt to regain her composure.

Annabel tried to wave him off. "Mishap...with a raspberry." She indicated to her throat before taking another sip of water.

"You do know you're supposed to chew your food, right?" Mayven asked kneeling to refill her cup.

Despite the tickle at the back of her throat she managed a disgruntled glare before she took another swallow of water. Lady Cierra giggled before stifling it with the back of her hand. Her cheeks were a shade darker as she opened her fan to hide behind it and a thought popped into her head. Her brother would soon regret his earlier barb.

"I believe I just need a moment to rest," Annabel said, sliding to the side as she lounged back. "Could you be so kind as to escort my ladies-in-waiting to the gardens? It is nearly time for the viewing."

Mayven's playful expression vanished in an instant. His gaze landed on Lady Phoebe who nodded eagerly—her eyes wide with excitement. Her brother visibly paled, but Annabel played at being blissfully unaware.

"Lady Zerwin, would you mind remaining here with me?" Annabel reaching for her. "I will need some assistance, as this coughing fit has made me lightheaded." She put her knuckles against her forehead in a dramatic play.

"If that is what you wish," Lady Zerwin replied solemnly. Mayven appeared trapped as Annabel just smiled. She'd pay for it later, but for now she enjoyed her victory.

Lady Ariah stood and began walking towards the gardens on her own. Which left the remaining two ladies to take Mayven's arms, one on each side. Her brother played the diplomat, but she could see how uncomfortable he was. It didn't matter that he would likely end up in a contract marriage that best benefited the kingdom—every girl hoped to catch his eye.

"Oh, and brother," Mayven turned back with a spark of hope. "If you see Cousin Var, send him this way. I'd like to speak with him."

Lady Zerwin paused as she was leaning forward. A thoughtful expression passed over her features before she picked up a little pastry. Mayven's frown deepened before he played the reluctant escort like a man ordered to walk the plank. Annabel would feel guilty if she didn't have ulterior motives. So much for not interfering—she really should work on her self-control. Perhaps another day.

"Tell me Lady Zerwin," Annabel said, attempting to put on an air of indifference. "How have you enjoyed your month here?"

Lady Zerwin had been the first to arrive nearly a month earlier. Although she was a serious person, Annabel quite liked her. She was straightforward, mature, and levelheaded, albeit a little judgmental. Her prim and proper nature hid a caring heart; one that deserved the happiness she hoped Varen would bestow upon her.

"I have been content here, your grace," Lady Zerwin replied, her gaze wistful before she turned in Annabel's direction. "What has prompted such an inquiry?"

Annabel shifted, glancing around for her cousin. "I only ask so that I might know you better. I believe you said you were the eldest of four girls." Annabel wondered if she'd have a hard time remaining in a foreign place.

"Indeed, I also have a younger brother," Lady Zerwin said with a nod. "It is kind of you to inquire."

"It is no kindness. I should have attempted such a conversation when you first arrived." It would matter more so, if she was to become family. "I was distracted by my duty and the following arrival of Lady Phoebe."

"I believe we were both…caught off guard when Lady Phoebe arrived," Lady Zerwin replied without even a hint of a smile. "I was surprised when I was selected. Why did you choose me?"

Annabel felt suddenly embarrassed that she'd left all matters to her mother. Though to be honest she'd only given her mother one parameter. "You were not the youngest in a large family." Annabel shrugged. "I thought you, like the others, might give me a wider perspective."

"Lady Ariah and Lady Phoebe have large families? Lady Cierra has spoken of her two brothers, but the others have not." Lady Zerwin leaned closer, for the first time she appeared fully engaged in the conversation.

"Oh yes. You are the oldest of your siblings. Lady Ariah is the second daughter in a family of four, and Lady Phoebe is the youngest girl but has two younger brothers in a family of six. Lady Cierra has two brothers, as you know, but also has two cousins who live with them as their parents have passed on," Annabel confirmed. Then she caught sight of Varen coming their way and perked up. "It seems our escort has arrived."

When Lady Zerwin spotted him, her pale cheeks became rosy. Annabel slowly stood as her cousin approached. He was rather dapper in his dress and with the way he'd slicked back his hair. He looked even finer than he had at the ball. As though he'd paid particular attention to his appearance...

How telling.

"Cousin!" Annabel lifted a hand in greeting.

"Cousin Annabel," Varen replied, kissing her on the cheek, before bowing to her lady-in-waiting. "Lady Zerwin, you look lovely. That is, you always look lovely." He seemed extremely nervous and wiped his hands on his pants before offering them each an arm. "Mayven said you needed to speak with me."

Annabel blinked, remembering she'd said that, but truthfully hadn't thought of anything to speak about. As both of her companions stared at her expectantly Annabel considered how convincing she'd be if she pretended to faint. Sighing as she abandoned the idea Annabel decided to take a risky gamble.

"I wanted to make sure Lady Zerwin had you as her first dance," Annabel replied and watched as their eyes widened and cheeks became pink. "It is customary to honor our guests and as she was the first, I wanted to make sure the honor was yours. My brother will have to make do with someone else."

"That is very kind of you, cousin," Varen said as Lady Zerwin took his arm. Annabel reluctantly took his other arm as they walked towards the atrium. "Do you accept?"

"Yes," Lady Zerwin said with a smile that somehow brightened an already sunny day. "Most ardently."

As they approached the hedgerow that stood an easy ten feet tall, Annabel considered how best to approach the subject. Though it seemed from the way they were chatting in their own little world that she needn't do much of anything. As they entered the open-air auditorium, Annabel remembered why this was one of her favorite places. This theater-in-the-round sported a magical island stage surrounded by water with only two ways in.

Everyone was seated in four rows of seats, each higher than the last, rising up to be encased by the hedgerow that stood higher than the topmost tier of seating. The Seat of the Sea; a clam-like structure where the royal family sat, was positioned between the two entry/exit points for the attendees. The members of the court streamed in like the water to take their seats. Anabel imagined they looked like an ornate ring from above, with the crowd being the band and they the gem.

The music rose up around them as they entered, dancers in pleated tulle spun in choreographed flourishes to the melody. Annabel purposely released her cousin's arm and hurried to her seat, her mother's gaze upon her. Once seated she found her focus bouncing between the graceful performers and the pair that she had entered with. They gave no indication that any promises of matrimony had been exchanged—no matter how many times she'd spared them a searching glance.

When the music ended Annabel quickly joined in the clapping. Her brother, Mayven, rose and offered Lady Cierra his hand. Lady Zerwin joined her cousin as was to be expected. An older man, whose name had slipped Annabel's memory, offered a hand to Lady Phoebe.

"Princess." Her attention snapped away before she could see who approached Lady Ariah. In front of her was a young man, a year or two older than her at most, offering his hand. "May I request this dance?"

Annabel glanced at her mother who nodded in encouragement. Apparently, this was her first obligatory partner—even if Annabel found his gaze a little too eager. She pressed her lips into a smile as she accepted his hand.

"With pleasure, Lord Tetra." Annabel stood and let herself be led to the dance floor. The beautiful opalescent tiles made the centerpiece appear to be that of a pearl. The designer had obviously been going for such a distinctly oceanic theme and had succeeded tenfold.

The music commenced and Annabel started to dance but kept a close eye on the couple to her left. She saw their lips moving, but still no exclamation. Perhaps her dream had been wrong—just her subconscious at work.

"You dance wonderfully, your grace," Lord Tetra said as they moved closer together.

"As do you," Annabel said with a short grin.

He shook his head. "None can hold a candle to your beauty."

They parted and it took all her willpower not to roll her eyes. She turned on the dancefloor with several other men, following the necessary steps of the dance, before returning to her original dance partner. Lord Tetra reflected on the weather, and she provided the requisite response. As wild as it had ended, Lord Cain had proved to be better company. Lord Tetra by contrast, complimented her appearance thrice more before the music ended.

"I hope you will accept another dance with me," Lord Tetra said, bowing over her hand.

"I would consider it, but you must understand I already have a full evening of obligations." As she made the statement, she caught sight of her cousin bowed over Lady Zerwin's hand. Her legs carried her closer to the couple.

Annabel held her breath at her cousin's words. "You must know I have no other thoughts but of you."

"Even as I am?" Lady Zerwin asked as other dancers looked in their direction.

"You are perfect as you are. Perfect for me," Varen stated, lifting her hand to his lips. "Will you do me the honor in accepting my hand?"

Annabel didn't have to keep listening—she already knew the answer. Worse, now her suspicions had become reality. She was dreaming of the future.

Chapter 10

"Pack those." Annabel pointed to a pile of dresses. "And my warmer cloak. It may still have a chill in the evenings or early mornings."

"You don't see early mornings," Heddie said under her breath. Annabel let it pass because she was right, and she quite enjoyed her maid's sarcastic wit.

Heddie picked up the dresses and placed them into one of her two open traveling trunks. They would be traveling soon to the hunting grounds. Annabel had kept busy with preparations, hoping every night before she closed her eyes not to dream. She didn't want another one to come and after a few days that was, thankfully, the case.

"Princess," Lady Cierra stuck her head around the open door. "You called for me?"

Annabel gestured for her to come in. "Yes, yes, please come in. How is your packing going?"

"Well, my brother is much more organized and has handled most of the arrangements," Lady Cierra replied as she took tentative steps into the room.

"I am glad to hear it, as you shall be joining Lenora and I in our carriage. Lady Zerwin will be with us as well. My sister is busy preparing and bid me

50

invite you." Annabel picked up a green bonnet and set it on the bed to indicate it would come with them. "I hope that is amenable to you."

"Yes, your sister mentioned she hoped we could continue our embroidery exchange," Lady Cierra replied with a twinkle in her eyes. Annabel would never understand their love of such a dull activity but did admire them for it. "I am sure Lady Zerwin will keep us entertained with plans of her coming nuptials."

"My thoughts exactly," Annabel replied with a nod. "Until then."

Lady Cierra made a brief curtsy before she hurried off, likely to pack more ribbons and thread. She really was a darling girl. Content, Annabel resumed packing, making notes of items to follow up on the next day. She'd arranged for a jousting tournament—a forgotten sport that had sounded fun in the history books. She'd prepared a golden arrow as a prize for whoever was crowned King of the Hunt. The menu had been planned, the tents arranged, and the rules finalized. All was in order, and she'd only gotten help on half of it. She would have asked Mayven for more assistance with the Huntsman's Ball but had felt guilty over her stunt at the imperial picnic. A self-imposed punishment seemed better than what her brother may ask of her.

Soon after the Annual Hunting Tournament they'd have a two-day celebration, the Huntsman's Ball. The winner would get her first dance and could claim any dance that followed. She truly hoped it was someone she could stomach.

There was a soft knock, and she looked up to find Dalus at the door. "Brother!" She hugged him as he clapped her on the back. Then she noticed Baltus behind him. "You, too?" She hugged her stiff brother as well, who smiled weakly at her.

"Nearly packed?" Annabel asked.

"We're here to say good-bye. There have been sightings of gremlins past the northern wall. Father has sent us to deal with it," Dalus said pointedly.

Baltus cleared this throat before adding. "We know that this is an important time, but if the gremlins nest before we can root them out, we could have an infestation." He put a hand on her shoulder. "I am sure you understand that we...that is you shall still have Lenora and Mayven to keep you company since we..."

She could tell he was struggling to break the bad news.

"...cannot come?" Annabel shook her head. "Do not worry about me and my silly dances and parties. Saving people is far more important." Then she sighed heavily on purpose. "Though you could make it up to me by taking me along."

Dalus laughed loudly, and Annabel glanced back as Heddie dropped something in the room. Her gaze focused on Heddie, she normally wasn't so clumsy, until Dalus put an arm around her shoulders and squished her against him squeezing the curiosity out of her. She glanced up at him as he beamed happily.

"She'll be fine," Dalus said confidently.

Baltus didn't seem as certain. "Promise me you'll be back by the Masquerade Ball. I'd at least like to spend time with you both during the Season's break." Annabel did her best to reassure him.

"We shall try." Then Baltus kissed her cheek affectionately. "You make a beautiful debutante."

"I already said it was fine," Annabel replied slyly. "I don't need further flattery."

"Princess, what about this?" Heddie asked, holding up the dress her father had commissioned for her birthday.

"Pack it for the Huntsman's Ball," Annabel replied to Heddie before turning back to her brothers. "Since you aren't coming with, I have packing to be done. Off with you both!"

Dalus was already out of the room with Baltus trailing behind. "If all is willing, we'll see you in a few weeks," Baltus said with a slight bow.

Annabel shooed him out playfully, before picking up black pearl pins for her hair. "Add these as well."

"Those will look lovely against your pale locks," Heddie replied, before packing them.

"Are you sure you don't wish to come along?" Annabel asked, now feeling even more forlorn that her brothers wouldn't be there.

"Goodness me, you know I don't travel well." Heddie busied herself with fixing her hair. "Best I manage things here."

"You do handle this well." Annabel indicated around the room with a sigh, wondering how she'd manage without Heddie's tending. "Though I shall miss you."

Heddie harrumphed. "You aren't fooling anyone. You are going to miss that I let you sleep in."

"That is true." Annabel crossed the room and wrapped her arms around her lady's maid's shoulders from behind. "Though I'll also miss the way you make my tea just right."

Heddie patted her arm. "You'll manage."

"It will be a hardship," Annabel replied, resting her chin on Heddie's shoulder. "I do not know how I shall bear it."

"With a few complaints I imagine," Heddie said, letting her hand rest on Annabel's arm.

"More than a few likely." Annabel purposely let out a heavy sigh. "It will at least give me something to look forward to when I return." Then she had a thought. "That and my parents, of course. Though the tea is a close second."

"I am honored," Heddie replied. "Can you promise me something?"

"I won't throw pillows in the morning at the other maids," Annabel conceded.

Heddie chuckled. "Try to have fun."

Annabel felt a sly smile cross her lips. "Don't I always?"

Except maybe on carriage rides. Why in the world hadn't they figured out how to use teleportation carriages like she'd heard Mavrid had? Perhaps her dreams would point her to a way to acquire one. They had figured out how to make teleportation orbs for emergencies, but those only went short distances and could only manage two people at most. Unfortunately, the hatred of being bored to tears in a carriage was not deemed an emergency by anyone but her.

"We've already set a date for next month." Lady Zerwin beamed as she responded to Lady Cierra. Annabel had already heard such news from her brother—plus she'd already seen the ceremony in her dreams.

"We are very happy for you," Annabel replied, sincerely delighted for the couple knowing that they were genuinely fond of each other. Even though she had no intention of walking down the aisle didn't mean she was against that idea entirely. Other people seemed to get great joy from the arrangement.

"I cannot believe it at times, I did not think Lord Varen would ask so quickly," Lady Cierra commented, her eyes lively.

"My cousin is many things; patient is not at the top of the list. Especially when he sets his mind to do something." Annabel laughed. "Do you remember when he decided he'd learn to play the piano?" She asked Lenora.

"He played it for a month straight!" Lenora replied, clapping her hands together. "Your mother was the only one who remained throughout while the rest of us fled."

"The queen is such a kind soul," Lady Zerwin commented.

A thought struck Annabel in that instant. "Join me the next time we have tea. I am sure she will want to meet the soon to be addition to our family."

Lady Zerwin beamed, and Annabel realized how warm she could be. No wonder Varen was quite taken with her. "That would be lovely," she said, shyly.

"And do not worry, you shall have the loveliest of weddings." Annabel could imagine everything from her dream with clarity.

"You say it with such certainty." Lady Zerwin blushed.

Annabel felt daring as she stated, "Perhaps it's because I've seen the future." She widened her eyes for emphasis. Everyone in the carriage erupted in laughter.

As the carriage slowed, Annabel was flooded with relief. She was out the door before the attendant could open it or offer assistance. The summer manor was just as she remembered it. Ivy scaled the walls and the white columns, while massive stairs led up to the veranda and into the beautiful house. Though to call it a house diminished its size. It had twenty bedrooms, three kitchens, a steam room, and a library. Not to mention a music hall, a full ballroom, and a conservatory that abutted a greenhouse.

It was the second largest home the imperial family owned and her favorite. She looked forward to visiting every year when her family hosted the Annual Hunting Tournament and subsequent Huntsman's Ball.

"Annabel!" Lenora called after her before following her out as the stunned footman sprang into action.

Hurrying up the stairs Annabel greeted the servants as she rushed by. "Grandma!" Annabel called when she saw the older woman on the back veranda.

Of all her family, she had always felt a special connection to her father's mother. The former queen was every bit the royal in her fine gown and immaculate presentation. The moment she was called, her face lit up and she slowly stood.

"Ann." Her grandmother opened her arms as Annabel embraced her. "My goodness, how are you, my dear?"

"Nana." She melted into her embrace; the one person who she felt truly understood her. "I missed you."

When Annabel eased back her grandmother captured her chin in her fingers. "I missed you, my dear. It is hard to imagine you have debuted. I swore just yesterday you were sneaking into the stables to feed the horses sugar cubes."

After the former king's death, her grandmother had moved to the countryside. She had settled into managing their summer manor, staying far away from palace life. Annabel once asked her why. Her only response was that she'd had a lifetime's worth of it and desired no more. Spending time at their summer home had been some of her happiest memories thanks to her Nana.

"Are the sugar cubes still hidden on the top shelf?" Annabel asked, with every intention of repeating her earlier antics.

"I am sure they are, Ann." Her grandmother laughed and hugged her again. "Come, delight me with everything that's been happening."

Chapter 11

It was a few hours east to the edge of the Black Forest. At the designated site, the tents had already been assembled and other makeshift buildings, like the stables, were being put to use. Only the royal box remained to be finished, and the stands for the spectator—those waiting to see what quarry the hunters returned with—were still being worked on. She was watching them complete the center box that the royal family would be using. It would be the place they would not only be viewing the proceedings of the hunt, but also the evening's entertainment. Thankfully the two dining tents had been set up, plus a private one for their family. She could only hope that it was enough.

Her ladies-in-waiting were all seeing to the final details, all dressed in their finest riding habits for this sporting event. Annabel was surprised to see Lady Ariah so engaged—she was issuing orders like a seasoned general. What wasn't surprising was Lady Phoebe who was surrounded by a small group of eligible bachelors and from the expression on her face, they were flirting with her.

"How many chairs?" A laborer asked.

"Three," Annabel confirmed; one each for Mayven, Lenora, and her.

"Cousin!" Varen called, with a wave. "I have just signed up for the hunt."

Annabel accepted a kiss on the cheek. "If you are participating, good luck to anyone else. You're the country's finest marksman."

"Coming from you that is a compliment." Varen patted her shoulders, affectionately. "Though there are a fair number of competitors this year. Your brother is seeing to them now, explaining we may not allow everyone to go out at once."

"Even with that many people, I am sure Lady Zerwin shall be queen of the hunt," Annabel laughed, patting his arm, then stopped as she suddenly felt sick to her stomach at the sight of a face that she was all too familiar with. Thankfully, he hadn't seen her yet as he was conversing with her brother, Mayven. She took a shaky step back; the memory of the dream causing her hand to flutter to her throat. She hadn't believed he existed, but now that she'd seen him, she had to admit to herself—Lawrence was real.

"Is something wrong?" Varen asked. "You're as pale as death."

Annabel shook her head. "I just realized I completely forgot something. Please oversee this while I attend to the other matter."

"With pleasure," Varen replied, before turning to the task at hand.

Her legs began to carry her away, first in stilted steps and then at a run once she was sure Varen couldn't see her anymore. The moment she realized she was in the makeshift stables she rushed to mount her horse. Spurring him into a run her horse nearly trampled a man. Her eyes met the surprised Lord Cain. Normally she might have told him off, but she was shaken to the core.

"Princess Annabel?" Lord Cain appeared worried, but Annabel couldn't manage a response.

She kicked her horse into a run, leaning close against his mane as he dashed along the wooded lane. The path cut through the forest, and she followed it until she could breathe again. It didn't matter that night was coming or that it was starting to rain. She needed to feel the sting of the wind on her face to grapple with her rising fear. The rush calmed her, centered her, as she tried to find reason for Lawrence's sudden appearance.

Annabel finally slowed her horse, taking him to a trot as she tried to catch her breath and calm her racing heart. Tipping her head back she closed her eyes and let the rain drench her face. A warm summer shower, that was more a misting, slid down her neck as she inhaled deeply.

Could she have been mistaken? Annabel thought. She'd only gotten a look at him from the side, but she suspected her first assessment was the correct one. Lawrence was real and he was interacting with her family. How much longer would she be able to deny what was right in front of her?

"Princess Annabel?"

Annabel was jolted out of her thoughts at the sound of Lord Cain's voice. He'd come after her in his full armor, including his knight's helmet. He must be participating in the jousting event. If it wasn't for his voice, she wouldn't have recognized him.

"What are you doing here?" Annabel asked, utterly confused.

There was an awkward pause. "You seemed distressed. I thought something might be wrong."

Not yet, but perhaps soon, Annabel thought, wondering if Lawrence was as terrible as her dreams had predicted.

"It's nothing," Annabel replied, hiding behind a stoic expression. "I was just hoping for a moment alone."

"I see." Cain sounded distracted.

"If you'll excuse me, I should return." She dug her heels into the horse forcing him forward. She jerked the reigns to move her mount around the gentleman, and headed back to the camp. She must have pulled too hard on the worn leather, as they suddenly went slack.

Her body kept moving as she screamed and tumbled off the horse. She tried to catch herself, but only succeeded in managing to land on her back, instead of face first. Her vision was blurry as she lay stunned on the ground. She was trying to catch her breath and failing.

Something clanked heavily against the rocks on the ground as she tried to focus. Without warning, there were hands as hard as rocks touching her, and she felt battered and bruised as someone lifted her up. Her head lulled as she tried to remember how to control it. Then, all at once she came back to her senses. When she looked up and saw a very stern Cain, she reacted on impulse.

Her hand pushed against his face as she tried to move away from the odious man. Just as he had at the ball, he jerked away from her, his eyes wild as he took a few stumbling steps back, nearly tripping over his own helmet. She stared in shock at his reaction, his face a mask of horror. Was she truly so terrible? That's when she felt the pain in her back and a sudden rush of emotions caused tears to bubble up. Determined not to cry in front of this hateful man she instead chose an easier emotion—anger.

"You don't have to be so rude," Annabel said, glaring at him as she brushed her hands on her riding pants.

"You aren't afraid?" He asked, confused.

"Why would I be afraid?" Annabel asked, slowly getting to her feet on wobbly legs. When she took a step, she nearly fell, feeling lightheaded from the pain in her leg, and suddenly he was there holding her up.

"What do you see?" Cain whispered, his voice tight.

Annabel fixed her best appraising gaze on him. "An unmitigated ass."

His eyes were assessing her. "Are you not afraid of anything?"

"I don't like bees," Annabel tried to take a step away from his support, but her leg threatened to buckle from the pain. "Or rude men."

"It doesn't work on you?" He sounded bewildered and that caught her attention. She'd never heard him sound so out of sorts, almost human.

Their noses almost touched as she turned back to try to understand. To her shock he brushed his nose against hers on purpose. She blinked as he searched her face, his entire body tensed. It was like he was expecting something to happen.

Realizing what he'd done she reacted to the impropriety and slapped him. Taking a step back, her leg screamed with pain as he caught her arm before she fell. Their eyes met and despite her confusion Annabel laughed. The absurdity of the situation finally caught up with her—this man was the strangest she'd ever encountered. He was making her react in almost barbaric ways because she'd set herself against him for the way he'd snubbed her.

He was looking at her as though she was crazy as he helped her back to her feet. "Are you hurt?" His voice was low, distracted.

"My leg. I can't walk," she admitted.

He whistled loudly and it didn't take long for his black horse to come trotting up. She was about to tell him she had no intention of getting onto another horse when he lifted her up into the saddle with nary a word. He was so caught up in his own thoughts that it was like he wasn't actually there with her.

She watched him retrieve his helmet, and he sent her a hesitant glance back before putting it on. As he strode back over towards her, she realized he was going to mount behind her. She started to shake her head, to protest, but realized the faster they returned, the better for them both. At least she wouldn't have to look at his stupid handsome face.

Chapter 12

"Our first contender for this jousting tournament," the announcer called, his voice booming over the din of the crowd. "Lord Tetra of house Vadimir."

There were scattered cheers and the women chiming dainty bells. Their sound pierced the air with excitement. The announcer waved his arms as though the quiet the group. Annabel glanced at the tent that housed the waiting participants as Lord Tetra made his appearance, his horse was brought to him by a servant.

He bowed in her direction before mounting the horse. Annabel did roll her eyes—one innocent dance and now the man was acting like he had a chance. "How shocking."

Lenora laughed behind her hand as Mayven cleared his throat. "Annabel," he scolded her, though it wasn't pointed.

"His contender," the announcer picked up an envelope at random. "Lord Halic of house Bren."

If Lord Tetra hadn't been on the horse, the man who exited the tent would have dwarfed him. He practically jumped right onto his horse's back. Annabel had not seen Lord Halic at the balls—she would have remembered a man of that size.

"Two coins says Lord Tetra is unhorsed on the first pass." Annabel craned her neck. Jousting hadn't been practiced for a long time—passed over for more equestrian sports over the last century.

"That isn't very sportsman like," Lenora whispered.

"Then it is good that Mayven is the Lord of Honour and not I." Annabel watched with batted breath as the two took their position.

On the first pass the lance struck Tetra's shield and shattered. There were gasps all around as Lord Tetra jerked to the side but stayed mounted. He'd completely missed Lord Halic who went to the end of his side of the tilt. Everyone clapped and a few cheered, Annabel's heart was pounding in her chest.

Annabel frowned. "You should have taken by bet." She had been so sure.

A new lance in hand the two lords faced each other for the next pass. Annabel was perched on the edge of her seat. She was pleased to have put together such an event—every year not all of the Lords participated in the Annual Hunting Tournament. At least this way there was another prize and event for everyone to enjoy.

This time Lord Tetra's lance struck true but so did Lord Halic's. The combined force pushed Lord Tetra off the back of his steed before he landed on the ground with a loud clank. She gave a triumphant cry as others applauded Lord Halic's win.

"Not so loud," Lenora said, glancing around as others eyed their group.

"It's a tournament, it is supposed to be loud," Annabel replied clapping her hands.

Two more were called to the field. She watched the next match, but it came down to points and broken lances. She glanced towards her ladies-in-waiting, to Lady Zerwin's right was Cousin Varen. They all seemed to be enjoying themselves; except for Lady Ariah who had the same look of indifference on her face. Her cousin had opted not to participate, wishing to have all his energy for the hunt. After watching the brutality of the breaking lances, she understood why.

"Lord Cain of the Southern Isles," the announcer called, and Annabel's attention swiveled back. Unlike other armor that was silver, his was black. He was like a walking shadow as he mounted his equally dark horse.

"That is a sight to behold," Mayven said before glancing back. "Do you also wish for him to be unhorsed?"

Annabel felt conflicted—his reaction to her had been bothering her. She suspected more was going on with Lord Cain than she knew. "I've already failed that bet once. You shall not entice me a second time."

The other man had been called and taken his place. They made their first pass and Lord Cain's lance struck true, knocking his opponent from his horse. Cheering rose up and she joined them, impressed at his ability. However, Annabel watched man after man fall to Lord Halic's size and strength. When the last pair was called, she sighed in relief—perhaps the man she'd seen was not Lawrence at all. She refused to ask her brother for fear he'd confirm what she'd seen, and her day would be ruined.

Others were called and they were eventually eliminated by the master jouster. Part of her wished Dalus wasn't busy dealing with monsters in the north—just so someone could best this giant at tilting. As runners picked up the broken pieces from the most recently shattered lance, Annabel settled back in her chair. Others were winning, like Lord Cain, but none had Lord Halic's complete dominance of the list field.

"There cannot be too many left for him to face," Annabel replied.

"Lord Cain is doing well, perhaps he shall prove to be an able challenger," Lenora replied, her hand on the railing as she watched eagerly. "Or Lord Jispen of house Barus. He had won by points many times. He seems very consistent."

"It is too bad Dalus could not be here," Mayven said absentmindedly. Further proof they were siblings.

"There are only three left," Annabel commented when she saw one of the marshals raise the marker indicating the three coins purses would now be claimed.

"Lord Halic," the announcer called him back to the lists. "Shall face Lord Cain."

"It seems we shall see soon enough if he is an able challenger to Lord Halic's strength," Annabel commented.

Despite her comment she waited with bated breath for the first pass. A pair of lances shattered but each man remained mounted. Annabel fanned herself, barely daring to breathe as the field was cleared. Once more they took their blunted sticks and passed a second time, splintered wood rained over them; to their eyes the knight marshal was passing even points. With only one final pass, they may end up tying and then it would come down to Mayven to make the final call as Lord of Honour.

The riders spurred their horses into action. The crowd fell into a tense hush as they all waited on pins and needles for the moment to come. To everyone's shock Lord Halic's lance swung across Lord Cain and acted like a tree branch; catching him in such a way that he was literally pushed off of his horse as the lance exploded from the impact.

Annabel stood as he crashed to the ground, his armor dented slightly from the impact. The marshals were yelling as Lady Cierra screamed and rushed down. Shocked by her lady-in-waiting's reaction she instinctively gripped Mayven's sleeve.

She was calling for them to leave him be as they pulled his helmet off. He was trying to push them off himself. The surprised helpers backed away as Lady Cierra cradled Lord Cain's head in her hands. He was nodding as he held fast to her, her face twisted in concern.

"Call it," Annabel whispered. "Call the match in Lord Cain's favor. That was not a clean strike."

Mayven stood; his voice boomed over the chaos. "Final point tally in favor of Lord Cain."

There was a cheer as Lord Cain gained his feet. He glanced in their direction, clearly still stunned by his fall. He leaned slightly on his sister as the Van Brandt siblings approached their box.

Lord Cain's armor hung loose off of him, his hair was wild around his face and dripping with sweat. "I concede the match to Lord Jispen who is the only remaining competitor." All eyes turned to Mayven, to see if such a statement would be upheld.

"It seems we have a winner!" Mayven called lifting his arms. "Lord Jispen, come claim your prize."

The crowd cheered as Lenora stood. She joined the men on the field as the three drawstring bags were carried over by a servant. She presented each of them as their names were called. Lady Cierra took Lord Cain's winnings before the pair retreated. Annabel had a nose for secrets, and she suspected Lord Cain had a big one. The only question remained in what manner she would sus it out.

Chapter 13

"Two hours remaining," an attendant announced outside the private dining tent.

She'd kept scanning the faces of the crowd, but Lawrence had yet to appear again. Her brother had too many duties to attend to as the crown prince, so she'd been unable to ask about his interaction with Lawrence. Though if she was being honest, she was stalling. Now that he'd appeared that first dream mattered more than ever, every detail and word. None of that mattered until he tried something; but if her dream was right, he would try to court her.

Yet despite that she'd been playing the conversation with Lord Cain in her head over and over again. Remembering Lady Cierra's strong reaction to others trying to help her brother. The more she thought of it, the more she was certain it was a mystery and not a foretold tragedy. Not to mention the dream she'd had where it indicated they'd overcome their differences at some point. Perhaps that was why she was hiding in their family's private dining tent, picking at her lunch, when she should have been in their box, verbally congratulating the hunters as they returned. The healer had seen to her leg from when she'd fallen from the horse, so there wasn't any excuse for her hermit-like behavior.

Not to mention she wasn't sure how she'd manage to handle Lawrence if she bumped into him by accident. She stabbed at a particularly slippery blueberry with more gusto than was needed. If only she could have a moment alone with her brother!

Mayven plopped down next to her like she'd summoned him out of thin air. Was that an innate ability siblings had? To feel a disturbance in their countenance and appear like magic? Or perhaps that was exclusive to her brother since he'd been doing it most of her life.

"I'm starved," Mayven said as he waved a servant over. "Has anyone returned yet?"

"Only a few lesser lords," Annabel replied, though she couldn't recall much at all since she'd been so absorbed with her thoughts and been hiding the better part of an hour.

"Our cousin was in the lead last I'd heard." Mayven picked up his fork as the servant set a plate down in front of him.

"That's good news. No doubt Lady Zerwin will be named Queen of the Hunt if that is the case—how romantic." Annabel let her voice trail off.

Mayven nodded as he was handed a letter from his attendant. "I am sure that will be a relief to you since you are fond of them both."

"I am indeed." Annabel set her fork down since she was just picking at her food. "By the way who was that man you were speaking to earlier?" Annabel asked, trying to appear only partially interested.

"Which one?" Mayven asked as he picked the blueberries off his plate.

Annabel waved her hand close to her head. "With the pretty blond hair."

"Lord Haywood?" Mayven asked.

Annabel's heart was hammering wildly in her chest. "Yes, how do you know him?"

"He's visiting in place of his father, Viscount Haywood," Mayven replied, his gaze suddenly direct. "Why?"

"No reason." Annabel shrugged. "I just didn't recognize him, and I know most of the courtiers. Is he also competing?"

"In fact, he is," Mayven's eyes narrowed. "You seem upset. Did something happen with him?"

Annabel blinked in surprise—she would have to be more cautious when dealing with her brother. She forced a laugh out of her that was meant to disarm him. "Goodness no, I haven't even met the man. You are becoming as terrible as Mother. Imagining attachments that aren't even there." She leaned over and patted his shoulder. "Rest assured that is the furthest notion from my mind. Actually, I didn't like the look of him."

Mayven's expression was serious a moment before it softened. "Don't be too harsh until you meet him. He seems like a nice enough fellow. Charming even."

Annabel leaned back in her chair and crossed her legs. "Yes, well so did Lord Cain and we know how that turned out."

"The final hunters are returning," Lenora said, craning her neck.

Annabel gripped the golden arrow tightly when she saw Lawrence Haywood come in with a wagon. She could see a crown of antlers signifying a large elk and a massive wolf. She was staring so intently at him at their eyes briefly met. Annabel held her breath as he smiled; it would have been captivating if not for the dream that had forewarned her of his true nature.

Averting her gaze, she scanned the rest of those returning and their prizes. Then she saw her cousin coming up the rear with two beautiful white-tailed deer. It was very likely that those magnificent beasts would be enough to take the prize away from Lawrence...Lord Haywood but it would be close. It would come down to their marksmanship.

"Five minutes," the announcer called and then played the hunting horn to signal time was running out.

"My lady," Varen stopped before the box where Lady Zerwin was seated. "I present all of my winnings to you."

A soft blush touched Lady Zerwin's cheeks and made her seem less severe. It was amazing how the power of love could alter someone so much. Many expressed their excitement and adoration for his gesture. They were turning out to be the love story of the season.

"Princess Annabel." Her blood ran cold at the sound of his voice. She slowly turned around to face the man from her nightmares. "As the honored lady, it is only right that I present these trophies to you."

Her throat was suddenly dry as she tried to gather her wits. She should have seen this coming—no doubt this is what began their relationship. She could see how, if she'd had no prior knowledge, someone like him defying the rules might have charmed her. With him, though, it just sickened her.

"Though I am flattered," her voice sounded so hoarse that she had to clear it and repeat her words before continuing. "It defies the rules."

There was an awkward moment where Lord Haywood seemed shocked by her response. He cleared his throat. "Here I thought you would waive the rules." He seemed uncomfortable; good. She wanted him to squirm like the worm he was.

"Not for a man I don't know," Annabel kept her tone cold; she didn't want to give him even a hair of wiggle room. "I suggest, sir, you look elsewhere, as your...gifts are wasted here." As were his attentions.

He blinked and then glanced to her right. Lenora gripped her arm and whispered, "You are causing a scene."

There were suddenly murmurs all around them as someone approached from the forest. Annabel swallowed as the armored man approached. In his hand was a white furred creature that Annabel couldn't make out. Yet she recognized that armor—since she'd rode on a horse with it only a day earlier.

"Is that a white fox?" Mayven whispered, glancing behind him to his attendant.

A white fox? Annabel couldn't believe her ears. They were legendary and impossible to hunt. How had Lord Cain managed it?

"Princess Annabel." Lord Cain bowed. "May you accept this kit as an apology for any disservice I have done to you."

A baby? He'd killed a baby fox? Annabel felt outraged until he lifted up his arm and the animal let out a yip and tried to scurry free from its ties. She shot up, dumping the arrow into Lenora's lap as she hurried to the field. As she approached Lord Cain pushed up the visor on his helmet.

In his armor he struck an imposing figure. The kit dangling in his hand had quieted, its feet folded under its body. She flipped her shawl around and held it out for the creature. Bundling it up she glanced up at Lord Cain who had waited patiently for her.

The whole field was quietly waiting on her. "I accept. On all counts." Annabel glanced at Lord Haywood before responding. "There are no rules on my acceptance of living animals. Only those hunted."

"It is rather unorthodox, but such a rare find, living or not, leaves me no other choice," Mayven declared before motioning Lenora forward. "With the hunt ended, I declare Lord Cain, King of the Hunt. Lady Zerwin, I name Queen of the Hunt. Congratulations to all those who participated."

Lord Cain hesitated before taking the arrow from Lenora who had to lean over the side to present it. He glanced at Annabel who curtsied to him. Despite her best efforts, Annabel glanced at Lord Haywood expecting to find outrage—instead she only found a stunned man who was utterly perplexed. Struggling to keep the smugness off her face—Annabel instead hugged the kit closer to her chest and rocked him back and forth. Today had turned out to be a very good day indeed.

Chapter 14

Annabel was draped over a branch reading a book, her head lulling to the side as she stared blankly at the page. She had come here often as a child when her siblings and cousins were being too loud, and she wanted a moment to read or think. It had been the strangest day yesterday. For some reason she couldn't get his reaction out of her head. Now that she'd calmed down about Lawrence's appearance, Annabel couldn't stop thinking about her odd encounter with Lord Cain. Why had he expected her to be afraid of him? He hadn't been asking out of a possibly but a sense of certainty that something was going to terrify her. What secret could he possibly have that would make him react like that?

She knew she should be focusing on Lawrence and how best to deal with him, but she'd bought herself some time. No doubt her future had already been changed by her open rejection of his attempt to win her favor. In a way she should thank Lord Cain for his unintended assistance. It had proven to be a meaningful diversion from Lord Haywood's attempts and a successful avoidance of having her first dance with Lawrence. Not to mention her darling pet fox that was presently being cleaned and inspected by the animal handler. Now she need only think of a name.

71

"Princess Annabel," Lady Cierra's voice suddenly and sharply broke through her thoughts.

When she glanced up, she was startled to see Lady Cierra approaching with Lord Cain. Momentarily forgetting her unladylike position over the branch, she attempted to lean back, lost her balance, and fell backwards the short distance to the ground. She was lying on her back looking up at the canopy of trees when Lady Cierra's concerned face hovered over hers, it was shortly joined by Lord Cain's. Why did she keep making a fool of herself in front of him? It was like the entire universe was transpiring against her. Rather rude of it, really.

"I didn't mean to startle you," Lady Cierra said, sounding concerned. "I called your name a few times."

Two sets of hands appeared to help her up. Annabel ignored Lord Cain's offered gloved hand and took Lady Cierra's. Her back and hips protested from a second jostling in as many days, but she managed well enough.

"What did you need?" Annabel asked, putting some distance between them as she retrieved her book from the ground.

The Van Brandt siblings exchanged a knowing glance, as though they were communicating about something that was between them. Annabel crossed her arms as they came to a consensus and finally turned to her.

"We weren't entirely truthful about the reason Cain came here," Lady Cierra said as Lord Cain averted his eyes. "My brother was set to inherit the dukedom, but…was cursed."

"Cursed?" Annabel eyed Lord Cain who appeared characteristically solemn.

"Whenever someone not of my blood comes into direct contact with my skin, they see their greatest fear," Lord Cain explained, awkwardly. "That is…until you."

Annabel frowned. Curses weren't unheard of, but they were rare. Though it would explain his behavior—why he kept people at arm's length. "Then we need to test it. To make sure it wasn't a fluke." She held out her hand.

Cain appeared uncomfortable for a moment as he glanced around before shaking his head. "We're too exposed here."

Then he stared at her hand, and she saw a flicker of hope. Suddenly, all of his rudeness was forgotten in the face of that kind of desperate want. How long had he suffered?

"If you react everyone will come running," Lady Cierra added, examining the area around them. "Is there somewhere we can go?"

Annabel glanced back at the summer manor that was barely visible through the trees. She scanned the grounds before nodding. "Perhaps the old, abandoned church."

"Lead the way!" Lady Cierra said, taking her brother's arm in one of her own and reaching out for Annabel with the other. After a moment's hesitation, she took the offered arm—linking them together in a sort of awkward chain. She noticed Lord Cain was not as formally dressed with only an ornately embroidered vest over his white shirt.

"Where to?" Lord Cain asked, clearing his throat.

"Across the clearing to that road there." Annabel pointed towards the tree line in front of them.

Lady Cierra was practically skipping between them as they walked across the well-maintained grass. For some reason, Annabel felt uncomfortable being so close to him with only his sister between them. It didn't help that she was internally groaning as she thought of all their interactions and realized that the recent revelation rewrote them all. It made her feel petty and even childish— not a sensation she enjoyed or was familiar with. Typically, she was very intentional when she was being immature.

Her guilt gnawed uncomfortably as the awkward silence grew. "It may not mean anything, but I apologize for my...behavior," Annabel finally said. She glanced at his shocked expression and felt her cheeks burn that he found it so surprising.

Lady Cierra elbowed her brother who cleared his throat. "If anything, it is my actions that need your forgiveness."

"It is given," Annabel replied. "I had thought you knew that from my acceptance of your gift."

Lady Cierra was smiling widely between them as they reached the tree line. Annabel waved off her guard when he began to follow them—she couldn't completely get rid of him, but at least they could have a moment of privacy. They would assume she was just giving them a tour of the old church—it was famous for how long it had existed.

"This way," Annabel said pointing down the path. Through the trees the stone ruins could just be seen. As they approached, the sun shone off the broken stained glass at the top of the caved in bell tower.

"My guard is following us," Annabel said, although she suspected Lord Cain was already alerted to his presence. "Lady Cierra, I'll take your brother within to show him, while you stay outside in the doorway to keep watch."

Lady Cierra nodded. When they reached the church Annabel let go of her arm and entered first. The air was stagnant with half rotted, forgotten furniture and decaying leaves that had found their way in over the years. She paused once inside the dimly lit area before Lord Cain ducked through the doorway.

"What if it was a fluke?" Lady Cierra said, sounding nervous.

"Tell them I saw a bee," Annabel replied before turning the corner to where the side chamber was, which just blocked the view of her from the doorway.

Lord Cain appeared uncomfortable, but she held a hand aloft. "Are you more afraid that I won't have a reaction or that I will?"

"I don't know," he replied while slowly taking off his glove. He put his hand over hers without touching, she could see how conflicted he was.

Before he could react, she clasped onto his wrist. He jerked back his eyes wide, but she just waited, his warm hand resting against her forearm. After a few tense moments of silence, Annabel shook her head. Relief flooded his features as his fingers curled around her arm.

"You are immune," Lord Cain said in wonder. "Why?"

"I have no idea. I want to help you, but I don't even know how I'm doing this," Annabel said with a sigh.

Cain's eyebrows arched in surprise. "Just like that? You'll help me?"

"I may seem silly to you, but I am not heartless. You have suffered greatly and if there is anything I can do to ease your suffering, I would do it." Annabel met his gaze with determination. She needed to rewrite their relationship, she knew it would take time, but it was only a matter of will.

When she went to pull her hand away, he held fast. "It seems I have more to atone for. I misjudged you and for that I am sorry."

"We have done plenty to mischaracterize each other. I am glad to get a new start." Annabel glanced at their joined hands. "But perhaps we should start with you returning my hand to me."

He seemed surprised before releasing her and taking a step back. "Forgive me. It has been a long time since I've…felt another person I was not related to. I overstepped."

"I do not mind," Annabel replied, honestly no longer repulsed by him since learning of his hardships. "But the guard who will soon check on me will. I would not want to give them reason to report any impropriety to my father. That is something my father will not overlook. Even for me."

"Then we should return." He held his arm out, indicating she should lead the way.

Annabel walked past him, but then paused and turned back. "How long have you had your…affliction?"

There was a flash of pain in his eyes before he masked it. The words were tight, almost whispered when he responded. "Eleven years."

Chapter 15

Annabel was in a daze as she sat at tea with her grandmother and Lenora. She'd been thinking about the eleven years that he'd suffered, and it made her heart hurt. She understood his anguish more than he'd ever know. Her thoughts turned to her mother and how she had become a broken person. Damaged by one mistake.

Suddenly a hand was on her arm. "Ann?" Her grandmother appeared worried.

"Did you say something, Nana?" Annabel asked, realizing she'd been lost in her thoughts and hadn't been paying attention.

"I only asked if you were happy with the outcome of the hunt," her grandmother said, shifting towards her. "It has been a long time since I've seen such a solemn expression on your face. What has happened, my dear?"

Annabel shook her head. "Just a lot to think about. I am sure I've forgotten some detail for the ball tomorrow." She had no intention of revealing Cain's secret to anyone.

"Lady Zerwin, Lady Cierra, and I all checked, and found nothing needing to be followed up on," Lenora assured her. "You have seemed morose. Is it because of Lord Cain?" For a moment Annabel was startled at her sister's astute deduction, until she added. "He seemed repentant; I do not believe he'll be offensive again."

"Offensive?" Her grandmother asked, her voice already with an edge of outrage. "What kind of offense did he give?"

"It was a misunderstanding," Annabel said quickly, not wishing anyone to think ill of Lord Cain for a condition he couldn't control. "I am certain it will never happen again. I was partially at fault for being so unaware."

Lenora's eyebrows rose at her words. "That is very…mature of you."

"Who is this Lord Cain?" Their grandmother finally interjected. "Anyone of consequence?"

"He's Lady Cierra's brother. She's one of my ladies-in-waiting," Annabel explained, feeling suddenly conspicuous. She waved a hand as though to ward away all negative thoughts. "He's a noble from the Southern Isles."

"Ah, the dark-skinned girl. She seemed sweet," their grandmother replied.

"We both like her," Lenora agreed with their grandmother's assessment.

"Though Lady Zerwin seems very capable. A good match for your cousin. His good sense comes and goes with the wind, but it seems she might be of heartier stock," her grandmother said before taking a sip of tea.

Annabel sighed. "My mother has spoken of little else. The sparkle in her eye was very intentional for Mayven and me. Most likely she shall begin searching for a match for Mayven."

"Still no interest in anyone?" Her grandmother asked.

"Just his love of paper," Annabel replied with a shrug.

Lenora frowned. "We have not had an arranged marriage in some time. Not since the first queen."

Lenora's mother and hers were both love matches. Their father had married Lenora's mother fairly quickly after the first queen had passed. After she'd died, it took well over a year, and some pushing from the noblemen, before her father considered a third match for himself. That was when her mother had come of age. She was much younger than him and yet they seemed so naturally happy that Annabel had never questioned it.

"And what of you, my dear. The same?"

"You know marriage is not part of the plan," Annabel said firmly.

"It is rare that everything goes perfectly according to plan," her grandmother countered with a wag of her finger. "For your sake I hope it doesn't. And you, Lenora?"

Annabel smirked. "I am sure there is someone who has caught your attention."

Lenora wrinkled her nose. "It was a flirtation, nothing more. Though I am very hopeful to find a love match soon. Perhaps even at the Huntsman's Ball." Her eyes were shining, and for just a moment, Annabel wanted that—that easy hope for more—without the guilt.

"What theme did you select in the end?" Her grandmother asked, sipping her tea daintily.

"Starlight," Annabel replied. "Tomorrow's ball shall take everyone's breath away."

Annabel was reading a letter from her sister, Yenni, who was busy making preparations in the capital for the Solstice Festival. Annabel felt a sting of remorse at not making more time for her and vowed to do so when she returned. Thankfully the festival was the last major event for a few weeks. A nice reprieve that Annabel planned to take full advantage of.

The door opened and the attendant announced. "Lord Cain."

Setting the letter down, Annabel straightened on the couch. She'd lost track of time and hadn't expected him yet. Straightening her skirts as he entered, she took note of his reserved manners. He likely hadn't put together why she'd requested his presence.

"I hope I have not inconvenienced you by asking you to come from town." Annabel gestured to the seat across from her. "Tea?"

"No, thank you." Lord Cain waved off the tea before sitting down stiffly.

"Are you recovered from the joust?" Annabel asked, pouring a cup for herself. It didn't even steam when it entered the cup, but she hoped it still had some warmth.

"It was only a minor inconvenience," he responded stiffly, his eyes appraising.

"It is best if we have a plan of action in place," Annabel said, adding some sugar before stirring.

"Regarding...?"

She tapped the spoon on the side of the teacup with a clink. "The dance. You are the King of the Hunt and as such you and I shall have to partake in that first dance. There are traditions to uphold after all." Annabel brought the cup to her lips so she could hide her smile behind the rim. The tea was over steeped and bitter, so she set it aside.

The way his face contorted into surprise nearly made her laugh aloud. "It is necessary?"

"Mandatory, I'm afraid. We have managed to dance once before," Annabel replied before standing to gather a pile of four books from the end table. "I believe it will be to our advantage if we appear to be...preoccupied with each other."

His eyes narrowed as she set the books down in front of him on the shorter table. "Preoccupied, as in courting?"

"It will make researching and spending time together appear less...suspicious. Plus, less suitors are apt to bother me, which pleases me to no end." Annabel put her hand on top of the stack of books as she sat down next to him. "These are all the books I could find on curses and magic. There are a few kept here that you will likely not find in the imperial library. Mostly those that are considered too salacious to keep close at hand, therefore, they may prove more insightful than others. Unfortunately, I cannot permit them to leave the grounds, but you are welcome to read them now and then come again tomorrow before we depart."

"You want me to pretend to be courting you so that we can research my curse?" Lord Cain asked, shaking his head in astonishment. "I do not understand. Are you that opposed to marriage?"

"I am averse to its...restricting nature," Annabel replied with a smirk. "Do not be concerned, I have no desire to marry anyone. Thus, this entire farce shall only serve to give us privacy."

79

After a moment he shifted to face her. "You shall need a chaperone once it is made known this evening. Will that not hamper our endeavors?"

"I thought you more astute than that," Annabel replied laying her hands in her lap.

She saw the light in his eyes as he lifted his chin. "My sister."

"Who else but one of my lady's-in-waiting?" Annabel felt pride in her plan. "It shall work perfectly."

His gloved hand touched the top of the books as he seemed to be reading their spines. "Why all of this effort?" Lord Cain asked, his voice hushed. "I offended you in a way that should not have garnered your favor."

"Now that I know the cause of it, how could I not?" Annabel wondered what kind of life he had led to make him so unwilling to accept her help at face value. "Besides, your imitation courtship shall relieve me of the pressures of the season. So, if it comforts you, think of it as a good turn."

The genuine nature of the following smile caught her unawares. The entire manner of his face was transformed in that instance. The ache of the thought of how acutely he must have borne the loneliness and fear, brought a newfound closeness to this man. It seemed once more her dream was correct.

"Very well," Lord Cain said before tipping his head to her.

Annabel clasped her hands together and brought them against her breasts. "So, what dance shall we do to cement our plan?"

Chapter 16

Candles of every size flickered under glass containers. Holes around the base ensured the flames stayed lit while protecting the decorations from damage and the air from smoke. The soft glow filled the entire garden and the greenhouse. Already the area was filling with guests as Annabel peered out from behind a curtain. The soft melody of a pair of cellos filled the air, setting the scene with their deep tones.

Crystals hung from the trees and navy-blue ribbons were set against gems that caught the light and twinkled. Annabel's fingers trailed over the beads of her own dress, knowing that she would shimmer with every step as the bottom of her dress was as black as the night sky.

Lady Cierra appeared suddenly, her face pale. "What is it?" Annabel asked, drawing her closer.

"Lady Zerwin's dress was...destroyed." She seemed shaken as she spoke.

"Destroyed how?"

"Shredded," Lady Cierra replied, tears glistening in her eyes. "Who would do such a thing?"

81

Annabel gripped her shoulders. "Go and tell Lady Zerwin to come to my room. I have a solution. Do you think you can manage that?"

Lady Cierra nodded. "Yes."

"Good, go," Annabel said, pushing her back towards the door as she followed her into the hall.

Making off in the other direction, Annabel went to the one person who could help. Lenora was overseeing the final preparations for dinner and laughing with the cook at something she'd said.

"Sister," Annabel called out as she lifted her long dress to come down the few steps into the massive kitchen. "I have need of your help."

"Excuse me," Lenora said before coming closer. "What is it?"

"I need your needle and thread. Lady Zerwin's dress is damaged, between you and Lady Cierra, I hope it can be mended," Annabel whispered, knowing full well it was sabotage.

"That's terrible," Lenora replied, already moving into action. "I shall get my sewing kit posthaste."

Annabel followed her from the kitchen, moving with her as they made their way towards the royal wing. Her grandmother stayed on the first floor, but the upper wing towards the back of the house that overlooked the sprawling grounds, and lake had been used for many generations. The decorations depicted a long line, all the way back to the usurper.

"You should let me tend to the dress, otherwise you'll be late," Lenora said as they climbed the stairs. "My dance with Lord Jispen is after yours with Lord Cain."

"I'm going out with all my ladies-in-waiting, late or not. Especially since she is the Queen of the Hunt." Annabel didn't care about what everyone thought, only that Lady Zerwin would not be left behind. "If they are gentleman, then they shall understand."

"I am sure it will not waylay us long," Lenora replied as they turned the corner to enter the hallway of the royal wing.

Lady Cierra was coming down the hallway towards them, a red nosed Lady Zerwin leaning into her. Lady Zerwin had a handkerchief pressed against her lips and Annabel could see the tear trails and her defeated posture—Lady

Cierra had likely under assessed the damage. It was horrible to see the normally unflappable Lady Zerwin so distraught. Then she saw the dress Lady Cierra was carrying—saw how tattered it was. Who would do something so cruel?

There would have to be an inquiry with the maids. Her grandmother would handle it, but this area was not restricted. I could have been anyone. Though if she was to wager a guess, Lady Pheobe would be at the top of that list.

"In here," Annabel said, putting her arm around Lady Zerwin as Lenora opened the door. "We'll get it mended."

"It's ruined," Lady Zerwin wailed, turning against Annabel as she cried on her shoulder. "The dress Varen gifted me is ruined."

Annabel patted her back and hugged her, understanding why she was upset. Something like that shouldn't happen, there shouldn't be any animosity amongst anyone and yet there they were. It vexed her but now was not the time for her to lose her temper—at least not yet.

Lady Cierra and Lenora were speaking in hushed tones as they inspected the dress. Annabel could see them holding up sections of ripped fabric. She didn't like how often they were shaking their heads as they moved the fabric one way and then another. In her heart Annabel knew it was a lost cause. There was only one thing to do.

"Cierra," Annabel dropped the formality, hoping her lady-in-waiting understood the urgency of her request. "Go to my floral chest and pull out the blue dress."

Lady Cierra moved quickly to comply as Lady Zerwin matted her face with the already damp handkerchief. "Is it fixable?" Lady Zerwin asked, sniffling.

Lenora opened her mouth, but Annabel shook her head, cutting her off. "Don't worry about that. My sister is going to take your measurements and we're going to make sure everything is right as rain." Annabel ushered her towards her sister as Lady Cierra carried the blue dress over.

"Here it is," Lady Cierra said, holding up the dress. "What do you want me to do with it?"

"We're going to take the under layer from this dress and stitch it up underneath to make it a full-length dress. With its adjustable waist and separate skirt, we should be able to modify it to her size. What do you think?" Annabel asked, trying to keep her voice quiet in case it wouldn't work.

Lady Cierra inspected the two dresses, looking back and forth as she rolled her bottom lip between her teeth. Finally, after a few suspenseful moments she nodded. "I think I can manage that pretty quickly."

"Good. Do whatever needs to be done and don't worry about destroying this dress to make it fit her," Annabel said, patting her arm before joining the other two. "All done?"

"I have 30 on the waist and I'm done," Lenora said, as she stood. "Have a plan?"

"Lady Cierra will fill you in, do your best Len, we'll be back," Annabel said, linking her arm with Lady Zerwin. She led her out of the door and down the hall. "Which room is yours?"

Lady Zerwin pointed to the one on the right as she sniffled, seeming calmer. "I'm with Lady Cierra."

Annabel marched them to the room and immediately sat her down. "Let's get you cleaned up, wash all the sadness away and rewrite all those tears."

Lady Zerwin chuckled. "Why are you being so kind?"

Annabel put her hand on her shoulders. "You're going to be family and you shall find this is what our family does. Now clear that nose and let's get to work."

"Ready?" Annabel asked, her arm linked with Lady Zerwin to show her support. She would not have anything else go awry.

"Thanks to you, I am." Lady Zerwin shined with newfound confidence.

The tea length blue dress now had a gathering with the lace from her dress that cascaded down like a shimmering waterfall. There were a few layers of lace underneath and a darker blue fabric that looked like it had always been there. It truly had turned out stunning.

They could all wait as long as necessary as far as she was concerned — Annabel had other matters to settle. No one harassed her lady's-in-waiting;

they were hers to protect, and she would do so with vigor. She may not wish to debut, but she had grown fond of them, well most of them, and they didn't deserve such negative attention.

The crowd turned to them as they entered. From their surprised expressions Annabel knew that the stunning dresses with their elaborate adornments had the desired effect. They approached the center of the room as a group approached them.

"Your dress is stunning, your highness," a woman in a bright pink dress said.

"Lady Zerwin, who designed your dress? It is exquisite," Lady Kadence said, one of the most prominent women in the region.

"Friends of mine," Lady Zerwin replied, beaming as she shared a knowing glance with Annabel. "It is one of a kind."

"It is remarkable to be sure," Lady Kadence said, fanning herself.

That is when Annabel saw Lord Cain approaching them. She stiffened for a moment, realizing belatedly she'd kept him waiting without a word of explanation. How thoughtless of her!

"Your grace," — Lord Cain extended a gloved hand — "I believe we are keeping everyone waiting."

He didn't seem at all displeased with her and she let out the breath she'd been holding. Putting her hand into his, she acquiesced to his request. "We must rectify the situation."

"With haste," Lord Cain replied, and she thought she caught a slight grin before he turned to lead her to the dance floor.

Once they were in position, the music started. They moved slowly, almost too close for what was proper if the dance hadn't called for it. It was a popular dance from the Southern Isles, known for its romantic undertones. A perfect pick for their plan.

"You're late," Lord Cain said as they moved effortlessly through the slow portion of the dance. "I thought you might have reconsidered."

"There was a...mishap with a dress," Annabel explained as they parted, and the tempo increased slightly before they drew close once more.

"All is well now?" Lord Cain asked, genuinely concerned.

Annabel was surprised at how…warm he appeared. For a moment she saw what Lady Cierra meant—the curse had altered this man so completely he was hardly recognizable from who he used to be. She felt in her heart he had not always been so solemn and for the first time, Annabel liked what she saw.

"Yes…" Annabel let the word trail off, nearly tripping over the next few dance moves.

When they shifted and dipped through the next set, Annabel focused on the steps. It was a traditional dance, but she was out of practice. She wanted to explain further, even apologize, but was more afraid she'd make a fool of herself.

"You're nervous." Lord Cain chuckled into her ear; one set of their arms almost fully extended as they tipped their heads away from each other.

"Woefully out of practice," Annabel replied as they switched sides.

"We both are," Lord Cain responded, and for the first time she realized he seemed to be relishing their dance. It struck a chord with her; he was acting hopeful and alive. Was this the real Cain?

Their noses almost touched as the music ended. "You seemed to manage just fine."

"Thanks to you," his voice was low, and it made Annabel's heart thud in her chest. Then he took a step away from her before lifting her fingers towards his face. He hesitated only a moment before she felt the brush of his lips across her knuckles.

"May I take other slots on your dance card?" Cain asked.

Annabel lifted her other arm where her dance card dangled from her wrist. "You may have them all."

There was a gasp behind her, and murmurs sprung up at her words—dances more than three were liable to indicate an engagement. No one would ever believe that this exchange was borne from an arrangement. Even Annabel had to admit she was having fun—this Cain was far more enjoyable than the somber one she'd first met. He was more like his sister than she'd originally supposed.

"Shall we?" He asked, offering his arm.

She took it, a feeling of triumph spreading through her. "We shall." She nodded to Lenora who joined Lord Jispen as she passed by, noting her sister's stunned expression.

Chapter 17

Annabel clapped as they finished another dance. She took Lord Cain's arm as they left the dance floor together. Hours had passed since their first dance, and yet they had all been as enjoyable. She was finding a friend in Cain, furthermore, he was proving to be an amusing ally.

"I thought Lady Gwenie was quite taken with you," Annabel said, trying to keep her lips from curling into a smile.

"She was rather vocal." Cain shot her a coy look. "I thank you for insisting on taking her spot."

"I did promise you all of my dance slots." Annabel leaned in close as she spoke, going up on her tiptoes. "This arrangement shall prove advantageous for us both. I believe we have everyone fooled."

Cain nodded before turning his head towards her and leaning equally as close. "Thank you for suggesting it."

As she settled back on her heel, her laughter died in her throat. Lord Haywood was speaking to her brother. Would he try something here? Her brother and cousin were the most logical first targets.

"Princess?" Cain asked, concerned. She'd gripped his arm harder than she'd intended to on instinct when she'd spotted Lawrence.

"I'll explain later," Annabel whispered, "I just need to interfere."

She went to pull away, but his hand clasped over hers, stopping her from doing so. His gaze moved from the two men, before going back to her. "I'll go with you."

Relieved, Annabel nodded as she tried to calm herself. It would do no good to give herself away. There were other ways to get rid of unwanted people.

Marching over to them, Annabel forced a smile onto her face. "Brother, you seem to have made a new friend."

"Oh yes, Lord Haywood was just explaining his plans to visit the capital," Mayven explained. "Lord Haywood, my sister Princess Annabel, Annabel, this is Lawrence Haywood."

Annabel lifted her hand. "Charmed."

Lord Haywood bowed over it. "Might I say that you are breathtaking in that dress?"

"You may say it, as many others have done so tonight," Annabel purposely snubbed him in a subtle way, most would not notice. "What business brings you to the capital, Lord Haywood?"

He seemed uncertain, like her very words unnerved him. Good, whatever plans he had, she fully intended to sever them. The easiest way to keep him far away from her family was by showing an outward, but subtle disdain for him. Her brother would recognize it, and he valued her opinion on people, even if he'd never admit it. No doubt Lord Haywood had used that to his advantage when he'd courted her. Her siblings would all follow their brother, if he didn't make Lawrence welcome, neither would they.

"My father had business in the capital that I shall now tend to. I was just discussing the best places to visit with the crown prince, but perhaps you would have better insight," Lawrence's grin should have been charming but to Annabel it was just sinister.

"Have you never been to the capital before?" Annabel asked, pinning him in place with her gaze.

"Only once, long ago," Lawrence replied, his smile becoming more strained.

"The city itself offers many interesting distractions," Annabel said, waving a dismissive hand. "Why, just outside the city is Bunker Hill, excellent views of the city." That was far enough away that he'd have to travel a good distance to see it. Plus, it was known to rain there in the afternoons—perhaps he would get drenched.

"I see." Lawrence's voice trailed off before he turned to Mayven. "I shall take you up on your offer to visit the palace while I am in the capital."

Mayven was staring at Annabel and was slow to respond. "Certainly."

"I do hope we'll have time." Annabel held fast to Cain's arm. "Our schedule is so full you see."

Lord Haywood shifted before bowing. "May you think of me should a free moment arise."

Annabel's grip tightened on Cain's arm on impulse as her stomach clenched. "Are you thirsty?" Cain asked, leaning close.

"Yes. I'm parched from all the dancing," Annabel replied, purposely turning away to dismiss Lawrence.

"It would be my pleasure to get it for you." Cain glanced up at her brother. "Excuse me, crown prince."

"Brother," Annabel said, shifting to take his arm, still ignoring Lawrence. "What do you think of my decorations?"

Mayven took the hint and turned them around, pointing at the hanging crystals. "They are quite lovely. The theme was aptly selected."

Annabel peered over her shoulder to confirm Lord Haywood was gone. She could see his back as he retreated into the crowd. Only then did she let out a sigh of relief. The worse part as he walked away was Annabel had to admit that he would have easily charmed her in the past. His bending of the rules, witty remarks, and attention would have been enough to have her interested. Once her family started to pass away one by one, his comfort would have made her blind to everything that was wrong. She knew in that instant, if she hadn't dreamt how horrible he was, he would have wormed his way in.

"Why the sudden change?" Mayven asked.

"It isn't sudden, I disliked Lord Haywood from the first if you'll recall," Annabel said, facing forward. "Do not bring him to the palace."

"I was speaking about Lord Cain," Mayven replied, jostling her shoulder affectionately.

"Oh!" Annabel felt silly that her entire focus had been on Lawrence. "We've made amends and found we have quite a bit in common."

Mayven eyed her closely. "This isn't some ploy?"

"If it was, do you think I'd ever admit it?" Annabel replied, being purposely cheeky though their conversation with Lawrence had left her a little shaken.

"No, but I hope for your sake that it isn't. You both seem happier with each other, ruse or not, the first I've seen you that way with any man who wasn't family," Mayven commented as Cain weaved through the crowd, drinks in hand.

"Perhaps," Annabel replied as she took in Cain's striking figure as he approached. "Only time will tell."

Chapter 18

Lenora cornered her in the carriage as they loaded in preparation for the capital. "You danced the entire night with Lord Cain," her sister slid up next to her. "Enlighten me."

"What is there to divulge?" Annabel replied, smoothing her skirts. "We have turned over a new leaf."

"That's it?" Lenora pressed.

"Too early to say is all," Annabel replied with a non-comital shrug. "I like spending time with him, and he is an accomplished dancer. He is surprisingly agreeable."

Lenora gasped. "You have rarely complimented anyone so much. Especially a man. Is it for real?"

"Len, please," Annabel replied fixing a few stray hairs. "You will not speak of your secret courtship; I wish to do the same." Lenora's cheeks became rosy, and Annabel latched onto her reaction. "Unless that has changed. What happened?"

"He spoke sweet words to me after we danced." Lenora pressed her fingers to her cheeks. "He spoke so highly of me I believe he is interested."

She'd seen Lenora with Lord Jispen off and on throughout the night. He did live in the northern territories. Could he be her secret courter? She would have to look into him at once.

"Will you tell me who he is now?" Unlike Annabel who was relatively open about her life, Lenora was much more reserved. Many times, keeping things to herself until she was certain or assured in what she was sharing. Despite that, Annabel had hope that enough had changed that the secret would be shared. Likely a result of their nosy tendencies and their collective need to protect each other.

Lenora shook her head, thus dashing her hopes once more. "Not yet."

"Soon?"

"Once he makes his sentiments known. He indicated he'd be in the capital soon and I shall see him then." Lenora leaned on her shoulder, snuggling close with a contented sigh. "I do hope we are both happily in love like Lady Zerwin."

Annabel glanced out of the window where Lady Zerwin and Lady Cierra were approaching the carriage. "We can only hope."

At their weekly teatime, her mother was laughing at something Mayven had said. She honestly couldn't focus on the conversation at all. Something about Lord Cain's suffering had brought up so many memories, leaving her lost in her thoughts. Mainly those that had led to her mother's current state. Yet she seemed so unburdened by her current circumstances. It was as though she could get up from that chair and walk around; but that wasn't the case. Despite what Annabel wanted, her mother would never walk unaided again. Did she hope to find a means to cure Cain because if she did, it would feel like there were some things she could affect positively? Even if the one thing she wanted to change she could not.

A hand clasped over her wrist. "Annabel, darling." Her mother's worried expression brought her out of her thoughts. "Is something the matter?"

Annabel inhaled before forcing a smile on her face. "Just reflecting on the events of the hunt."

"Yes, I heard," her mother said with a knowing smile. "It seems Lord Van Brandt has made amends."

Annabel nodded. "I am quite pleased even if Mayven is making me leave Edur with the animal trainer until I have time to housebreak him." She sipped her tea as she considered if she should visit her new pet or her new 'friend.'

"And you told your father you weren't interested." Her mother leaned on her hand and tipped her head to the side.

Annabel shook her head, but then remembered their plan. "It is too early to tell, but I do enjoy his company."

Annabel would never tell her mother that she had no interest in marriage. Once her brother was secure in his, she planned to tour the country—perhaps even some of the other kingdoms. Now if only her brother was half as interested in women as he was in paperwork.

"Perhaps you should consider visiting Yvette. Your grandchildren would be a good distraction," Mayven suggested, and Annabel felt conflicted. On one hand her brother was right, but on another her mother would have to travel a long distance in her fragile state.

"That is a marvelous idea once the season is done." Her mother took another sip of her tea.

Annabel set down her empty teacup. "Perhaps I'll join you."

"That would be lovely dear." Her mother patted her hand affectionately.

"We can discuss plans later, I think I'll go and see Lady Cierra before the day is completely gone," Annabel said, bending over to kiss her mother's cheek.

The halls were busy with preparations for the engagement party. Too many flowers in vases and not enough garlands. A few people greeted her but must have sensed how focused she was on her way to the library.

Annabel had to walk the many shelves and search a few alcoves before she found the Van Brandt siblings tucked away on the upper landing where the sunlight slanted across their makeshift workstation. Lady Cierra was seated with an open book in front of her while Lord Cain stood, looking over her shoulder. As she approached, he turned to her slowly and she saw his focused expression soften into hopefulness at the sight of her. It caused an odd tingling sensation in the pit of her stomach—not all together unpleasant, just undesirable.

"Princess." Cain bowed to her.

Annabel waved a hand. "Let's dispense with the formalities. I do believe when it is just us, you both can call me by my given name."

"I don't know if I can," Lady Cierra replied with a warm smile. "Though I shall try...Miss Annabel."

Lord Cain just appeared uncomfortable. Now that she was getting to know him better, his unreadable expression was slowly becoming less cryptic. A part of her even wanted to tease him but held herself back—just narrowly.

"May I join you?" Cain moved silently to pull a chair out for her, which she accepted graciously, and waited until he was seated before launching into her reason for hunting them down. "I believe the best way to come at this is to understand everything about this curse. What you've uncovered or anything that caused a change."

"Very little on all accounts," Lady Cierra replied with a heavy sigh.

"Did you feel anything when the curse happened?"

Lord Cain nodded. "Energy. A stirring of emotions."

"Nothing else? No dark feeling?" Annabel asked, finding it odd from other curses she'd heard about. Someone with an ability to cause such misfortune would no doubt leave a trace.

"No," Cain replied.

"Did you eat anything or did your family cause any issues with another family?" Annabel asked, picking up the closest book to read the title—*A History of the Southern Isles*.

"We thought the same," Lady Cierra said, picking up a piece of paper. "We detailed all of the possibilities and have found none to be the cause."

Annabel took the list and read through them. It contained all of the usual possibilities—ones her tutors had warned her to keep watch for. They were taught about abilities and the possibility to inflict them on others in a lasting way; in the event they needed to find the person who had done it and lift the affliction.

95

They ran through how they'd removed each item from the list. Annabel listened and asked the occasional question. No strange food. They'd removed every person who might have wanted to harm them and cause a curse. No cursed object since no one else had been affected. It wasn't a venerated animal or the result of a monster—they didn't have many of either on the Southern Isles. Most sea monsters were further out in deep waters.

"You have been thorough," Annabel stretched and then saw the hour. "Perhaps we should see to dinner. I can return tomorrow in the afternoon, but the concert is in the evening."

"I've been so looking forward to it. The music here is so…refined." Lady Cierra sighed. Then to Annabel's surprise she nudged her brother.

Rubbing his side he asked, "Might I accompany you?"

Annabel felt amusement blossom in her chest as she leaned forward on her elbows. "You would risk rumors spreading even further?"

His lips twitched. "Isn't that just as you planned?"

"True enough." Annabel giggled despite herself. That's when Annabel noticed one very important possibility was missing from the list. "And you've already ruled out the possibility you're a Mystic?"

Annabel had been looking at the paper, her comment had been half conceived. Her finger tapped on the table as she considered all the possibilities they might not have. When there was only silence to her question, she met the gazes of the confused siblings.

"What is a Mystic?" Lady Cierra asked.

Annabel sat up straight. "You don't know what a Mystic is?"

They exchanged a glance as they shook their heads. "What is that?"

"Someone who has an ability," Annabel replied leaning forward as she lowered her voice. "You know, magic?"

Cain shook his head. "That is only found on the continent. Not on the Isles."

Annabel scanned their faces for any measure of jest. "It is a matter of blood. If your family ever married someone with an ability—known or unknown—they could pass it on. Sometimes it skips generations."

The siblings were shaking their heads. "It has to be a curse," Cierra insisted. "He was a teenager the first time it happened. It didn't start from birth."

"They rarely do," Annabel said, suddenly putting the pieces together. "Most happen to children around puberty, but sometimes they come later when certain events trigger them. To be honest it's mostly random."

"Then how do you know for sure?" Cain asked, frowning.

"The palace Mage has an orb that tests it," Annabel explained. "I could go and get it; we could see if that is the cause."

"Then it could be removed?" Cain appeared hopeful and she was startled for a moment.

"No," Annabel replied, shaking her head. "But you could learn to control it."

He thought for a moment, then nodded. "When can I test?" Cain asked, grimly.

Annabel stood up. "I can go now. It may take me a moment, but I remember where it was."

"I'll wait," Cain replied nodding his head, his gaze unfocused. "I'll wait." The second was more forceful and stared at her fervently.

"I'll be back." Annabel didn't wait for an answer as she rushed towards the magic tower.

Chapter 19

Annabel had forgotten how busy the Magic Tower could be. There were people strolling in and out in a continuous flow. It took Annabel a moment to think of a reason to visit; an excuse to get inside. After a while she finally had formed a decent plan and strode towards the entrance with purpose.

The guard opened the door for her with a nod. "Princess."

"Thank you." Annabel smiled at him, as she stiffly entered.

The circular tower was filled with parchment, bottles that were all manner of colors, herbs, and, further up, books. It had been a long time since she'd been there; not since she'd been tested. She made her way towards the stairs, taking them to the second level where a smaller room sat. In its center was the orb, about the size of an orange. Although people had been milling around downstairs, there was no one in that room.

Her fingers grazed the smooth surface of the orb, and she saw the same soft yellow glow she'd seen all those years ago, but this time it changed. Her breath caught in her throat as within the orb, she saw a single strand of thread break in two. *What did that mean?*

"Princess?"

Annabel snatched her hand back as she swirled around. "Master Wil, just who I was looking for."

"Is something the matter?" Master Wil came towards her, a set of scrolls in his arms.

"I was hoping for something that would help me sleep. I've been restless and finding myself waking earlier and earlier," Annabel said, which wasn't untrue. "Is there something that could help?"

"Valerian root would be best," Master Wil replied, adjusting his hold on the scrolls. "Would you like some?"

"Yes," Annabel waved her arm, "Lead the way."

When he turned his back and exited the room, she snatched the orb up and tucked it into one of the hidden pockets of her long flowing skirts. She quickly followed Master Wil so he wouldn't suspect anything.

"Is there something else you needed?" Master Wil inquired.

"No," Annabel answered quickly, "Why would you ask?"

"You've never come in person before, you've always just sent your maid," Master Wil replied, his sharp eyes appraising her.

"I was curious," Annabel replied with a purposeful sigh. "I haven't been here in so long. Should I not have come?"

"You are always welcome on the main floor but be careful you stay there. There are dangerous items further up, that should not be trifled with," Master Wil explained.

"I shall take that to heart," Annabel said as they reached the main floor. "May I return later for the valerian root?"

"Certainly, your highness," Master Wil said, but his gaze told her he was suspicious of her. Annabel's intuition told her he'd soon discover what she'd taken and her time to test it out would be short.

"Later today?" Annabel asked, planning to return the orb once Cain had been able to use it.

"If that is what you wish," Master Wil said as she started to back towards the door.

"Until then." Annabel swirled around, her skirts a flurry as she made haste towards the library.

They were gathered around the table staring at it, Cain's expression distrustful. "And I just touch it?"

"Yes, if you have an ability the orb will light up." Aside from her own testing, Annabel had only ever seen dormant results. Now, she couldn't stop thinking of the breaking string it had shown her. Was that her ability, to see and break the future?

She could see Cain was conflicted as his hand hovered over the orb, but then his sister's hand touched his arm. "It is going to be all right," Lady Cierra said, nodded to him encouragingly.

"Why don't you try first?" Annabel told Cierra.

Nodding, she hesitated only a moment before her fingers touched the orb. It didn't respond, remaining only a circle of clear glass. Annabel looked to Cain, wondering if a curse or an ability would be better.

"Now you," Annabel said, gesturing encouragingly towards the seemingly innocuous crystal.

The moment the tips of his fingers touched the orb, a pale light started to glow, then shine. Within the glass itself there was a person's face, that was out of focus, but the open mouth and placement of the eyebrows denoted fear. Cain snatched his hand away, eyes wide as he looked at Annabel for answers. She didn't blame him, that happened the first time to her as well—the feeling of denial that it could be true.

Annabel leaned back on her heel. "You're a Mystic."

Her declaration was met with stunned silence. Cierra was watching Cain closely as Annabel picked the orb back up, careful to use her handkerchief so as not to touch it. That was a secret she was not quite ready to reveal. Perhaps with time and trust.

"What does this mean?" Cierra asked as Cain sat down heavily in a chair.

Annabel picked up one of the books from the pile. It laid out all the different types, different ways abilities were woken, and the truth about how they were passed from parents to children through the blood. She turned to a

100

page she was familiar with from her early education after she'd tested, and it had been discovered she had the ability to become a Mystic...or more.

"It means you have an ability," Annabel explained as she turned the pages.

Cain swallowed heavily. "It isn't an ability. It's a curse. I want it gone."

Annabel set the book down in front of him. "There is no way to remove the power. It is in your very blood."

Cain put his hand over the book's pages, as though to hide their truth. He turned away and then stood abruptly. Annabel glanced at Lady Cierra who appeared confused. Motioning for her to sit down, Annabel followed after Cain as he fled deeper into the older sections of the library, sensing his distress.

"Please wait," Annabel called after him. He didn't stop. "Stop running," Annabel snapped as she moved to get in his way. "You need to face what this gift has done to you."

"It's a curse," Cain replied, his features dark. "You wouldn't understand since you can't take anything seriously."

Annabel jerked back like he'd hit her. To her surprise his words carried more weight than she was expecting as her heart hurt and her skin tingled on her upper arms. She immediately took a step back from him, trying to put some distance between them as she worked to rein in her emotions.

"I know very well what you think of me," Annabel whispered, unexpected tears threatening. "That won't stop me from trying to help you." He seemed stunned so she pressed on. "We are more alike than you realize but have just chosen different ways to deal with the darker sides of life."

"What darker sides of life could you have possibly seen?" Cain replied with a scoff. "You are doted on by your siblings. No one fears you. You are responsible for no one but yourself. No one has abandoned you because they think you are damned by the gods. No one has suffered at your hands while you were powerless to stop it."

His chest was heaving by the time he was done. Despite the passion in his words, he'd never raised his voice, yet that didn't diminish their sting. When she'd decided to confront him, she'd considered he might have attacked her, yet she hadn't expected his words to cause such anguish.

"You are right." She felt suddenly very tried. "On all counts except one." She lifted her head up and met his judgmental gaze. "Have you never wondered what happened to the queen? How she came to be bound to her wheelchair?"

He hesitated a moment. "I'd heard it was an accident."

"In a way it was," Annabel replied, her throat dry. She swallowed heavily before continuing. "But none of it would have happened if it wasn't for me. I'm the reason she's like that." The secret she'd been carrying for so long, it threatened to strangle her as she felt tears slide down her cheeks.

He shifted onto his heels, his gaze less judgmental. "Why are you telling me this?"

"Because you are more than your ability and I am more than one bad decision." Annabel swiped her tears away. "If you keep running, you'll end up like me, but instead of a flake, you'll be a blackguard."

"Why does it matter to you?" Cain replied, his voice hard.

Annabel swallowed her emotions as best she could. "Because I thought we'd become friends. And that is what friends do."

Cain's eyes widened at her words. "You have helped me. For that I am grateful, but you are overstepping."

"That is something you should have already figured out." Annabel took a step forward, challenging him by proximity. "Whatever line you try to draw or box you try to put me in, I shall never conform to it."

His lips twitched and then slowly curled into a reluctant grin. "There at least we can agree. You push all boundaries."

Annabel laughed aloud and it did not take long for Cain to join her. It was ridiculous but so freeing that she gave into the wave of emotions. They laughed so hard that Annabel's earlier tears of woe were overwritten with ones of merriment, both eventually having to be dashed away from her lashes.

When they were done Cain held out his hand. "Friends?"

"Friends," Annabel shook his hand. "You didn't let me finish. Will you now?"

"I apologize that I lost my temper," Cain replied with a nod. "I shall listen 'til the end."

"There is no way to remove it, like I said, but you can learn to control it," Annabel explained, gesturing that they should return. "It will take time and dedication but soon I will not be the only person you can interact with. Then eventually it'll be like second nature, and you can lead a normal life."

"How can you possibly know that for sure?" Cain asked as they slowly returned to where Cierra was waiting.

"I cannot reveal who, only that I know someone who overcame it and lives every day without concern." Annabel sent a silent apology to her brother—certain he would forgive her. "If they can, so can you." Alas, she didn't know for certain if Cain was the only person she was trying to convince.

Chapter 20

Annabel stood awkwardly on the first floor of the Magic Tower. She waited while one of the younger apprentices fetched Master Wil. Cierra and Cain, who accompanied her, seemed interested in everything they saw, as apparently, they did not have such places on the isles. How strange it must have been to all of them.

"Princess," Master Wil called, tucking his hands into his sleeves. "You come back sooner than I thought. Are you prepared to return the orb?"

Feeling sheepish, Annabel held the object in question out. "Apologies, I didn't think you'd let me borrow it without explanation."

"You are my princess, you need but ask," Master Wil said before holding out his hands and taking the orb from her. "Yet I sense you are ready now."

"Yes," Annabel said, glancing around at the other people in the room. "Might we have a moment of privacy?" Lord Cain and Lady Cierra moved to follow but Annabel stopped them. "I just need a moment."

They nodded as Master Wil took her to a small room to the right. It was filled with herbs and bottles that were crammed in every nook and cranny, but it gave them the privacy she'd requested. Master Wil closed the door behind him before indicating he was ready.

"Ready to explain yourself?" Master Wil asked, before folding his arms.

"I am going to bring Lord Cain and Lady Cierra in here to explain further, but before I do, I wanted to stress the importance of your discretion. At no time are you to reveal that I have any potential for abilities, or mention anything about Dalus. I hope you understand now is not the time." Annabel felt protective of her brother and was not yet ready to speak of her own abilities.

"Here I thought you'd finally awoken," Master Wil said, furrowing his brow. "That does not seem to be the case."

"No, I am here to help someone who has suffered a long time." Annabel thought of all those years he must have struggled. "Will you help them?"

"At your request, I shall endeavor to do so," Master Wil replied. "Which one is it?"

Annabel opened the door and waved them in. They reluctantly crowded into the already small room before closing the door again.

"Master Wil, this is Lord Cain Van Brandt and his sister, Lady Cierra. They are visiting from the Southern Isles," Annabel said before pausing. When the Van Brandt siblings said nothing, she opened her eyes wide and nodded her head in Master Wil's direction.

"I thought I was cursed..." Cain's voice trailed off.

"You are not the first, nor will you be the last. Is it a bad one?" Master Wil asked, tipping his head to the side in sympathy.

"I manifest fears." Cain seemed tense but the moment he spoke his shoulder slumped. Like a weight had been lifted from them. "Whenever someone comes into contact with my skin who isn't family, they see their greatest fear." Cain glanced at Annabel. "That is except for her."

"Those with royal blood are special. Many of them are immune even though they don't have any powers of their own," Master Wil lied through his teeth and Annabel was shocked at how easily he did it. That kind of loyalty was not easily found. "Unfortunately, the only way to test it is to try it, and that is ill advised."

"I had no idea," Cain said, regarding her closely. "How fortunate that you are immune."

Annabel felt uncomfortable withholding information and quickly deflected. "Can you help him?" She asked Master Wil.

"Most definitely," Master Wil said, swinging his arm around to move his sleeves away. "Tomorrow, come here alone. I shall clear the tower, and we shall test your ability."

"Just like that?" Cain asked, glancing between them.

Master Wil chuckled. "It won't be easy."

"Will I...will I be able to interact with others again?"

"Yes. Most assuredly. Soon you shall know the full extent of your abilities as a Mystic and begin taking steps to control them," Master Wil assured him. Cain appeared to be in shock at his words.

"My father is not to be told until I am ready," Annabel declared. Master Wil's loyalty was to her father, not necessarily to her. "Until Cain...until Lord Cain has better control. I do not want to cause him any harm, you understand." It wasn't a question.

"Until I know more about what Lord Cain can do, I have nothing to report." The wrinkles on Master Wil's face deepened as he grinned softly. There was something so comforting about his words. "Though I cannot put it off forever. He will have to be told."

"I understand." Annabel glanced at Lord Cain who appeared conflicted. Perhaps that is when she, too, should come clean with her family.

"What will happen when the King learns of this?" Cain asked, Annabel not at all surprised by the direction nature of his question.

"He will ask you to join the Magic Tower," Annabel replied, having seen it happen again and again.

"Will he...force me?" Cain sounded uncertain and she didn't blame him for his line of questioning.

Annabel sighed. "Absolutely not. Perhaps if you were our countryman, he would make it difficult for you to decline, but you are nobility from the Southern Isles. It would be too great of a diplomatic risk." Annabel shrugged dismissively. "If you are anxious after Master Wil is able to help you, then you can always leave before my father learns everything."

"Won't that cause issues for you?" Cierra asked, touching a hand to Annabel's arm in concern.

"Even if it does, my father doesn't have great expectations of me. He is more likely to be disappointed—a notion I'm used to," Annabel replied with a laugh, trying to make their heavy conversation lighter.

Cain suddenly put a hand out, causing both of them to stop. "I must ask once more for your forgiveness." He swallowed and she saw true remorse on his face. "I regret the words I spoke to you in haste. You have done far more to earn my trust then I have done in return."

"You've already apologized once," Annabel reminded him. "You need not do it again."

"I think that I should," Cain replied. "It was small of me to disparage you the way that I did. Your suffering is not less than mine. It was wrong of me to make such unfounded assumptions."

"My brother, apologizing," Cierra said, her eyebrows raised. "It has been a long time since I've seen that."

Annabel took a step, but he moved to stop her again. "Please, Princess, ask anything of me and I shall endeavor to fulfill it."

She knew he would not stop; he perceived a debt was owed and he would see the scales balanced. "Annabel," she replied raising her chin. "Friends do not call each other by their titles." She made her way around his hand before stopping at the junction at the hall to look back at them. "Friendship is all that I ask, a true one. Do you think you can manage?"

A soft smile touched his lips. "If I cannot, I know you will correct me."

Annabel felt her heart thud louder—an odd sensation. "Good. Do not be late for the concert tonight." And then she continued down the hall to return to her private rooms.

Chapter 21

Annabel had escaped after Lady Zerwin had made a delivery of more paperwork. Under the pretext of wanting more tea, she'd slipped out to the gardens and was hiding in the furthest gazebo with a good book. Slipping further down into her chair, Annabel covered her face as though she was thoroughly preoccupied with the tome when she noticed Yenni in the garden, cutting a direct path towards her.

"How could you not tell me?" Yenni asked, pushing the top of her book down.

Annabel's heart raced—had she discovered her secret? How could she know about the dreams? Feeling a little overwhelmed at the possibility of admitting she was a Mystic, she carefully inquired, "Tell you what exactly?"

She leaned forward, their noses only a hand length away. "Lord Cain." Each word was said with unnecessary emphasis. "Is this why you wanted to see me tomorrow? To tell me that he's courting you."

"No!" Annabel jumped up, nearly banging their heads together. Although her confessing their courtship would make sense now that she thought of it. "I just missed you."

Yenni crossed her arms and rested on her heel. "Well, are you going to tell me about it now?"

"How did you find me?" Annabel glanced around, wondering if someone else would come and drag her back.

"I know all your favorite hiding spots," Yenni reminded her.

Annabel frowned. "You are the only one who truly does. I do hate how good you are at figuring out…people." Then a thought occurred to her. "How would you expose someone's true motives?"

"Put them in a situation where they think they've won," Yenni replied without skipping a beat and then her eyes narrowed. "What is Lord Cain doing? Has he tried something?"

"Not him, someone else. Someone I'm worried about," Annabel replied before waving her hand as though swatting away the thought. "Lord Cain is the opposite of what I thought." That much was unavoidably true. "I like his company."

"Is that it?" Yenni asked, half collapsing into the white metal chair. "Here I thought you'd finally fallen in love."

Annabel laughed as she closed the book and joined her sister at the table. "Goodness, no. Though I don't dislike him."

"That is a first." Yenni said leaning forward. "Is he a shield?" Yenni rested her cheek on her fist. "Please tell me you are not dragging this poor man along because you don't want anyone else to bother you."

"Perhaps. It is more that others are less likely to try but also that he is…" Annabel was surprised at her lack of words.

Yenni sat up. "Do you fancy him?"

Annabel blinked in surprise, did she? When had that happened? She tried to rationalize the barrage of emotions, chalking them up to fondness, but felt her heart waver in a way she wasn't prepared for. Fear gripped her and she locked down anything that was beyond general care. He was a good man, one she felt a kinship to, nothing more. She would not put him in a difficult position because of one small quiver in her heart.

"I find him diverting," Annabel replied, leaning back in the chair. "He and his sister are both so refreshing." Yenni studied her closely and Annabel kept her expression carefully neutral. "Is Lord Euros visiting?"

"Don't think I am so easily swayed from this topic. We shall return to it soon, but yes," Yenni's face transformed in an instant to giddiness. "He promised."

"Have you picked a day?"

Yenni sighed heavily. "Father will still not give his consent." Lord Euros had been married once before and their father had been putting off accepting a date. "Our cousin gets to have his wedding within a fortnight of his engagement, and we've had to wait nearly a year. I fear Euros shall lose patience with me."

"That is precisely what father is waiting on. Confirmation of a steely resolve or a half-hearted attempt." Annabel shrugged. "It is not common for a man with one failed marriage to do well in another one. No doubt father does this for your own good."

"Euros' first wife was nearly twice his age and forced upon him by his father. They had an amicable relationship, and when his father passed away, they'd separated quietly. She's living quite happily in the south last I heard," Yenni replied with a sigh. "How much longer will father make me wait?"

"Ask him again, after the wedding, he may be in a more willing mood," Annabel said, trying to give her sister hope.

"It is difficult to steal kisses and know that no matter how much I long for more, I shall be barred from it until we are wed." Yenni sighed before leaning back, tilting her head back as she inhaled deeply.

"You haven't…" Annabel asked, genuinely curious.

Yenni met her gaze and then raised her eyebrows. "Oh heavens no. Last thing we need is a scandal involving a child conceived out of wedlock. Though we have gotten close." A sweetness touched her entire being, like a flower blooming in sunlight. She seemed to glow at the memory, her cheeks rosy and her lips parted slightly. Annabel felt a sudden yearning to experience such happiness, despite its costs, before she quickly discarded the thought.

"I do not know if I ever fell in love that I'd be so reserved," Annabel commented absentmindedly. "Even at such a risk." Then her gaze snapped up to Yenni. "Though I would never advise such a risk."

"There are many other things..." Yenni giggled; her fingers pressed against her mouth. "You can enjoy each other without crossing such a sacred line."

"Yen!" Annabel said, slapping the table, but laughed heartily. "I do not need to imagine my sister doing such indecent things."

Yenni only laughed harder, clenching her stomach. When she finally gained some composure, she leaned forward and tapped Annabel's book. "If you'd like a more exciting read, go to the western part of the library and pick up *A Rose in the Garden*."

"You read such rubbish, Yenni? Reprehensible!" Annabel had to wipe away tears as she gasped dramatically. "What would father think if he knew?" Annabel tried to make her tone more chiding but wasn't doing well. "What color did you say the spine was? I must see that this horrid book is properly...properly handled."

Yen snorted slightly as she gasped for air. "Annabel! Enough. It's green, dark green with a single rose on the cover."

"It shall be dealt with posthaste," Annabel assured her, straightening her spine and trying to put a serious expression on her face. "I wouldn't want such a salacious book to fall into the wrong hands."

Yenni was waving her hand in front of her face. "That is if Len returned it."

Annabel burst out laughing. "Why'd you tell her?" She could barely get the words out.

"For her beau, he apparently reappeared with vigor and is pursuing her again," Yenni leaned back as she let out a few final chuckles. "How I have missed you sister."

"We cannot go so long without making time," Annabel said, realizing she'd been so busy as of late.

The Promise of Dreams

"That is true. Visiting Yvette reminded me that we will not always be together as we are." Yenni nodded and put her hand on Annabel's arm. "Though, no matter what we will always be sisters."

Unlike Yvette who was quite a bit older since she was the oldest of all siblings, Annabel was close with Yenni and Lenora. Now it was easy to see them, but soon they would marry and have families of their own. Likely far away like her eldest sister. She would have her mother and brother, but that was not the same.

"I do not like growing up." Annabel sighed, suddenly morose.

Yenni patted her arm. "That is the thing with time; it doesn't care. Even less than you."

Annabel stuck her tongue out, causing both of them to laugh and break the spell of sadness that had threatened to take hold. At least for now she could see her sisters, even if that was to change, it would be in the future. For now, she could talk of dresses and the upcoming solstice festival with Yenni, pretending that this is how it would always be. At least for now.

Annabel had attended multiple musical concerts in her life. She'd neither disliked nor liked them, they were simply a way to pass the time. Plus, Mayven loved them. She glanced at her brother who was practically perched at the edge of his seat. There was a way his eyes shined as he listened—one would think her brother, who was good at everything and loved music, would be at least moderately proficient. Sadly, it was the one area he had struggled with all his life. The one thing her brother wasn't good at. Well, that…and finding a wife.

For some reason that thought brought her back to her escort. Lord Cain was dressed in a traditional black robe from the isles. It had a high collar and was decorated over the shoulders with a hand stitched pattern that Annabel had never seen before. His dark curls were gathered tightly to the top of his head yet appeared perfectly maintained. Perhaps that was due to his beard being sculpted in such a way to artfully enhance his striking attributes. Despite every feature, from his well-placed nose to his noble brow, creating a stunning overall visage, her attention was drawn only to a single location. There was a kindness in his eyes she'd missed when he'd first arrived.

'Missed' was not the correct term. She'd only focused on his behavior and overlooked that, despite his direct gaze, there was an inherent goodness behind it. He was a good person. It left her feeling lucky that she'd met him.

He leaned towards her and whispered. "Are you not enjoying the concert?"

Annabel realized she'd been staring and immediately turned forward as her cheeks warmed. "I was trying to determine if you were."

"I am."

She met his gaze, smiling at him in comfortable comradery. "Do you play an instrument?"

"Yes. Music was very comforting when I was…alone." He cleared his throat. "The pianoforte was my favorite. Do you play?"

"Shush," a woman said from somewhere behind them.

Annabel glanced back and realized they were disturbing others. Her gaze passed over the faces of those closest, who appeared nervous at her attention. Cain was staring forward again, focused on the musicians. Annabel put her hand on his shoulder and leaned in intimately close.

"No. The only thing I play is cards and games." Annabel sat straight again but continued to lean close. She wanted everyone to know how keenly they were courting.

The rest of the concert went with little excitement. The music was pleasant enough, but Annabel was distracted by her thoughts. No matter how much she endeavored not to think of the growing attraction between them…she failed miserably. At the conclusion of the performance, Cain escorted her, in front of everyone, to the end of the concert hall. The party would continue, but they'd agreed to part early so that Annabel could make more of an impact with a larger group.

"Will you visit me tomorrow?" Annabel asked loudly, as she held her hand out. "For tea."

"As you wish," Cain replied, kissing the back of her gloved hand. "I am at your disposal, princess."

And just like that they had declared that Annabel had accepted his courting, and they were exclusively interested in each other. As she returned to her room, Annabel tried not to think about the way her heart was thudding in her chest.

Chapter 22

He slid her hand across his face, kissing her palm. "You taste just as I imagined."
His tongue slid along his lips, drawing her in. "Sweet."

Somehow, she'd found herself pressed against him, eager for his touch. The tips of
his fingers caressed the back of her neck as she tipped her head to the side. He nibbled
along her jaw then down her neck. His lips tracked kisses across her collarbone,
promising more as his hands cupped her supple mounds. They pined for him, straining
against the fabric, as his deft fingers pulled at her corset laces.

Once free he took her nipple in his mouth…

"Miss Annabel?" Annabel gasped at the sound of Lady Cierra's voice, the
book sliding off her lap before it snapped shut on the floor.

Her heart was in her throat, racing like a wild horse, as she met the
concerned expressions of the Van Brandt siblings. She felt like a child who'd
been caught stealing sweets. Her cheeks felt warm as she tried to gather some
modicum of decorum by straightening her skirts. She should have known
better than to start reading *A Rose in the Garden* the night before. Yenni had a
mischievous streak that was only matched by her uncanny ability to see
through to people's true natures.

"Yes, what is it?" Annabel asked, moving so her skirts concealed the immoral tome.

"Forgotten already that we're courting?" Cain asked, his gaze laughing.

She had, in fact, forgotten all about the appointment. Curse Yenni and her sinful tastes in literature. There was no way in the world that she would admit their plans had completely escaped her. It was not to be borne.

"I simply lost track of time," Annabel replied with a wave of her hand, hoping to push the conversation forward—and the book under the couch. "Please come in."

Cain sat down across from her as Cierra closed the door and joined them. She glanced at the cold tea and forgotten snacks that were too long in the room. Annabel leaned forward and picked up a jellied sandwich. The bread had begun to harden but beyond that it was still edible—the peaches were sweet.

"Shall we call for more tea?" Annabel suggested as she sat on the edge of the seat; still trying to unobtrusively shift the wicked volume further under her seat, while attempting to keep the book concealed with her skirts as best she could. "I want to hear all about how things are going with Master Wil."

"Progressing," Cain replied, with a hopeful smile.

"Tea sounds lovely." Cierra stood and left the room.

"She does know what a chaperone is, right?" Annabel asked, as Cain poured some lemon water from the pitcher. The condensation on the glass jug dripped onto the table.

"She has always been very trusting," Cain replied, raising the glass to his lips.

"Imagine if we were really courting," Annabel replied, tipping her head to the side as she used the toe of her shoe to finally slide the terribly, wonderful book under her couch and completely out of sight. "This would be the perfect opportunity to Hunt the Squirrel." Perhaps it was the book that made her say something so...naughty.

Cain choked on the water, struggling to swallow it. "You..." he waved a finger at her, but it was in good fun, "you are going to get me into trouble."

"With exacting pleasure," Annabel said with an internal squeal. He really was turning out to be an excellent companion. "It is what I am known for after all."

He chuckled. "You *are* known for your nonsense."

"Do not take me for a flibbertigibbet." Annabel crossed her arms in defiance. "I do not spout drivel, I'm—spirited."

"Then I shouldn't ask about the book you've been trying to hide." He gave her a cheeky grin.

Annabel tipped her head up as she shifted uncomfortably. "Certainly not. A gentleman wouldn't."

"I'm about as much of a refined gentleman as you are a proper lady," Cain said, and Annabel felt a surge of heat. Growing affection aside, she was very much enjoying their exchange.

"You don't give yourself enough credit," Annabel replied, suddenly serious.

If gazes could cause a fire, she would have gone up in flames. The door opened and in an instant the spell was broken. Cierra carried in a tray filled with sweets and a large teapot. It took Annabel a moment to get her bearings as she turned away and adjusted the pins in her hair.

"I didn't mean to take so long," Cierra said as Cain jumped up to help her. "Cook just kept adding more to the tray."

"Why don't we take this to the garden?" Cain said, still holding the tray. "The clouds have broken."

"That would be lovely." Annabel stood, suddenly feeling like the room was too small for the pair of them. She'd always been reckless but for once she wished her mouth had a little more discernment.

Annabel linked arms with Cierra as Cain made his way to the door. "The patio?" He asked, shouldering the door open.

"Perfect," Annabel replied, as she watched him leave—trying hard not to notice how fetching his physique was.

She was grateful for the soft breeze that brushed her cheeks as she made her way to the table where Cierra was unloading the tray. The happy green of the garden brought serenity when she needed it most. How fortunate that Cain should suggest such a setting.

"I forgot the jelly," Cierra said, before she tsked. "Do you mind, Cain?"

"Gladly." He patted his sister's arm before leaving them.

Annabel spotted the honey and lifted it. "We can make do with this."

Cierra sat down. "Let him get it. I wanted a moment with just us."

"Oh?" Annabel replied, careful to keep her composure. "For what reason?"

"I should ask you that." Cierra's gaze was surprisingly direct. "Is it possible we might become more intimately connected?"

Annabel leaned forward. "No doubt your brother told you the true manner of our courtship," Annabel whispered.

Cierra nodded. "My brother does not keep secrets from me."

Annabel inhaled deeply; the sweet aroma of the blossoms filled her senses. "Then you must know that what you suggest is...unlikely."

A curl bounced against Annabel's forehead as the wind picked up. She caught it in her fingers and pushed it back into place, waiting for the wind to die down. Cierra just studied her, as though appraising her every word and movement.

"What I know is that both of you are better having known each other," Cierra replied, the most cunning she'd ever displayed. "Are you telling me that is where it ends?"

"Friendship does not end so easily," Annabel countered, looking at the garden, its hedges and flowers, but not really focusing on anything. "Yours and mine also meets that threshold."

"Yes, we have become good friends." Cierra leaned towards her, shifting her chair so they were nearly knee to knee as she laid her hand across Annabel's arm. "So, listen to me, my friend, when I say that you deserve happiness." Annabel felt tears threaten as she fought back the lump in her throat. "As does my brother. And I think you can give it to him."

Annabel opened her mouth but found no words. Not a sensation she was used to. Slowly she closed her mouth as she recognized the determination on Cierra's face. Suddenly moved by her kindness Annabel hugged her.

"I will consider what you said." Annabel felt she owed her that much. "For you."

Cierra shook her head before they eased back, their hands on each other's shoulders. "Do not do it for me. Do it for yourself. For your future. Consider if it would be better alone or with Cain."

Annabel's heart cried out as she sat back in her chair. Cain was making his way towards them; she could see him through the glass doors. Though she wished for it, no immediate answer came. Only confusion and a swell of affection.

"I shall search my heart," Annabel whispered.

"May it be found wanting," Cierra said before she began to pour the tea.

Chapter 23

Edur yipped as he rolled around in the grass. Annabel laughed; it was wonderful to see her little fox so happy. Though a part of her was guilty over the age of the kit, she very much enjoyed having it as a pet. Besides a horse, she'd never had a pet before that was just hers.

Annabel picked up some of the sliced meat and held it aloft. The playful fox chattered at her but was focused on the food. When she dropped it, he caught it. Edur wasted no time in gobbling it up. When he was done, he hurried to her and rubbed against her legs, hidden under a thin summer dress.

She picked the fox up and lifted him into the air. His long ears almost looked like wings. With a cry of happiness, she brought him against her bosom. He cuddled in and seemed to almost purr against her. She never knew foxes could purr, only cats, but that was exactly what it was doing.

When she heard rustling, Annabel looked up, past the brim of her sunhat. Cain stood awkwardly in the hedgerow; a book cradled in his arms. She waved to him when she saw him, her other arm still holding tight to her fox who was cuddled against her.

"Cain."

He cleared his throat and came closer. "Miss Annabel."

"Why did you not call to me?"

"I didn't know you were alone," Cain replied, glancing around. "I thought your maid would be here."

That's when she noticed he was keeping a respectable distance. "Afraid to tarnish my reputation?" Annabel asked, petting Edur when his head popped up to see what was happening.

He smiled at her. "Yes."

Annabel waved over to the right. "My guard is at the building." She leaned forward. "So, we are technically not unchaperoned."

Cain confirmed for himself the guard was there. He nodded to Sir Harl whose frown only deepened. Annabel unsuccessfully tried to stifle a giggle. Cain really was very darling, positively adorable really.

"Were you looking for me?" Annabel asked, letting Edur rest in her lap.

"I was. If you have a moment, I have some questions." Cain hovered, still not coming any closer.

"Please," Annabel said, gesturing at the surrounding grass, "join me."

He didn't hesitate, despite the fact that she probably should have a blanket down. But she liked the feel of the grass, and her skirts protected her. He settled down next to her, coming to sit directly on her left and closer than she would have thought. She could smell his soap and lingering lavender.

Cain's expression was serious as he opened the book. "I was trying to understand what this means."

He showed her a passage from an older book. It was written in the ancient language and Annabel glanced at him in surprise. "You read old Itreian?"

"A little." Cain seemed embarrassed. "I used to have a lot of time on my hands. There was little else to do but learn." He glanced at her. "Can you read it?"

"Luckily it is a requirement of our royal education," Annabel said taking hold of one side of the large tome. She read the passage. "It is talking about the origin of our abilities. A lot was lost you see, forgotten with time. Some of it was recorded for prosperity. Specifically, the blessing."

"The blessing?"

121

"Yes." Annabel pointed at a passage. "It is believed that there is a well of magic. That in the heart of Valor, lays this enchanted spring. That it is the source of the Gods and Goddesses powers, not meant for man."

"Then how did we get them?" Cain asked, as Annabel turned the page.

Edar slipped off her lap and she glanced at him as he ate the last of the meat. Once it was done, he moved to the shade, curling up into a ball by the hedge. Once she knew he was settled, Annabel turned back to the book and Cain's question.

"The Prince Houdin had a wife who was sick. He prayed to the heavens for a way to save her and her unborn child. In answer, they told him the location of the well. He traveled to the well, determined to save her. He faced many hardships but returned. It cured the queen, and she bore two children." Annabel turned the page again, the old text and its large font made for a quick turning of pages, not to mention she was paraphrasing some of it. "A girl and boy."

"Are we all descended from them?" Cain asked, completely focused.

Fighting back the urge to touch him, Annabel put her hand on the book. "No. This is not the end of the story. Prince Houdin wanted the magic for himself. He took a group of knights with him to steal the magic from the well. In his greed he unleashed magic into the world, engraining it with his knights and the world around him. His actions not only created the first Mystics, but also monsters."

"How did he create monsters?" Cain sounded confused.

Annabel chuckled. "He didn't, his actions angered our deities and to protect the well of magic from further incursion, they brought monsters to guard it. It is believed it exists until today."

"I see." Cain's shoulders slumped.

"That is why most do not speak of their abilities open. They are born from a blemish on our history. Though it is often used to negotiate more advantageous marriages. Some abilities are quite handy." Annabel turned the page. "Do you want to know the rest of the story?"

"There is more?" Cain reached for the page at the same time as her. "Sorry," he said when their hands brushed.

Annabel didn't move her hand as he retracted his. It was unfortunate he was still wearing his gloves. "It's not a problem."

"Please continue."

"The monsters overtook Prince Houdin's home. They were forced south, to try and withstand the sudden attack on their people. Thankfully after a decade of suffering and bloodshed, Prince Houdin's children came of age. His offspring were the most powerful users. They quickly became magicians and protected the realm from the monsters." Annabel turned the page. "Each raised their own kingdom, to ensure the safety of their people. Mayrid was the kingdom born from the son, and Itreia came from the daughter. Each named after them."

"Then all magic users are descended from them?" Cain asked, seemly shocked.

A laugh exploded out of her as she pressed a hand to her mouth to try and stop it. "Oh goodness no. Few are descended from the old bloodline. Itreia only had two children, though Mayrid was known to have fathered a few more only a few can boast a direct linage from that line." Her father being one of her descendants. "Most were born from the knights that followed Prince Houdin. Many are noble houses, now and can be traced back. They were touched by the well, so their abilities were weaker but some married Itreia or Mayrid's children. Strengthening their abilities."

"So, I am a descendant from one of these knights?" Cain asked.

"Yes, that is most likely." Annabel glanced at Edur who was just where she left him.

"I had no idea," Cain replied, letting the book rest on his legs as he leaned back. "This explains why abilities are so rare in the Southern Isles and why I never even considered it." He turned his attention to her. "Thank you for explaining."

She reached back and put her hand over his. "Does it help to know where it comes from?" Annabel asked, wondering if he'd found comfort where she never had.

He sighed. "No, but it helps me forgive myself." He sent her a sad grin. "That all those years, before I could come here, weren't wasted."

She could feel the heat of his hand through the glove. "I don't think it was wasted. We would never have met and there was no certainty you would have discovered it even if you came. It was luck."

His expression became warm, and it caused her chest to tighten. "At least having met you was worth some of the hardship."

"Come to the Solstice Festival with me," Annabel blurted out.

Cain nodded. "Of course. We must keep up appearances." He picked up the book and stood. Annabel tried to ignore how much the words hurt her as he dusted off his pants. "I've taken up too much of your time. I shall see you tomorrow."

Annabel nodded. "Until tomorrow." She watched as he left realizing her heart was beginning to have a mind of its own when it came to Cain.

Chapter 24

Yenni linked arms with Lord Euros as she pointed at a massive kite. Its wings fluttered in the wind, shaped like an ornate sun. Many, of similar designs, graced the skies on the warm summer day. The Solstice Festival was in full swing, with vendors, entertainers, and visitors lining the streets. They would have blended in were it not for the gaggle of guards escorting them. Sighing, she tipped her head forward to block out the sun with her wide brimmed hat.

"Bored already?" Cain asked, sounding amused. "It seems I am not the company you seek."

Annabel glanced at him. "It isn't you. It's them." She pointed her chin at one of the guards. "Takes all the fun out of it."

"She does this every year," Lenora chimed in. "Don't even think of sneaking off. You must present the sun stone this year."

Annabel groaned at the thought. Festivals were only any fun because she could slip away and have a night of freedom. The prospect of being deprived of that weighed heavily on her. What other horrible things could happen? Out of the corner of her eye she thought she saw Lawrence across the street. When she tried to see over the crowd to confirm, a roving vendor went by and when he passed Lawrence was gone. She'd been certain her brother had not extended an invitation after she'd dissuaded him of the notion. It was likely a mistake. Her mind playing tricks on her.

"Unlike you, I am alone," Lenora pointed out, "So I'm going to go with Yenni to look at the ribbons." Yenni and Lord Euros were already making their way across the street when Len hurried to join them.

"Shall we?" Cain asked as he held out an arm.

"Anything, but ribbons," Annabel replied, hesitantly taking his arm. Trying hard not to notice how her dampened mood was lighter with him there. She didn't really know what these feelings meant, nor was she fully prepared to find out.

"Did you have anything in mind?" Cain asked as they walked by a vendor's stall selling windchimes. They tinged lightly in the warm breeze.

Annabel considered his request. "You came here earlier. Surprise me." Her words were more of a command than a request.

She could see him thinking until he turned back to her with excitement. "I think I know where to go."

He took them through the stalls, weaving through the crowd with careful precision. It was impressive if not a little sad. After eleven years of avoiding people, his expertise was showing. When they were nearly separated at one junction, she took his hand.

He glanced back, surprise etched into his features, but he said nothing, only gripping her hand back. They passed jewelry, ribbons, and carvings. Then they rounded another corner, and the buttery sweetness of fresh baked bread filled her senses. It was the food area in an open, circular square, a fountain at its center.

"Food?" Annabel asked, trying to sound offended. "What do you take me for?"

Cain shook his head and pointed to the other side of the square where the booths continued. At the far end there was a notable one on the square. Books were stacked high under a large tent. Her heart caught at the sight.

"How did you know?" Annabel could hardly manage the words.

"You've always had a book every time I see you," Cain replied with an embarrassed shrug.

Gripping his hand tighter she pulled him along. Laughing at her excitement, he followed without protest. They arrived at the books and Annabel lost herself in them. Reading spines and asked the owner questions. They were from far away, many old and worn but some new and fresh. She picked three, despite wanting more.

When they left, they stood in line for some fresh flaky bread. It was fluffy and warm in her mouth as she enjoyed it. The taste of butter was nearly overpowering.

"Thank you," Annabel said, feeling grateful.

"My pleasure," Cain replied.

"Is there something you'd like to see?" Cain shook his head. "Not a new saddle or instrument?" He declined again. She wished she'd tried to know as much about him as he'd proven to know about her. "There must be some secret wish."

"It is enough to enjoy the day through your eyes," Cain said simply, as though he was commenting on the weather.

His earnest response caused her heart to beat faster. A sensation that seemed to be happening more as of late. It shamed her to find out with each passing day that Cain was far superior to her in every way. In temperament, in thoughtfulness, and even in his straightforward honesty. He not only matched her but surpassed her. She found herself feeling undeserving of his kindness and attention.

Embarrassed, she glanced away, her gaze landing on Lord Jispen conversing with Lenora. She straightened when she saw them, feeling certain her earlier guess was coming true. Who else could be her sister's admirer?

"That I am glad to see," Annabel tipped her head in their direction.

"They seem preoccupied," Cain replied.

Annabel moved closer to Cain. "Not nearly as convincing as we are." Their noses nearly touching as she gazed into his eyes.

"We don't have anything to cripple us," Cain whispered.

"Like what?" Annabel replied coyly.

"Affections."

"We don't?" Annabel's breath felt constrained. "How convenient."

He moved closer, one movement and their lips would touch. She saw he was flirting, tempting fate in a way that thrilled her. "Is it?"

"Absolutely," Annabel replied, her heart pounding in her throat as she brushed her fingers against his wrist and into his glove. "It keeps us honest."

His lips spread into a genuine smile as his eyes seemed to shine. "You do recognize the contradictory nature of that statement, don't you?"

Annabel giggled as she eased back onto her heel, breaking the tension. "That's our little secret. We can be frank with each other."

He regarded her, his expression no longer playful. "Can we? Truthfully?"

Annabel opened her mouth but found she lacked the words. Did she want to know what he was going to say next? What did she want in the secret recesses of her heart?

"Annabel?" Yenni called. "We need to get to the ceremony!"

Annabel jerked away from Cain with a start. "Sister!" Her face felt warm at being caught. "I'd nearly forgotten."

Yenni slowed and glanced between them. "Am I interrupting?"

Annabel shook her head. "Not at all," then she held out a hand. Her sister took it as they made their way to the temple. "We were just discussing an important topic." She curtsied swiftly at Cain who bowed his head slightly.

Yenni's eyes were sharp, and Annabel knew she'd done nothing to convince her observant sister. To her credit she didn't press the topic. "We can talk more later." No way she was avoiding that discussion. "We mustn't be late."

Chapter 25

The music played softly as she inspected the last of the decorative flower arrangements for the engagement party. In narrowly a week they would be wed, but such a small evening of entertainment would celebrate the couple. Lenora was busy overseeing the kitchen preparations while Annabel was busy helping in the garden. At least that is what she was supposed to be doing instead of daydreaming about her last encounter with Cain.

"Higher," Lady Ariah said, pointing to a decorative ribbon. Lady Ariah had been an excellent choice to assist her; mostly because she'd taken over everything while Annabel just stood there in a daze.

She was chewing on her fingernail; a habit she hadn't done since she was a child. Annabel couldn't remember the last time she was this indecisive. On the one hand she very much wanted to explore the romance that was budding, but on the other she didn't want Cain to think she would marry him. Marriage was still something she didn't intend to pursue. How to have her cake and eat it too?

"There you are," Yenni said joining them. "The kitchen is ready, and the first guests are starting to arrive. Are we ready?"

129

"Ready?" Annabel replied before remembering herself. "Lady Ariah, are we close?"

"That's the last of it," Lady Ariah said, pointing to a pile of flowers. "They need to be placed at the entrance for guests to take as they arrive."

Yenni picked up the vase as Annabel collected the carnations in her arms. Their deep red was a symbol of the loving affection the couple shared with little ribbons embroidered with their name. Flowers had a language all their own; Annabel had never been interested or fluent in what they were, but Yenni was. Annabel may not have understood why, she just supported her sister's love of flowers by ensuring everything was covered in flowers. Especially her dresses. The one she was wearing had bluebells on them—which meant kindness apparently. Annabel just thought they were pretty.

"I like your dress," Yenni commented, eyeing Lady Ariah's dress. It had deep purple flowers on the bodice. "Irises are a lovely flower and a good choice for you."

"Thank you, Princess Yenni." Lady Ariah curtsied.

Annabel waited until they were out of earshot before asking, "What do they mean?"

"Wisdom," Yenni replied glancing back. "Trust, faith, hope, and even our planet's name – Valor."

Her head spun at all the different meanings. "That's a lot for one flower."

"Hmm." Yenni put the vase on the table. "Belladonna may be a better choice for her."

"Isn't that a poison?" Annabel asked, shocked at her sister's assessment. "That would be better for Lady Phoebe."

Yenni laughed as she helped put the carnations into place. "That is true, but it means silence. I've never met someone I couldn't read before."

"I much prefer her indifference to many others. She's quite amiable once you get to know her." Annabel felt the need to defend her lady-in-waiting.

"You are right sister," Yenni replied as they turned back to join Lenora who was overseeing the final food be set out. "Indifference is a better word for her, therefore, the Iberis would suit her best."

Annabel shook her head—deciding to change the subject before her sister started naming more flowers she didn't know. "Let's just focus on the engagement party. Once we get through this, it'll be on to the wedding in a week and then the masquerade ball. To mark the two-week hiatus."

"You must be counting the days," Yenni replied as they approach the food area.

"The hours," Annabel replied with a sigh. That's when she noticed the tension in Lenora's figure as she explained something to a servant.

"Are you in need to assistance, sister?" Yenni made a show with Lenora, exaggerating her curtsy.

A previously stressed Lenora laughed. "Most assuredly, Yen. They overcooked the mini pies. The top crusts are burned beyond eating." Lenora held one up.

"Can't we just take the tops off?" Annabel asked, eyeing the sweet.

Both of her siblings blinked at her. Lenora nodded eagerly before thrusting the pie towards the servant. "Take the tops off and add snow powder to make them presentable."

Yenni linked their arms together as they turned around to admire the splendor. "I do believe we've pulled it off."

"Indubitably." Annabel's response caused them all to laugh. It was going to be a good day.

Annabel was watching the happy couple as they danced together. The tempo of the music was lively and so was the atmosphere as night took hold. She was so happy for them as she sat with her lady's-in-waiting, having decided a break was in order.

"I am surprised at their quick marriage," Lady Phoebe said, seeming almost put out.

"She seems happier for it," Lady Ariah said with a smile. It was one of the few times Annabel had seen any expression on her face and suddenly her dream came back to her.

"To think they were only engaged a month." Lady Cierra sighed contently. "So romantic."

Annabel's heart hammered in her chest as she struggled to remember what she was supposed to say. What was it? The pressure of saying the right words paralyzed her momentarily.

Lenora sighed contently. "I am so happy for them."

"As am I!" Annabel exclaimed, louder than was necessary, drawing attention to herself from those nearby. "It's making everyone focus on them."

Lenora laughed. "That is true. When they first announced it, you seemed almost as happy as they were. Even insisting they not wait until the season ended, instead having their wedding before the Masquerade Ball."

"I feel indebted to them for taking all the attention away from me," Annabel said, hoping it was in line with what was said last time.

"Though my brother seems to have managed that as well," Lady Cierra said, with a knowing twinkle in her eye.

"That reminds me," Annabel said, realizing it was best to simply leave the conversation since she was struggling to remember what to say. "I promised your brother a tour of the gardens. Enjoy the evening."

Annabel stood without waiting for an answer and hurried towards Cain. He was speaking to Lord Jispen but turned his full attention to her as she approached.

Curtseying, she hurriedly explained, "Lord Cain, now is the perfect time for me to give you that tour I promised."

"Tour?" Cain asked momentarily confused.

"Forgive me, Lord Jispen, I had completely lost track of the hour," Annabel said with contrite smile. "Might I steal Lord Cain away from your company?"

"Most assuredly, Princess," he said with a bow.

Annabel maneuvered him towards the gardens. When they were a good distance away, still where people could see them but not where they could be heard, she relaxed with a sigh. This seeing the future business was very vexing on one's nerves.

"Did something happen?" Cain asked, seemingly concerned.

Annabel glanced up at him in surprise. She'd been so focused on getting away from the conversation that she'd used him as an excuse. Then standing there she realized she had nothing to say. Stumbling, she gestured towards a nearby bench.

"It was a long day is all," Annabel managed. "Lots to set up and prepare."

"Is that not normally left to servants?" Cain asked as they sat.

"Things are different here. When a royal weds, even a first cousin of a royal, it is considered the family's responsibility. Especially of those not married." Annabel crossed her ankles under her dress. "Are wedding's different on the Southern Isles?"

"The last wedding I attended was my aunt's," Cain told her, a sadness about him she had not seen in some time. "It was a happy event at the time."

"What happened?" Annabel could sense a sorrowful tale.

He sat up straighter. "Not appropriate for happy celebrations such as this. It is not a pleasant story. Another time perhaps."

Annabel put her hand over his. "I did not ask if it was pleasant, I asked what happened."

He appraised her before sighing heavily. "My uncle appeared faithful but had many illegitimate children in the first few years. It broke my aunt's heart when she found out. She was never the same." His gaze was as solemn as when they'd first met. "Like she'd lost all hope. She could be cruel to the children that weren't hers, only his."

"Is that why you value marriage so ardently?" Annabel asked, suddenly understanding why it had been such a serious topic.

"It is. I will not beget a child outside of matrimony." His fervor was a credit to his honor. Normally such talk would have been off-putting, instead it made her feel safe.

"I have no such desires," Annabel replied honestly. "Perhaps I fear that like your aunt my freedom will be taken as well as my dignity." That and she was undeserving, the last she dare not speak in the open. "Perhaps I am just selfish."

Cain shook his head. "Those fears are not unfounded. I have seen them happen with my own eyes."

She never thought anyone, let alone a man, would speak such words. "Cain, I..." what was she trying to say? "I am very glad you came here."

133

The Promise of Dreams

He covered her hand with his other one. "So am I."

Chapter 26

Dream

Even though Annabel did not intend to enter the bonds of holy matrimony, she was a wedding enthusiast. From the simple ceremonies to the happy celebratory breakfast, in general they were filled with such positivity. There were, of course, outliers, but those were few and far between. In love matches there was rarely a solemn word spoken.

The ceremony had been heartwarming, and the breakfast was already in full swing. By all accounts the marriage of the king's nephew and Lady Zerwin had been successful. Lady Zerwin's family had turned out to be her exact opposite—almost unruly in their manner. Annabel had adored their blatant speech instantly, especially enjoyed watching others squirm in the face of their directness.

"It must be difficult to part with your daughter," Annabel commented.

"It is an adventurous match to be sure," Lady Zerwin's mother said tapping a small spoon on the side of her teacup. "I didn't think my dear girl had it in her."

"I believe that is the case often with love matches," Lady Cierra replied earnestly. "They make you see the world differently."

They were standing off to the side of the garden area. Soft, light music played, bringing an extra level of enchantment to the morning. Behind them, the pavilion was packed with many guests who were enjoying the splendor. Among them the bride and groom were beaming at each other.

"Your daughter caught my cousin's eye almost instantly," Annabel remarked. "But even I could not have predicted how quickly he would propose."

"When I received word of the marriage and the quick manner in which it would occur, I thought it must have been a mistake," Lady Zerwin's mother remarked. "It was the first time she'd ever thrown caution to the wind."

"Love has that effect," Lenora commented, her voice trailing off.

The older woman chortled. "It cast a bloody spell on my daughter, that's to be sure."

Annabel laughed when she caught the shadow of someone sneaking into the temple. No one should have been in that area, so her gaze wandered to see who it was, and her heart stopped. Lawrence Haywood was leaving the gardens. A knot in her stomach, Annabel excused herself and hurried after him.

He went through the side of the temple that led to the entrance, making his way to the carriages. She watched him leave, conflicted about seeing him there. How had he gotten in? More importantly why was he there and why did he leave in such a hurry?

Annabel rushed back to the breakfast celebration, determined to have a word with her brother. Her shoes tapped on the stone steps as she entered the gardens. She scanned the faces of those that were in the direction that Lord Haywood had come from. Her gaze lingered longer than was necessary on Lord Cain—should she seek him out?

No, Mayven would be best. Annabel thought as she turned left towards her family's seating.

She only took two steps when someone screamed. From her vantage point she saw the reason for the commotion instantly. It was her uncle, Varen's father. He staggered out of the hedgerow, holding his heart.

"Help him!" Annabel called before hurrying down the garden path.

A group of guards surged towards him as she pushed her way through the stunned nobles. Then she was standing over him, his eyes were rolled back in his head and his hand gripping his chest with strained fingers. In her heart she knew who had done this. It wasn't until she felt someone holding onto her that she realized her legs had given out.

His voice was a siren's call in the chaos of her thoughts. "Don't look," he said as he turned her away, but it was too late. She'd seen everything.

Present

Annabel woke with a start. A cold sweat covered her as she felt sick to her stomach. The violent way her uncle had died had not been a normal heart issue. Ripping her covers off she hurried to splash cold water on her face. Tears erupted and slid down her cheeks unchecked as she came to the realization that she'd been foolhardy. It took her a moment to reign in her ragged breathing and just as long to put her thoughts in some semblance of an order. Her belief that if she rebuffed Lawrence Haywood, he wouldn't go forward with his plan had been foolhardy. She should have known better—a man willing to kill that many people to become king wouldn't be put off so easily.

Gripping the wood of the dresser she felt the twist in her gut turn to anger. She was going to have to change tactics. She'd tried the path of least resistance but should have recognized it was foolish at best. Annabel had purposely ignored the part of herself that demonstrated her true potential, that had been just below the surface. Now she was going to have to put it to full use.

She spent the remainder of the hours until dawn strategizing. To go on the offensive would require a complete reversal and putting Lord Haywood in a position of false security. Yenni had been right, the best way to force the truth to light was to give him exactly what he wanted. Make him believe he'd won or was on the verge of winning.

Annabel was staring out the window when Heddie opened the door. She'd been there for some time after she'd come to the inevitable conclusion that she was going to have to make a very difficult choice. She crept across the room, as always.

137

The Promise of Dreams

"Good morning," Annabel said, and Heddie gasped.

The pitcher was jerked around as Heddie whirled. Water sloshed onto the carpet and Heddie's dress as her maid's wide eyes locked onto her.

"For all that is holy, what are you doing awake?" Heddie pressed a hand to her chest.

"It isn't that surprising," Annabel replied, rolling her eyes as she crossed her arms. "I can wake up when I wish."

"Apparently. Here I thought those last two instances were flukes." Heddie shook her head. "Do you intend on making this a habit?"

"Unfortunately," Annabel glanced back out the window. The words were stuck in her throat before she managed to dislodge them. "Can you request that Lord Cain call upon me this morning?"

"Happily," Heddie replied, sounding pleased. There was a long pause before she spoke again. "Is something wrong?" Annabel felt conflicted in the face of her lady maid's concern. "Did you have a fight? I thought you were getting on well."

"We are friends, most assuredly," Annabel replied trying to smooth over her own troubled emotions. "I just have difficult news to share, that is all."

Heddie crossed the room to give her a pat on her shoulder. "You've really grown, I know you can handle it."

"Thank you, Heddie." Annabel patted her hand. "It was just what I needed to hear."

138

Chapter 27

"Lord Cain and Lady Cierra," the attendant announced.

Lord Cain tipped his head to the servant as he entered. It took everything within her not to turn away. She met his gaze head on as the door was closed behind them.

"Cierra, I know it is against protocol, but I must have a moment alone with your brother," Annabel informed them.

Cierra's gaze darted between them, but she eventually nodded, before going out onto the balcony. Once the door was closed behind her, Annabel turned to Cain. After a momentary struggle she found the courage to continue.

"I believe I've done you a great disservice," Annabel said earnestly.

He seemed shocked at her words before shaking his head. "You have given me my life back."

"Yes, but I asked you to court me, leveraging the appreciation I knew you felt," Annabel stated. "That was unfair. It took advantage of you and your situation." Annabel felt emotions swell at the words. "That is, I used you poorly and was not a very good friend."

Annabel waited patiently while Cain contemplated the words she'd said. "I had...not thought of it that way." Cain finally spoke after a lengthy pause.

"I believe it best if we end this farce." Annabel forced her fingers to uncurl when she realized she was clenching them in her dress. "Wouldn't you agree?"

"Did I do something wrong?"

Annabel felt dread form in the pit of her stomach. "It is for the sake of our friendship. You have become very dear to me, and as your...friend, I should stop placing you in a difficult position. Especially since it is keeping you here, away from your family and your life back home." She forced a smile on her face as the last use of 'friend' stuck her throat and did not want to dislodge. She needed to use another word, any alternate, but found herself grabbing hold to it like a drowning woman.

"Do you wish me to leave?" His eyes narrowed.

Had she pushed too hard? Annabel worried. "I only wish to free you from this obligation." She saw the conflict on his face and tried to keep her demeanor with an unaffected air. "I am sure your family misses you. And now that you are gaining control of your abilities, you are no longer restricted from finding a fine lady to marry."

Why were those words so hard? She tried to stifle any more discouraging thoughts from bubbling up.

His eyebrows arched further above his eyes. "I had not considered it."

She clapped her hands together. "Truly the world is open to you. So now you understand why I feel this arrangement is unfair."

The room became still, his gaze seemed to be searching for something. A lifetime of hiding her emotions meant he would find nothing. Even if her heart wavered, her face remained unchanged. She waited patiently, her hands poised in her lap, for his response.

"Is this because of what I said yesterday?" He asked, his words barely audible.

"Yes," Annabel replied, "I realized I was being selfish. That you have become someone I hold dear and that you should now finally seek out that honorable marriage you desire." Annabel clasped her hands tightly together.

"I want that happiness for you." She forced the next words out. "As your friend."

It was momentary but he appeared disappointed. "I see."

"I am glad that you do," Annabel replied shifting forward. "I have given it some thought and at the masquerade ball, we should make a public break. I do not intend it to be a dramatic affair, simply an amicable end to our supposed courtship."

He seemed so disheartened, and she had to fight every instinct to pretend that she wasn't seeing it. "You've given this much thought."

"I would never wish to tarnish your reputation," Annabel replied, feeling like she wanted to reach out to him but refrained from doing so. "You are my dear...friend after all." She cleared her throat. "Do you find my plan sufficient?"

He nodded. "If it is what you wish, I shall see it through."

She forced a cheerful disposition as she folded her hands together. "I am so glad you understand." She stood and went towards the terrace to retrieve Lady Cierra.

"Annabel."

She stopped in the middle of the room; it was the first time he'd said her name. No titles, no barrier, just her name. The lump she had to swallow down made her lower lip quiver a bit before she managed to gather her composure. How had he gotten so good at breaking down her barriers?

Annabel turned around with a smile on her face, as though the way he'd said her name with yearning hadn't affected her. "You've finally said my name."

Cain was standing and his brows were furrowed. She felt her smile falter and struggled to keep it in place. If she'd had any doubt before, she could no longer deny it; she was in love with him. Despite that she had to move forward. It was the only way to draw Lawrence into a trap and to keep her family safe.

It was cruel, but she saw no other way. "Is something wrong?" Annabel asked, tipping her head to the side.

It was like she'd slapped him in the face. He straightened, she saw him physically gather himself, before he shook his head.

"No," Cain answered, his expression as solemn as when he'd first arrived. "Nothing is wrong. I simply believe I don't have to wait for the ball. If I leave now the message will be clear that our courtship has ended."

"I see," Annabel replied, keeping herself in check. "Have a safe trip."

They stared at each other, neither moving for a few moments. Then he bowed deeply to her. When he stood, she felt the wall he'd built between them and tried not to acknowledge how much its presence hurt. "Thank you for all that you have done, I am forever in your debt. Should you need me, I am but a letter away."

Annabel didn't reply as he left the room. She watched the door long after he was gone—wondering if she'd ever see him again. With a start, she glanced at Cierra when the other woman touched a hand to her arm. She was holding up a handkerchief. It was only then that Annabel realized she was crying.

"Do you wish to discuss it?" Lady Cierra asked, as Annabel took the offered cloth.

"Do not tell him." Annabel's voice hitched at the end. "He must never know. No matter what he says, it is best if he leaves."

"I will not pretend to understand," Lady Cierra replied her brows furrowed, "but encourage you to reconsider."

Sniffling, she gathered herself. Wiping away her tears she focused on what she must do next. "I would not begrudge you if you wished to leave with him."

Lady Cierra sighed. "I shall stay." Then she curtsied and left.

Annabel went to her bedroom on wobbly legs. When she closed the door, she leaned against it as a quiet sob escaped. Sliding to the floor she put her head in her arms as she set all of her emotions free. She let herself experience regret and accept that she'd just sent away the man she was in love with. She acknowledged that she risked never seeing him again based on a dream. It was the only way she could possibly face what she was going to have to do next.

Chapter 28

Annabel purposely extended an invitation to Lord Haywood. In her letter she wrote that since the Annual Hunt she had thought of little else. She invited him to meet her to take a turn about the park the next day. The morning had turned out to be rather dreary. It matched her mood perfectly though she'd have to pretend otherwise. Heddie had informed her earlier that morning that Lord Cain had departed for the Southern Isles rather suddenly. He'd done just as he'd said, left prior to the ball which was in a few days. In a way she should thank him for making the next steps of her plan easier to take. Though her heart did not agree with her head on this matter.

With Lady Zerwin soon to be married and Lady Cierra an unneeded reminder, she'd decided to take Lady Ariah as her chaperone. Especially since she was the one who would say the least. A notable trait that Annabel had discounted until that morning.

Holding an umbrella, Annabel made her way to the benches on the northern side of the park. Normally a servant or groom would carry the umbrella but for what was to come next, she wanted as little wagging of tongues as possible.

She spotted him already at the benches when she approached. Her stomach twisted in knots at the memory of his sword slicing across her throat. Forcing that down she went to the water's edge. Stopping beside him, she smiled as he took his top hat off and bowed.

"Greetings, Princess Annabel," Lawrence said as he put the hat back on his head.

"Lord Haywood, what an unexpected pleasure." Annabel feigned astonishment as she offered her hand.

He seemed surprised but took it and kissed her gloved knuckles. She pretended to enjoy the exchange as he straightened. It seemed it would be easier to ensnare him than she thought.

"The pleasure is mine."

Annabel giggled in a flirty way. "It seems the weather is leaving you quite exposed." Annabel purposely reached out and wiped at the rain on his jacket. An intimate exchange that would be viewed by many as inappropriate. "Might you share my umbrella?" She hid her hatred behind her lashes.

"That would be lovely," Lawrence replied offering his arm.

She took his offered arm as they turned to take a turn about the park. "Are you intending to go to the ball?"

"I am," Lawrence replied. She already knew that since she'd found out her forgetful brother had extended him an invitation. "And Lord Varen's wedding."

"Do you have a lady that you are set upon?" Annabel asked, brazenly pushing the boundaries of propriety.

"Perhaps," Lawrence replied. "Though she is already being courted. So, I find myself attending alone."

"I have it under good authority that has ended," Annabel replied, trying not to think of Cain at all. "Would that change your plans?"

He smiled in her direction, and she forced herself to match it. Her chest felt tight as she pretended to be enamored with him. It seemed he wasn't questioning her sudden change at all. Either her letter or behavior had quickly turned the tide in their relationship.

"I believe it would," he said as they followed the horseshoe shaped path around, back towards where they started.

"Then it seems you must make a formal request, I am sure news of her unattachment shall spread quickly," Annabel said glancing over her shoulder. "Isn't that right, Lady Ariah?"

"If her highness says so," Lady Ariah replied without a hint of expression.

"See," Annabel hurried over the less than supporting statement. "It'll be well known by the evening." Annabel sighed heavily. "What am I to do?"

Lawrence chuckled charmingly, but it felt grating to her ears. "Might I be able to remedy it?"

"Perhaps with a well-timed letter." Annabel felt like she'd laid the groundwork. When they reached the end of the path she paused and purposely let his arm go to reach back for Lady Ariah. "I've lingered long enough. Though it was a pleasure seeing you again, Lord Haywood."

Lord Haywood bowed to her, deeply. "Until next time, your highness."

Annabel took Lady Ariah's hand and let the other girl's quiet nature act as a balm. To reinforce her intent, she paused at the carriage and glanced back. Lawrence was right where she'd left him on the path. He seemed quite pleased with himself and tipped his head to her. She pretended to be shy as her stomach rolled.

Once they were safely inside the carriage Annabel stared out the window into the dreary weather. "Aren't you going to ask what I'm doing?" Annabel felt a lump in her throat as she asked.

"Do I have any right to know, your highness?" Lady Ariah countered.

"That is true." A part of her wanted to be told to stop.

"When I am unsure, I speak to my sister's," Lady Ariah said, her gaze almost eerily sharp.

Annabel sighed. "Family is complicated."

She may be acting with intent, but part of her felt out of control. Her uncle's dying face was the only thing that steeled her resolve. She would not let it come to pass or any of the other tragedies her first dream had predicted.

No matter the personal cost.

Annabel was staring out the window at the rain as it coated the window. It had gone from a slight rain to a downpour. She took a sip from her tea, warmed by the beverage but not comforted. It had only been a few hours since she'd met Lord Haywood and that should have been her focus, but all she could think about was Cain. Had he gotten caught in the rain? What if he took ill?

"Annabel?" Yenni's voice roused her.

"Yes?" She replied, glancing at her sister. She sat across from her with a book open in her lap.

"When you sought me out, I thought you wanted to talk, but all you've managed is to sigh." Yenni's knowing stare attempted to break down her defenses. "Is this about Lord Cain?"

Annabel stopped herself from heaving yet another sigh. She was going to have to be careful with those—they were become an unfortunate habit. "We broke our courtship." The next part was going to be difficult to sell to her clever sister. "I went for a walk in the park to clear my head and happened upon Lord Haywood. I am expecting a letter." This time she pushed out a fake heavy exhale. "I do hope it comes soon."

Yenni's gaze sharpened. "Lord Haywood?"

"He is quite...charming." Annabel took a sip of her tea.

"You seemed quite taken with Lord Cain," Yenni replied. "Did something happen?"

Why was her sister so perceptive? Annabel thought. "Marriage. He made it quite clear, that was his end goal, and it is not mine." That at least was the truth.

To her surprise Yenni snapped the book closed. "I never thought I'd say this, but I'm very disappointed in you. I didn't think you so cowardly."

Annabel blinked at her sister in shock. Yenni was not one to speak a cross word about anyone, let alone her family. Annabel realized she was slack jawed and slowly closed it. She stayed silent, having no retort for her sister's attack. Instead, a sense of defeat overcame her despite her resolve. It seemed Lady Ariah's suggestion was a poor one.

"Especially for such petty reasons," Yenni continued when Annabel said nothing. "Lord Haywood is not someone you've ever expressed an interest in."

Annabel stood so quickly that her teacup fell to the carpet and splashed across it. "It seems you don't know me at all." Then she stormed out before Yenni could see her tears.

The wedding hall was filled as they all took their seats. Weddings were simple affairs compared to engagement parties. Annabel sat down, glancing around for Lord Haywood. His letter had indicated that he would arrive at the ceremony and then ask to escort her to the masquerade ball at the wedding breakfast. Despite the extra steps she'd taken to safeguard her uncle, she felt uneasy. Not willing to leave anything to chance, she'd convinced Master Wil to let her borrow one of the Mage healers. She'd made up some excuse, but Master Wil had taken little convincing.

When the wedding started, she focused on the proceedings. Lady Zerwin made a perfect bride, and Varen couldn't seem to take his eyes off her. Lady Zerwin's father was a portly man who had tears in his eyes as he handed his daughter to her future husband. Apparently, that is where Lady Zerwin had inherited her temperament from.

The clergyman recited the rites. Once that was complete, the happy couple read from the holy book and in quick order the rings were exchanged. Annabel found herself so completely distracted that she felt like she'd missed it all. With the ceremony complete they entered the marriage into the temple's register. The register served as legal proof that the wedding had taken place.

Once done, the happy couple walked down the aisle and out into the garden just beyond the palace temple. The royal family, including herself, followed suit. Outside, pavilions were laid out with breakfast already set out. She scanned the area but found no sign of Lord Haywood. Had he changed his mind?

To the right of the food were plates filled with the wedding cake, and one untouched for the newlyweds to dole out to family and friends. Unlike the ceremony which had limited attendance, the garden was already full of nobility wishing to participate in the celebration. When she continued to find no sign of him, her stomach turned.

Normally Annabel was quick to sample the wedding cake as often as she could with its fruit and copious amounts of libations drizzled on top. As was normal for the royal family, it was wrapped in a thin white sugar icing. She loved that part more than anything but now it would only hurt her sour stomach. Where was he?

Annabel fidgeted with her parasol as she slowly made her way towards her seat. Servants had laid out food for them. Carefully she picked up her cup and swapped it with her uncle's—she wasn't taking any chances. Turning the swapped glass onto its head indicated it needed to be replaced, as she took her seat. She barely tasted the sweet, buttery roll as she nibbled on it. She kept glancing at her uncle, keeping him and his food within her sight.

Comparing what she remembered from her dream to what was unfolding, much of it was the same. The only major difference being the lack of Lord Cain. She didn't know if it was his absence or Lord Haywood's tardiness that made it all feel wrong. She felt lightheaded, her breathing was increasing, and Annabel realized that she was having trouble focusing.

"Princess," Lord Haywood said, bowing to her. Her world came into focus, and she swallowed down her panic as best she could. "I appreciate the invitation."

"You honor me." They were turning heads when Annabel stood. Her legs wobbled as she stood, and Lord Haywood caught her as she felt her world narrow. She didn't have time to feel anything as she faded out.

A moment later she inhaled sharply, coming out of it. "Annabel?" Mayven's face came into view.

"Brother? What?" Annabel asked, confused by the angle in which was she viewing the world.

"You fainted, are you well?" He asked, helping her sit up.

Annabel glanced around at the crowd and then noticed that Lord Haywood was kneeling beside her still. Despite her half-conscious state, she reached out a hand. Everyone watched as Lord Haywood took it.

"You saved me." It was not a question.

"It was my duty to come to your aid," his false charm affective for those watching.

"I am in your debt, sir." Annabel leaned heavily into her brother as she decided it would be best to feign falling asleep to end this exchange. "Would you honor me with...the ball?" She slumped against her brother, letting her hand droop as she pretended to faint like her life depended on it.

Chapter 29

Annabel smoothed the front of her dress as she waited for Lord Haywood to arrive. To avoid any interference in the days leading up to the ball, she'd insisted she'd spent too much time in the sun, slept poorly after Lord Cain's sudden departure, and hadn't eaten enough despite the excitement. Though her ladies-in-waiting were the only ones who visited her. Despite asking for both Yenni and Len, neither came. Perhaps Yenni had shared with their sister what Annabel had done and now they were both mad at her. Add to that the nagging guilt at worrying her mother, it had been a miserable few days. Even if her accidental fainting episode had proved to be the perfect cover. Now all that was left was to lure Lawrence in, and spring the trap.

"Is something wrong?" Lady Cierra asked as they waited in the side hall. She was stunning in her emerald-green dress, as was Lady Phoebe in her bright pink one. Lady Ariah had opted for a simpler attire with a powder blue, but still cut a fetching figure.

"Princess Annabel," Lawrence approached, escorted by a royal guard. "You are breathtaking."

She took his hands as he held them up as though admiring her. Her deep purple dress made her pale blond locks seem almost white. Amethysts adorned her hair and were draped across her throat in an elegant arrangement. She did not doubt his compliment was true, she'd made sure it was.

"I am glad it had the desired effect," Annabel replied, her gaze purposely direct.

Lord Haywood was momentarily surprised. "This was for me?"

"Who else?" Annabel asked. "Shall we?"

He firmly tucked her gloved hand into his arm. "Yes, we must."

They were announced and entered the hall. Heads turned, tongues waged, and whispers filled the hall. The escorts for her entourage were waiting and were announced as they entered. To her surprise Lord Jespin was with Lady Cierra. Apparently, she'd thought too highly of him if he'd moved on from Len so soon.

"Shall we dance?" Lawrence asked.

"With pleasure," Annabel replied.

They danced and at every turn, Annabel insisted he bring them another drink. What he didn't know is she'd taken a tonic and eaten a meal that would help her withstand the effects of alcohol. She could have drunk him under the table if she wanted. All her life she knew what libations did to a man's judgement. She hoped Lawrence was no different. Plying him with compliments as well as drinks, progressed through the night.

"He never left her side again!" Lawrence finished the punchline.

Laughing harder than was necessary, Annabel fluttered her fan. "Oh, Lawrence you are too much."

He blinked at her. "Lawrence?"

Annabel covered her mouth as though shocked. "Was that too forward?"

He moved closer than polite society would normally allow. "Not at all." She smelled the liquor on his breath.

"I'm feeling so warm." Annabel fanned herself with her hand to escape the sudden lack of personal space. "Can you get another drink and meet me on the terrace?" She paused for effect. "My private terrace?"

The princesses were granted a private terrace during such events. The princes could use it as well, but they rarely did. Annabel made haste to the terrace. She dismissed the guard, making sure no one would stop him. Once there she went to the railing and took a deep breath of the warm evening. She only had one shot at this.

The door opened behind her, and she turned around with a smile firmly planted on her face only to freeze. Instead of Lawrence, Lord Cain stood on the threshold. The door closed quietly behind him as she forgot how to breathe.

"I know you asked me to leave." Cain came closer to her, his expression pained.

Her happiness at seeing him again when she was certain she never would, immediately devolved into panic. He had to leave!

She shook her head, and it caused him to stop. "You shouldn't be here."

He swallowed heavily as her heartbeat rapidly. "I know, but I had to see you. I had to talk to you one last time." Her gaze slid towards the terrace to her left, as her heart felt like a trapped bird. "To tell you, what I feel for you."

Annabel forgot everything else at those words. "What you feel for me?"

"You are without equal. I may have left you, but you never left me. You were always in my thoughts, and further I rode away, the worse it became." He reached a hand towards her. "End my agony."

"I don't understand."

"I want to court you for real." Annabel's heart blossomed at the words.

"Cain," Annabel felt herself lean forward. "I—"

Before she could complete her reply, the glass door closed loudly. Standing with two glasses, one in each hand, Lord Haywood examined the scene with obvious surprise. Reality slapped her in the face, and she drew back, physically moving away from Cain and the words her traitorous mouth had tried to speak.

"Lawrence," Annabel called out and watched Cain flinch at the word.

"Am I interrupting?" Lawrence asked, his gaze sweeping between them.

Cain's gaze fixed on her. Filled with desperation that nearly made her weep on the spot, Annabel steeled herself. The next words broke her heart.

"No." It was like she'd cut his strings; she watched as all hope slid out of Cain. "Lord Van Brandt was just leaving." She had failed to keep the quiver completely out of her voice.

"Is this what you really want?" Cain shifted towards her.

"Yes." She stepped towards Lord Haywood as he came to her side, setting the glasses on a table on his way. "You and I want different things. I will never want what you want. Please accept that."

"I can't," Cain replied, his voice resolute. "Just as I cannot accept that he'll make you happier than I could."

"You heard her," Lawrence replied, his voice as sharp as his gaze. "Leave."

She watched as his longing turned to despair. "Once I leave, I'll never return." His gaze was so sincere, so sure, that Annabel couldn't keep her lip from quivering.

Annabel curled her fingers in her dress so tightly it hurt. It was necessary. It was for her family. She must say the words. They were needed to ensure what came next. "I don't want you. I want him." Why was breathing so hard? It was like someone had stabbed something into her lungs.

Cain searched her face one last time and then said nothing more to her as he left. She saw him slip through the door. She never knew a person leaving could make the world feel smaller and emptier, but that is what happened. Would he ever forgive her? Would she ever see him again?

"Do you mean it?" Lawrence asked.

"I did not mean to reveal it so soon, you must think I'm silly," Annabel said, her voice high-pitched with emotion. "We've known each other such a short period of time."

He hugged her then. She tried to get better footing, and her shoe caught a crack in the floor, her shoe sliding awkwardly to the side as she felt her entire world shift. Annabel let tears slip down her cheeks unchecked.

"Yes, though my father will never allow it." She wiped at them, letting the pain of possibly losing the only man she'd ever loved feed her frustrated voice. "He doesn't think anyone I choose is good enough. I sometimes wish he was gone."

Lawrence's charming smile suddenly grew in intensity. She tipped her head forward and covered her face as though grieving, but it was to hide the disgust on her face. Leaning into him he stroked her hair.

"I can take care of him," Lord Haywood said.

"What?" Annabel replied, purposely sniffling. "How?"

"Don't you worry your little head about it." Lawrence patted her back, and she fought down the urge to claw his eyes out.

"He's the king," Annabel pressed, what he said hadn't been enough. "How can you take care of him?"

He sighed heavily as though dealing with a child. "I'll make sure he isn't the king that much longer."

The certainty in his voice was chilling, making her heart start to thud in her ribcage like a galloping horse. She had to take a steadying breath and remember the expression on her uncle's dying face before she could manage to steel herself for the next part. Annabel was going to have to say something she thought she'd never say in her life.

She tilted her head to the side and asked as though a dullard. "But my father's so young. He'll oppose us as long as he lives."

"Do you wish to marry me?" He brought her hand towards his face before turning her wrist and kissing it. "Tell me Annabel."

She hesitated only a moment. "Of course." *Only in his dreams.*

"I knew you would agree." His confidence was astounding.

Annabel sighed heavily. "That doesn't change what my father will say."

"A simple accident could fix all that." Lawrence patted her cheek lovingly. "My dear sweet Annabel, we shall be wed in a fortnight."

"Even if my father is dethroned, my brother will also oppose it," Annabel cried, covering her face with her hands. That wasn't true at all, her brother would approve, if Annabel really insisted. "I am without hope."

He parted her wrists and came so close their noses were nearly touching. "Then let me restore your hope. I will remove every obstacle towards our marriage, even if it is by force."

"Permanently remove them?" Annabel asked, as though finally understanding his words.

"Yes. Even if they have to be wiped from this world," Lawrence said, menacingly. "Now that you have agreed to marry me, we shall announce to everyone our intent."

"Right now?" Annabel asked, taken aback.

"Yes, it will allow me more access to the palace," Lawrence replied, dragging her out of the terrace and back into the dance hall.

He wasted no time in getting them before the king. After Lord Haywood bowed, Annabel thought to curtsy to her father. She glanced desperately behind her, hoping her plan had worked. Had his words been enough?

"Your highness," Lawrence declared, going against every decorum. "I have just asked for your daughter's hand in marriage, and she has accepted."

Gasps filled the hall as Annabel felt herself shrinking under her father's gaze. "Annabel. Explain yourself."

"Its...that is, I..." Annabel wasn't sure how to stall for time.

Thankfully she didn't have to as the crowd parted for Sir Jeorge with a squad of royal guards. "Lord Haywood, you are under arrest for treason against the crown."

Annabel sighed in relief. Apparently, Sir Jeorge had heard their exchange loud and clear from the other terrace. Her relief was so great, she nearly started crying again on the spot. Lord Haywood was completely shocked as he shook his head. They took hold of him as he tried to jerk free.

"Unhand me." Lawrence struggled in their hold. "You have no proof."

"I heard you proclaim it myself."

"Nonsense, Annabel, tell them it is nonsense," Lawrence said, turning to her.

"Do not address me so intimately." Annabel lifted her head. "You were going to kill my family," Annabel replied. "Do you think I would accept that?" Then she had a thought. "You aren't the man I thought you were."

Her betrayal shocked him as he went still. Annabel held his gaze as it turned to hate, and she felt only relief. It was finally over.

"Take him away," the king ordered. Annabel watched him resist momentarily before letting himself be hauled away. "You have some explaining to do."

"I suspected for some time that Lord Haywood had designs on our family." Annabel declared, causing a ripple of whispers to span out.

"Father!" Lenora joined them. "I ask for clemency for Lord Haywood." Her gaze sharpened on Annabel. "We all know how Annabel can be."

Annabel gasped in shock. Who was this person? Certainly not her sister. "Len?"

Her only response was a glare so full of loathing that Annabel didn't recognize her. "Please father, give him a fair trial. I have known him far longer and can vouch for his character. I am sure whatever was said was at Annabel's manipulation."

Annabel suddenly realized Len's secret man was none other than Lord Haywood. All this time he'd been focusing not on one princess, but on two. Annabel suddenly felt sick to her stomach. How had she not seen it?

"I shall investigate the matter." His gaze slid over to Annabel. "Thoroughly." He waved his hands. "This ball is over, return home."

Lenora sent her a horrible sneer before turning on her heels. Annabel immediately pursued her and asked her to stop. Yet her sister showed no signs of listening to her pleas.

Chapter 30

"Len, wait," Annabel tried to catch her arm, but her sister jerked free. "Let me explain."

"I don't want to hear it. Whatever you touch gets ruined," Lenora said, her face twisted. "You are a curse upon this family, and I wish you had never been born."

Annabel was shocked as her sister rushed away, angry tears in her eyes. Everything she had been trying to prevent had happened. The very people she wanted to protect, were the very people she was hurting—Yenni, Len, and Cain. Who else had she hurt? Why have this power if she had no way to prevent the outcome?

"Annabel?" Cain's voice cut into her thoughts.

She whirled around in shock. "You're still here?" Then she glanced towards where Len had fled. "How much did you hear?"

There was a flicker of pity in his gaze. "Enough." He drew closer to her. "I was about to leave forever, when I heard the commotion."

Annabel lifted her head high and took a step back. "I...don't know what to say." She'd hurt him in every possible way. On purpose to stop Lawrence, but that couldn't take back the words.

He seemed perplexed by her answer and took a step closer. "It doesn't matter."

"How can you say that? I have wronged you." Annabel felt tears threatened. "In every possible way. How can you ever believe anything I say?"

"You are a lot of things, Annabel," Cain said moving closer to her, "A liar is not one of them."

"And you think you know me so well?" Annabel replied. "I do break everything I touch. Len is right, I'm a curse."

He tipped his head to the side and shifted in intimately close. She could smell the clean scent of soap and lavender. For some reason something so simple as his smell made her heart beat wildly.

"I know a thing about curses. You are not one." Cain's voice was but a whisper, yet it was firm. "You try to hide your good and caring heart behind mischief and a façade of unruliness."

Annabel swallowed at his assessment as she felt tears prick her eyes. How dare he say something so...wonderful. Her strong foundation shuddered in the face of his assault on her sensitivities. She shook her head as though that would ward him off. Instead, he put a hand on her cheek.

"You have been there for me, when I was lost and desperate. You sought to understand not just the curse, but the man behind it. You broke down my walls, please let me do the same." Cain's thumb caressed her cheek. "There is nothing you could say that would make me hate you. Even when you told me no, I couldn't hate you. I don't think I ever will."

"How can you say that with such conviction?" Annabel asked, her voice shaking as she averted her gaze.

"Because," he said, sounding so tender, "I'm in love with you. Tell me you did not mean what you said before. That I have some place in your heart."

Annabel just stared at him. Her hurt and fear left her in a snap as she opened her mouth to respond but found no words. It was everything she'd ever wanted and yet it came on the heels of ruining her sister's happiness and breaking his heart with falsehoods. Did she deserve to have this moment?

He leaned in, pressing his lips to her forehead. It shook her out of her state of shock. Before he could pull away Annabel gripped his collar and jerked his face towards hers.

"If you think after such a confession you are going to get away with a chaste kiss, you don't know me at all," Annabel said before thrusting her lips against his.

He chuckled, and it made her quiver with desire. He tipped his head to the side and urged her lips open. His tongue slid into her mouth, and she met his passion with her own. He tasted better than she could ever have imagined, and it left her feeling breathless. His hand slid to the back of her neck, bringing her even closer. She could feel how warm he was, his skin making her own feel flushed.

When he eased back, she felt light-headed. Her legs were wobbly, and she felt like she was in a daze. She'd tried to catch him off-guard, but it was she who was left stunned. With all she knew of him, from his solemn side to his kindness, she was unprepared for his desire.

"Why do you make everything topsy-turvy?" Annabel whispered, her thoughts escaping her lips unaltered.

"Does this mean you'll let me court you?" Cain asked, his hands on her waist, pulling her against him. "Properly?"

"Could I stop you?" Annabel replied before brushing her lips against his, feeling dizzy with longing. It didn't matter that everything they were doing went against what society expected.

He groaned and put his hand on the column behind her, leaning forward. "Not if you keep doing that."

"Good," she whispered, feeling wild as she craved his touch. "I don't want you to stop."

Pulling him close she opened herself to him. Her hands finding the contours of his body through his clothes, caressing him as she'd never imagined possible. The feelings she'd been trying to ignore were let loose like horses across the plains. He seemed hesitant at first, but she would not let him quell their heat, she was afraid he'd never let her do this again—explore this man she had fallen in love with.

"Annabel," her name said in desperation sent shivers down her spine.

"Cain." His name ripe with passion as he trailed kisses down her neck.

He grunted and put his hands on each side of her, his head resting on her shoulder. "We should stop."

Her hands caressed the contours of his face. "You're right," she said breathlessly.

Easing back, he glanced up at her. "This is risky."

She searched his face, completely overcome with yearning. "I know."

The unsaid words hung in the air between them before their lips met, arms entangled around each other, as they ignored reason. His tongue declared war on her mouth, conquering every region with vigor. Annabel moaned; her knees weak as she succumbed. How could she ever have thought life would be better if they were apart?

He gripped her arms, their breathing ragged as they stared into each other's eyes. "I cannot have a child out of wedlock."

Annabel blinked at him. She could see it distressed him, see the conflict within him, and what should have been a sobering statement instead strengthened her resolve. She'd almost lost him once; she would not allow it to happen again. Inhaling, she tried to see reason, but found only one answer.

"I won't let that happen," Annabel whispered.

He seemed shocked by her statement. "How would you prevent it? There is always a possibility."

"I do not mean preventing a child." Annabel lovingly touched a hand to his cheek. "I mean that I would ensure the child was legitimate."

"The only way to do that would be to…" his words stopped coming out of his mouth as his thoughts tried to catch up.

Then his eyes went wide, and she nodded. "Marriage." She confirmed aloud what he was realizing.

"You'd…you'd marry me?" Cain asked, as though he couldn't believe it.

"Yes." Neither her heart nor her head faltered at the declaration.

"Forget your independence?" He seemed so astonished she nearly burst out laughing.

"I know you would not ask me to forgo it all. It would be a…partnership." Annabel had never been more sure of anything in her life.

"Annabel!" He lifted her up and spun her around.

This time she did laugh as she clung to him. Her hands sought his face so she could plant her lips against his. He gripped her in his arms and kissed her fervently. She was thoroughly in love with him, she could not deny it any longer. His honest confession had turned her world upside down and all she could see was him.

She took his hand and led him through the palace gardens. She took all of the secret paths before happening upon her favorite place. The gazebo had been closed up, already prepared for when they would have departed in the coming days. She pushed it open and guided Cain inside. The moonlight came through the slats in the gazebo, providing just enough light for her to see him.

"Annabel." He sounded hesitant.

She reached out and took his hand. Pulling the glove off, she brought his knuckles to her lips. "I want to dispel any concerns. I am in love with you as well. I have been for longer than I care to admit. Even to myself." She moved closer to him, feeling the heat radiate from him. "I want you to imprint yourself on me in such a way that you will always be a part of me." She guided his hand to the back of her dress.

His lips found hers in the near darkness. Finger working the buttons as she explored his body, tugging as waistbands and removing his over jacket and vest to gain better access. When his fingers finally found her skin she gasped, pressing her body against his.

"Where should I touch?" He whispered, sounding lost.

"Everywhere." Annabel gained access to his shirt and slid her fingertips across his smooth skin. He had hair on his chest, and well-toned muscles. "Anywhere!"

Still, he hesitated but she was impatient. Pulling at her own outer dress she soon felt it fall away. He eased back and she could just make out the outline of his person in the darkness. Then in the haze of her desire, she realized he'd never touched someone like that before. How could he have with his curse?

Finding a modicum of patience, she found his hand and guided it to her breast. "These are supposed to feel good. Especially the nipples."

His fingers dipped below the fabric and freed one breast. His fingers moved across her nipple, almost clumsy as he tried to gain access. Then his mouth was on her breast, and she moaned, gripping his head. It was far better than anything she'd read in a book.

"You're so soft and taste…" he just let out a sigh of longing before returning to massage her breasts.

Annabel worked at her corset, trying to loosen the strings. She wanted to grant him better access to all of her. When he realized what she was doing, he helped her and soon it was on the ground with the rest of her clothes. Then she started to pull at his. When her hand brushed against the bulge in his clothing he groaned.

Encouraged by the sound she didn't hesitate to trail a hand down his stomach and to his manhood. Once she found the start of the shaft, she followed along the length of it. She could wrap her hand around it, but it seemed to go on forever. When she finally found the tip, her fingers explored his velvety softness. How could something so soft be so rigid?

Cain's arms went around her as he started to breathe heavily. The way he was completely at her mercy encouraged her to start moving up and down the impressive length of him. His hips started moving and he was whispering her name. The junction between her legs started to tingle. She wanted him to touch her too. Guiding his hand from her waist to her breast she continued her assault on his member.

"Annabel," he whispered. "Slow down. Please." Her excitement intensified at the desperation in his voice.

She could tell he was at his limit. "Do you want me to stop?" Annabel breathlessly asked. Trying to remember what those salacious books had said.

He was clinging to her as he muttered, "Yes?" Followed quickly by a pleading, "No!" when her thumb brushed across his velvety tip.

A moment later he shuddered, bucking wildly against her grip before stilling as he moaned softly. He held her tight as he quivered against her as she felt him breathing heavily. Her own desire building, desperate for his touch.

"That," he said, resting his forehead against hers, "was better than anything I'd ever experienced."

"Do you want to do it again?" Annabel asked, her cheeks hurt from how much she was smiling. How could this tall, imposing man be so adorable?

"No," he replied. "It's your turn."

"Do you know..." she gasped mid-sentence as he knelt in front of her, stripping off her drawers and stockings.

"I know enough," he said, as he lifted her leg over his shoulder and slid his tongue along— "Oh my!" She gasped at the feeling of him. Annabel forgot reason as pleasure washed over her, taking hold of her senses. He was sating raw aches with sharp gratification she'd never experienced before.

His fingers and his tongue were exploring every part of her, and she felt herself open to him. When he brushed against the top of her womanhood, she jerked in surprise with a breathy gasp as she felt her muscles clench at the wonderful sensation. He focused his attention there with vigor. Her legs started to quiver as she felt something building within her. His fingers, were barely penetrating her, began exploring deeper, while he sucked and licked her sensitive nub.

"Cain." She gasped, her hands gripping his shoulders as she tried to open herself wider to him. "More!"

Without hesitation, he happily obliged. As she whimpered in pleasure, the sounds, her moans, and the way he was touching her was too much. She began to rock back and forth, grinding against his mouth as she felt an unfamiliar sensation growing.

"Cain, something's coming." Annabel tried to pull away, uncertain what was happening.

He locked the arm he wasn't using around her leveraged leg, preventing her from moving, then he added another finger. She arched her back as something exploded within her, euphoria spreading through her very essence. Cain caught her as her legs gave way and helped her to the ground.

"Are you hurt?" Cain asked, panic in his voice.

"No...no...no...no..." Annabel felt herself shaking her head, saying the same word over and over as she tried to get her bearings. She felt intoxicated, like the time she'd stolen a bottle of wine when she was younger and drank it all. Yet this felt better—so much better—like her entire body was floating!

"Annabel?" He sounded so worried, but all she could do was giggle.

Pressing her forehead against his, she barely felt the evening chill start to set in against her feverish skin. "I love you."

"I love you." Although she couldn't see it, she could hear the smile in his voice.

"I want you to join us." Annabel kissed his lips softly. "Please, Cain. I want to be closer to you."

By way of answer, he laid her back slowly. He parted her legs and positioned himself but then paused. She waited, uncertain what was happening. Then she knew, in her heart, why he'd stopped.

She caressed his face as she said, "I'm sure. I won't change my mind. I won't run away. I want this and I want you."

He pressed himself against her opening. She opened her legs wider, inviting him in. His heat filled her, the further he pressed into her, the worse the pressure became. It had felt wonderful at the opening but further in, she felt discomfort, bordering on pain. Unexpected tears sprung to her eyes as she gripped his shoulders.

"Annabel," he whispered, his thumb brushed across her wet cheeks. "I'm hurting you." He was aghast.

He tried to move back, but she locked her legs around him. "I knew it would hurt the first time. All the books say so." Annabel exhaled shakily. "Move slowly, it only hurts a little." When he still didn't move, she whispered, "Please."

Slowly he started to shift back and forth, his hips making small motions. She felt both on fire and numb. She felt conflicted about whether to continue or not when he kissed her chest. Then her chin and her cheeks. He even kissed the tip of her nose. Every inch of her face was covered with kisses as he moved in and out of her. She sighed in contentment and then kissed him, wrapping her arms around his neck and they kissed deeply.

His thrusts were starting to gain speed, the pain was being replaced by pleasure. He began driving into her, and she found herself floating once more. Her entire sense of self was lost in the moment. The feeling of him inside of her, them being joined so intimately, fulfilled her.

"Cain!" Annabel called, trying against all reason to not cry out too loudly.

"Annabel." He grunted, his body shuddering again as he dug all the way into her, causing lightning to shoot through her.

She held him against her, feeling his weight as she basked in the glow of their love making. They laid embracing each other for a while. Then slowly they dressed, leaving kisses on the, normally hidden, parts of each other's bodies.

"I never thought this would be possible for me," Cain whispered, his fingers on her waist as he kissed the inside of her thigh, her stockings half up one leg. "You have altered my life in every possible way, and now I fear I cannot live without you."

A laugh filled with joy bubbled up her throat. "You continue to astonish me, my love. Who knew you had such a way with words?"

"It is you who inspires me to say such words." Cain helped her put her foot into her other stocking. "At times I fear this is a dream and I shall wake from it, to find I am alone once more."

She watched him finish quietly before kneeling in front of him, so they were nearly eye to eye. "You are far better than any dream, for I could not have imagined you on my own. You are more real to me then the moon and the stars."

They kissed passionately again, tongues entangled and arms embracing. It was torture to part after such a wonderous night, but it would be best if they returned. She should try to avoid some scandal after what she'd done publicly at the masquerade ball earlier that evening. When they opened the door, it leaned slightly off its hinges. It appeared to have broken at some point, how unfortunate. She'd have to send someone to repair it.

"I shall go to your father tomorrow," Cain told her, kissing her knuckles. "Ask to formally court you."

"I shall make him agree." Annabel brushed some short curls from his forehead.

He glanced at the looming castle behind her. "Are you sure I cannot walk you inside?"

Annabel shook her head. "We mustn't be seen together so late. It would be best if everyone assumed I'd hidden after what...happened." Reality was trying to invade their happy space.

"I understand."

One final kiss and she broke free. She nearly went back again for one more, but knew it was already impossibly late...or early the next morning. It was easy to slip through the corridors to return to her room. She only hoped Cain would be able to escape out the garden's side door in the morning when the guard changed over. Annabel had used that exact location multiple times to go on various adventures.

Annabel was still basking in the glow of their joining when she rounded the corner towards her room. She stopped in surprise as Sir Harl was standing guard at her door.

"Is something wrong?" Annabel asked, suddenly concerned.

Sir Harl's stern face betrayed nothing. "Your father wishes to speak with you."

Chapter 31

"First you cause a scene at the ball, then you disappear for hours. No one can find you. Your brothers are angry that you didn't come to any of them for help. Len is refusing to speak to anyone, and Yenni is with your mother since she thought you were dead or dying somewhere since no one could locate you." The king slammed his hand on the table and Annabel jumped. "What in the world were you thinking?"

Normally she would have said something silly or sarcastic about her not thinking, but not this time. This time she wanted her father to know how dead serious she was. "That Lord Haywood was going to kill uncle. Then all of you, one by one. He said as much when Sir Jeorge was listening."

He drew up with a sigh. "That is another matter entirely. I want to know where you have been."

"Len was angry with me. I was shocked when I realized that Lord Haywood was after her as well. He'd been trying to win my favor for some time, but apparently, she'd been his victim longer." Annabel felt tears when she remembered Len's words. "Len was...is angry with me."

"She's insisting he is innocent and if it wasn't for Jeorge's assurances that Lord Haywood had threatened not only my life but your brother's, I may not have taken this seriously." For the first time in her life, she watched her father fall back in his chair, seemingly defeated. "How did you know?"

"Know what?" Annabel was confused, she hadn't known about Len.

"About what Lord Haywood was planning," the king clarified.

"I didn't..." Annabel replied with a shrug. "I suspected he was up to no good, but I didn't know for sure he would go so far. I thought he might try something indecent or might be trying to steal." She had to force herself to stop rambling; she'd decided not to tell her father about her ability. Anyone finding out still terrified her.

"That was risky. A stupid gamble." Her father leaned forward and put his elbows on the desk. "You could have been hurt."

Real tears, ones she couldn't keep in check, blurred her vision. "He never threatened me. He wanted to use me to get close to all of you and kill you." She couldn't stop the tears, covering her face with her hands. The weeks of fear since the first dream were breaking loose.

Unexpectedly she felt his arms around her a few moments later. "You saved us all. Lord Haywood has been yelling he would kill us all since we put him in the dungeon."

"I was so scared." Annabel wrapped her arms around him, clinging to his clothes.

"You were brave. When I saw how unhinged the man was, I realized how narrowly we avoided tragedy." He kissed the side of her head. "You did that."

Annabel nodded. "It's over now."

He put her at arm's length and asked seriously, "Do you have anything else to tell me?"

"Well...um..." Annabel smiled weakly. "I don't know if this is the best time to tell you, but Lord Cain is going to court me...with marriage in mind."

Her father's brow furrowed. "Is he now? I thought you swore never to marry."

Annabel nodded her head with a smile. "I did. He changed my mind."

Her father shook his head with a little humph. "I have known you your whole life and I still can't predict what you're going to do." He shook her a little as though excited. "Your mother will be pleased to hear that you've found a love match."

"I didn't say it was a love match," Annabel countered, caught off-guard.

"You didn't have to. You and I are more alike than you realize. Why do you think I remarried twice? Love is a powerful motivator," her father said with a knowing smirk.

"Then you give your consent?" Annabel asked, hopeful.

"It will strengthen the alliance with the Southern Isles. For the king, you have found yourself a most advantageous match. But as for your father." He kissed her forehead. "I am happy to see you so in love that you have finally overcome your fear of losing your independence in favor of a partnership that will bring you more fulfillment than you could ever imagine." He stood straighter then and nodded. "I give my consent. Decide and you shall name a date for your engagement."

She squealed and threw her arms around her father. "Thank you, Papa!"

"You haven't called me that since you were a child." He patted her back.

Annabel kissed her father's cheek. "I can't wait to tell him."

Chuckling, her father muttered as she left the room. "Not at all how I imagined that conversation going..."

Annabel sat down for their family breakfast. Everyone was staring at her as she started to butter a biscuit. She noticed Len wasn't there, but that came as no surprise since her sister had sequestered herself in the temple. She'd apparently decided to fast while the injustice surrounding Lord Haywood was transpiring. It hurt her more than she cared to admit. Especially Lenora's harsh words that had been spoken in anger.

"How long?" Mayven asked, his gaze sharp.

"Whatever can you mean?" Annabel asked, setting her knife and biscuit down so she could add honey on top of the recently spread butter.

Mayven's hands curled into fists, a rare show of anger. "How long did you suspect Lord Haywood's murderous intent?"

Annabel sighed. "As I told father, I suspected he intended to do something horrible, I had no idea how horrid until he told me on the terrace." Part of her hadn't trusted the dream until he had spoken the words on the terrace.

"You could have told me." Mayven's fist pounded against the table, startling everyone. Annabel blinked in surprise; she'd never seen her brother so furious. "I would have helped you."

"I know, but we needed someone who wasn't family, someone above reproach," Annabel replied, though her voice trembled.

"Please don't fight," her mother said, appearing overwhelmed. That was when Annabel noticed how pale she was.

"Forgive me, mother," Mayven replied, standing. "I need to take a walk."

Annabel blinked in shock as he left. Glancing at her father, he had one raised eyebrow, which indicated he'd be no help. She'd made this bed, and he expected her to lie in it. Regardless of the fact that she'd saved them all, she had to remember they didn't know that there had been a future where he'd succeeded. Cruel irony were the words the came to mind.

"At least we are on season break," Annabel said weakly.

"Father," Yenni said, her expression serious. "Now seems to be the right time to remind you that you promised to consent to my engagement to Lord Euros after the Masquerade Ball. In light of recent events, you can hardly delay it again."

Her father stared at Yenni who stared him down without wavering. "Yenni, now is hardly the time…"

To everyone's surprise Yenni interrupted him. "Father." Her expression seemed to plead with him. "You promised."

He inhaled before nodding. "So, I did. You have been patient, and Lord Euros has proven to be a gentleman. I give my consent, at the end of the season, you may announce your engagement and begin all the preparations."

Yenni's entire face beamed with delight. "Thank you, father." She stood and kissed his cheek. "I must tell my betrothed immediately." Then she too left.

For the first time that she could remember, Annabel was alone with her parents. Her mother reached over and took her father's hand. She was nodding at him, as though approving of his choice. He seemed pleased until his gaze fell on Annabel.

"You do not have to stay, daughter," the king was with her now, not her father. "I am sure you would rather tell Lord Cain I have approved your official courtship."

Her mother gasped. "Official courtship?" She turned on Annabel like a pouncing cat. "Tell me my ears do not deceive me!"

"It's true," Annabel said, her cheeks burning. "And I think I'll remain, father. If that's alright."

Her father smiled at her and signaled for the servant to move her place setting closer. "You are always welcome, daughter." And with a newfound hope, Annabel felt comfortable.

Chapter 32

The moment breakfast was done, she kissed her parents' cheeks, cherishing them more easily, and with less worry, now that they were no longer in mortal danger. She hugged her mother as she commented for the hundredth time that Annabel's courtship was a miracle. Then, Annabel went in search of Cain. She had so much to tell him and had a bounce in her step. She was no longer weighed down by the threat of Lord Haywood.

She'd sent a messenger to bid Cain to meet her at their spot. The gazebo had always been her place, the one that had been her solace. Now it held so much more meaning. Something far better than she'd imagined from reading books. She understood Yenni's joy and Len's pain; the ways love seemed to make you stronger and weaker all at once.

As she approached the gazebo, Annabel saw Cain within. He was staring off in the distance as he turned something over in his hands. She stopped for a moment to just admire him. His dark skin was flawless, and his hair trimmed short. More than anything, it was his countenance that left a gentile aura Annabel had come to love. A part of her knew this was inevitable; that from the moment she'd met him her eyes had gravitated towards him.

Annabel entered the gazebo; the broken door was still leaning on its broken hinge. Cain turned around, and his entire face lit up as she approached. Her very being started to sing, reaching out into the world for the one person it resonated with. When he bowed and held out a hand, Annabel walked past it and threw her arms around him, holding him close.

"Yes, I still want what I wanted yesterday," Annabel said, her head resting against his chest. She tipped her head up so her nose was under his chin. "I love you more with each passing hour."

Cain had stiffened at first, but as she spoke, he wrapped his arms around her and held her close. Even though he hadn't said anything, she could sense he had been nervous. Perhaps even uncertain about where Annabel stood. His hesitation was expected after what she'd put him through. Annabel would do everything to make amends, to right the wrong she'd caused him the day before.

"I barely slept," Cain whispered, his voice barely audible. "For fear that I would find it all a dream."

Annabel put a hand on his head, her fingers running over the soft curls. "I am sorry," Annabel's voice shook as she fought back tears. "I didn't want to hurt you, but I knew no other way."

Cain eased back before putting a hand on her cheek, his thumb caressing her cheekbone. "I didn't even realize the depths in which I'd fallen for you until you asked me to leave. You became illusive, like water spilling through my fingers. Try as I might, I couldn't hold on."

Annabel put her hand over his. "I'm here. You have imprinted onto my very body." He rested his forehead against hers. "As long as I live you shall be a part of me."

"Annabel," he said softly as she closed her eyes. They stood there, intimately close, and just enjoying each other for a few moments. "We should part, we may be seen."

"It does not matter," Annabel said, as he pulled away and she took hold of his hand. "My father has consented to our courtship."

Cain's eyes widened before he blinked at her a few times. "Consented? When?"

"Last night." Annabel said softly, wishing very much to kiss him.

He swallowed heavily. "After we..."

Annabel's cheeks felt warm. "Yes." She tipped her head back.

Then someone cleared their throat and both her and Cain turned to the noise. Lady Cierra was trying to look away discreetly, clearly embarrassed. Annabel and Cain shared a private smile. Cain moved away from her, but Annabel pulled on his arm. When he dipped towards her, Annabel kissed his cheek.

"Princess!" Lady Cierra said, covering her eyes. "Please try to have some decorum."

Annabel laughed heartily. "That has never been a strong suit of mine. Is there something you need?"

"We are set to return to the orphanage." Lady Cierra was still acting bashful. "The final time before we depart for the north."

Annabel had forgotten during all the excitement. "Did Len say she'd come?"

Lady Cierra hesitated a moment. "No. She declined." That Len's decision was due to Annabel, went unsaid but hung heavy in the air.

"Then we had better depart." Annabel said, trying to be cheerful. She paused when Cain caught her fingers before she could move away. "Cain?"

"May I join you?" He seemed concerned. Her heart warmed when she realized he was worried about her.

Annabel opened her mouth to answer when she heard a happy squeak. Startled, she saw Cierra practically vibrating in place with her fists pressed to her chest and her eyes wide and bright. Her smile was so large it practically split her face in two.

The happy noise escaped her again before she managed to say, "It's really real!"

Annabel glanced at Cain in confusion, but he was slack jawed. Annabel had no idea what Cierra was talking about. Bouncing in place, her eyes ticking back and forth like a clock as she kept shifting her gaze from her friend to her brother, and back again.

"When you told me I didn't believe it was real this time, not really. That is, I always knew there was something there, something beyond," she waved a hand between them a few times. "But to see you both. Now that your courtship is official and real, I am just..." She sighed heavily and rested on her heels. "Overcome with joy to see *that* expression on each of your faces."

A little embarrassed Annabel was stunned by Cierra's outburst. It was Cain who spoke first. "Thank you. For sharing in our joy."

His outward contentment made Annabel stare at his face. He was handsome to be sure, but now he seemed even more so. How had that happened in mere moments? Not to mention she had a strange desire to continue to just marvel at it, like it was a piece of art. An odd sensation to be sure, but not unwelcome.

"Well, I knew you really loved her. I think I knew before you did, brother," Cierra said with a laugh. "And I suspected your attentions to Cain were not simply for show. Though I could never have imagined such a deep attachment." She pressed her fingers to her mouth, her excitement coming from her in waves.

Laughter burst out of Annabel. She held her stomach as tears formed in her eyes. Cain's eyebrows arched, but then he chuckled and shook his head.

"It isn't funny that I loved you first." Cain seemed almost bashful as he spoke.

"That isn't it. Everyone is going to wonder how someone as magnificent as you ever fell in love with the troublesome princess who no one takes seriously," Annabel said, her words stopping and starting she clenched her sides. "If your own sister doesn't believe you, that can only mean we have our work cut out for us." She wiped at her tears as she made her way towards the carriage. "What a debut this has been."

"Why are they staring like that?" Cain whispered; his eyes locked on the gaggle of children who were crowded around them.

They'd spent most of the morning helping the children learn their letters since Len wasn't there to do that part. Annabel was thankfully so busy that she couldn't think often of Len or her absence. It had a habit of making her feel

175

terrible, and she needed to keep a brave face for the children. After they'd had an afternoon meal, they'd go into the back garden to let the children play.

"Because I told them I was going to marry you." Annabel tried to keep any sign of her impish behavior from her smile.

"That doesn't explain why they're practically glaring." He turned sideways, as though to divert their sharp gazes.

"They asked if I was going with you." Annabel felt as warm as the sun shining down on them, barely blocked by the treetops. "I said that depended on you."

His wide eyes turned on her in disbelief. "Why would you tell them that?"

"Because it's true," Annabel said tipping her head to the side as though completely innocent. "It does depend on what you want."

She saw the corner of his lips twitch, suggesting he'd finally caught on. "Odd. I have a feeling you are telling me it depends on what you want."

Annabel could no longer suppress her grin as happiness seemed to bubble up within her. "It seems this marriage is going to work after all. Perhaps we'll travel for a time." Annabel clasped her hands in front of her as she leaned closer to Cain. "Or stay here after visiting your family for a time."

His expression became loving as he moved intimately close. "Whatever you wish, I never lived as free as when I'm with you. It does not matter where."

She momentarily forgot to breathe. "It seems I have met my match." Her eyes would not move away from his face. "There is nothing I wish for more than for you to kiss me."

Lady Cierra cleared her throat. The children were all wide eyed with giddy grins on their faces. Annabel realized they'd temporarily been in their own world, a temporary spectacle for two dozen orphans. Despite herself, her cheeks felt warm as she fanned herself against the embarrassment.

"The princess found her prince!" one of the girls yelled, her fists curled and shaking from excitement. "They're going to live in a castle together like in the story."

Some of the children made kissy sounds. A few boys made rude comments that made one of the caretakers try to hush them. A few disgusting faces mixed with moony ones to round out the group. Annabel decided, all in all, it had been a successful outing.

Chapter 33

Lady Cierra dozed against the carriage's wall as Annabel sat beside her. Annabel and Cain were staring intently, while also checking on his sister. When Cierra's eyes closed for a decent length of time, Annabel carefully joined him on the opposite side of the carriage. Her hand sought his, before interlocking their fingers together. She leaned her head on his shoulder and sighed contently. She didn't know how it was possible to love someone more, but it just kept happening. No wonder so many books were fixated on it—it was the most wonderful sensation in the world. He kissed the top of her head and she wanted to sink further into that moment.

"Annabel?" Cain whispered several minutes later.

"Hmm?"

"There is something we should…discuss." Cain sounded worried and her eyes popped open as she sat up.

"What is it?" Annabel asked, keeping her voice quiet even though she was alarmed.

He inhaled deeply as though bracing himself. "I have no intention of staking a claim on what is now rightfully my younger brother's. That is, I am without a title and thus cannot provide you with one. My brother generously provided a small country home to me when I abdicated the dukedom. I will not take it away from my brother or his family."

"Are you saying you no longer wish to marry me? For want of title?" Annabel asked and then had to cover her mouth as she turned away to try not to let her laughter come out too loudly lest she wake Cierra.

"Annabel," Cain said seriously, he was almost admonishing her, not for the last time she imagined. "I am in earnest."

Annabel shook her head. "Forgive me, I only meant to relieve your concerns." She hadn't intended to devalue his concerns, only assuage them. "I am a Princess. I have an extensive dowery that will pass in full to you once we marry. We shall have no needs left unmet so long as we do not live past our means. Which is a substantial amount each year, I assure you."

"Annabel," Cain said, shifting in his seat to take her hands. "Our children will have no promise of title." He sounded so disheartened as though he had done a great disservice.

"They will have something better," Annabel said touching a hand to his cheek. "The freedom to choose what they want. Without title, or restriction, or want of connection. We shall make it that in the event of my death, our deaths, my dowry passes to them in equal parts. I am sure father will agree. That way they have no wants and the freedom to decide what life they lead. It is better than anything I could imagine giving my children for their future."

He stared at her for a moment before a grin graced his face. "I had not thought of it that way."

"Then it is fortunate you have me." Annabel pecked his lips before settling in beside him.

He interlaced their fingers again. "On that we agree."

When Annabel entered the palace walls, there was a hushed tension. Annabel was instantly on edge as the Van Brandt siblings stood behind her. Her gaze swept over the people in the room as she called for dinner, knowing that they were getting back later than initially planned. The servant left, but one of the guards approached her.

"Prince Mayven asked that you be brought to this study," the guard informed her. The grave way he spoke made her heart crawl up into her throat.

"What happened?" Annabel asked, her stomach instantly in knots.

He hesitated; his expression conflicted. "It would be best if the crown prince explained."

"Lady Cierra you're excused," Annabel said, glancing back at the siblings. "Lord Cain, you're with me."

The guard interjected as Cain moved to her side. "He said you should go alone."

"My brother says a lot of things." Annabel linked her arm through Cain's. "I rarely listen to them."

Annabel marched them towards her brother's study. Eyes seemed to follow her on her journey, digging into her in such a way she felt sick to her stomach. Was it her mother? Had something happened to Len? The hushed silence coupled with the attentive stares was unnerving, until Cain covered her hand on his arm with his other one.

"Whatever has happened, we shall face it together." Cain's quiet confidence was an instant balm to her soul. She was not alone, no matter what it was.

"I know you regret what happened to bring you here," Annabel whispered as they reached the door to Mayven's study. "But I could not be more thankful."

She nodded to the attendant who opened the door for her. "Princess Annabel."

Mayven looked up from the desk, his expression bleak. Her fingers tightened on Cain's arm. She had seen her brother all her life, knew that face better than her own. Whatever had happened was going to be horrid.

"I asked that you come alone," Mayven said, staring at Cain.

"I asked that he be here."

Mayven sighed. "I hear I am to congratulate you." Mayven stood and offered his hand to Cain, who shook it.

"Apologies brother, I meant to tell you myself, but you seemed cross with me at breakfast," Annabel said, she could tell her brother was hesitating. "May-

may, what's happened? Is it mother?" She hadn't called him that nickname since they were children, but she was scared and could no longer wait.

"Sit down," Mayven said, as the two men helped her sit in a chair in front of the desk.

Mayven sat beside her, leaning towards her as Cain continued to stand behind her. "Mayven, you're scaring me."

Mayven sighed heavily, his face grim. "Lord Haywood has escaped."

Chapter 34

"Escaped?" Annabel felt the world close in on her.

"He simply walked out," Mayven said, dumbfounded. "I've never seen anything like it. The guards stated they just let him walk free."

How had she not seen this? How had she not dreamed something so vital to their future? A warm hand covered her own and she glanced at Cain. His support was both the most touching moment of her life and the most devastating. He needed to leave. She needed to send him far away from her. He was going to die. Lawrence would kill her and him if he remained.

Annabel suddenly started breathing heavily and couldn't catch her breath. Her chest felt tight as she started gasping for air. It was similar to how she felt at the wedding, only worse. She couldn't feel anything, but the damp sweat on her skin. She suddenly felt disoriented and dizzy as she slumped back. Mayven and Cain were by her side, they were speaking to her. To her surprise Cain's concerned eyes filled with fear and tenderness helped her focus.

"Breathe," his voice cut through the words. "That's right, Annabel, deep breaths through your nose and out of your mouth."

Tears slid unchecked down her cheeks, and she took a shaky breath. She felt hollow and exhausted as the shaking in her hands subsided. Reason was slowly returning to her though she still felt lightheaded.

"What's wrong with her?" Mayven's voice cut in, but she continued to focus on Cain as his thumb caressed the back of her hand.

"Melancholia," Cain replied, touching the side of her face to wipe away her tears. "I had them when I was younger. Usually when I was...distressed."

Without a care for proprietary Annabel threw her arms around Cain, gripping onto him like a drowning woman. After a moment she felt him hug her back, his strong hand rubbing her back. Squeezing her eyes closed she turned into his neck, taking in his scent. Lavender and clean linen.

"Annabel," Cain whispered, gathering her against him. "I'm fairly sure your brother is going to strike me down."

"Then I'll never let go," her voice came out in a croak.

Cain chuckled as he turned his cheek against her head. She knew she should gather herself. Knew she should compose herself and try to make excuses with her brother. Annabel recognized that she should be doing anything but what she was doing and didn't care.

Lawrence Haywood was going to come for her. He was going to hunt her down and murder her. When he did, whoever was beside her would be caught up in whatever strange ability he had to kill. Which meant the last place Cain should be was anywhere near her.

That was a problem for tomorrow, for today Annabel was going to stay in Cain's arms. She was going to be wrapped in the warmth of his love. Spill her passions onto him like a newly lit candle who felt the end of the wick was not far off.

"I won't let him hurt you," Cain said softly.

They should have been words of comfort, but they only filled her with anxiety. "I'm not the only one he is after." The words were barely a whisper, a frog in her throat and butterflies in her stomach.

"I've called a physician," Mayven said as he reentered the room. She hadn't even heard him leave. "Come, Annabel."

"Please don't leave me," Annabel said clinging shamelessly to Cain. "I don't want a physician."

"Annabel," Marven's voice was full of warning, but Annabel would not be swayed.

Cain's calm voice surrounded her. "I shall take her. You can escort us so that all is proper."

Her brother must have accented because the next thing she knew, Cain was lifting her into his arms. Annabel held fast like she was a dying woman and he her only solace. Despite her desire to stay awake, she felt herself fade as he took her through the palace and eventually laid her on the bed.

"Cain," she whispered when he tried to leave, reaching for him.

He returned, leaning closer to her. "Thank you," she said loudly before slipping her fingers to the back of his neck and pulling him dangerously close. "The terrace. I shall wait all night."

"You are welcome, Princess," Cain replied, diligently tucking her in as his eyes sparkled with understanding. "Rest now."

Annabel watched him leave; Mayven's gaze bore into her, but she did not turn away. Shame had never been her strong suit and as a result she did not shy from her brother's silent accusations. Instead as Cain left, she snuggled into the covers and let it seem like she was going to sleep. The moment the door clicked closed she opened her eyes.

Rolling onto her back she sighed and stared at the canopy over her bed. All her hard work, undone. All her hope for a happily ever after, shattered. Her chest felt tight again but she focused on her breathing and imagined Cain. Before long, her breathing settled, and she felt herself relaxing.

Unwilling to be paralyzed by her fear, Annabel hurried to the terrace. She undid the latch and opened the doors. Cain pulled it open as she gazed up at him, he appeared as impatient to see her as she was to see him.

His arms were around her, hugging her as she wrapped her arms around his neck. She shamelessly clung to him as he lifted her up. Carrying her inside she saw he'd closed the door behind him. They were alone in her room, and it felt so natural. As though he'd always been there.

Cain set her on the bed, her legs dangling over the side as he knelt in front of her. "I will not let him harm you."

"I do not wish to speak of it," Annabel said. She leaned forward and kissed him. He kissed her back, the moment filled with aching sweetness. "Will you hold me until I fall asleep?"

He removed his glove before touching the side of her face. "I shall do whatever you wish."

She smiled coyly at him, as though suggesting something else. "Anything?"

"Annabel!" He exclaimed in a hushed whisper.

She giggled as he lifted her up and laid her on the bed. Despite his protest he continued to kiss her, his lips brushing along her neck sent tingles down her spine. He let himself taste and touch every part of her as she ran her fingers through his hair. She felt parts of herself long to be connected with him again, but a larger piece was falling asleep.

When he tried to pull away, she clung to the back of his shirt. "Stay," she whispered as tears sprung to her eyes. "Stay with me."

Annabel tucked herself against him, taking in the soap and lavender that always seemed to surround him. She felt him kiss the top of her head and tell her to sleep. With nary a protest she let his warmth comfort her as she felt sleep take hold.

Annabel woke as Cain's warmth left her. She opened her eyes, feeling groggy as she glanced up at Cain. He stood, and she saw him stretch. Before he could move away from her, she reached out and caught the back of his shirt.

He stopped and glanced down. "Did I wake you?"

Annabel sat up and tugged on his sleeve. He sat down on the edge of the bed and smoothed her hair back from her forehead. "I must look a fright," Annabel whispered.

"I prefer you this way," Cain replied with a chuckle. "Though I must go, I am sure it will be harder as morning comes to sneak back." He bent down to brush his lips across hers. "Rest well."

Annabel's hand shot out and wrapped around the side of his neck. "I don't want to rest." She pulled him towards her, kissing him passionately. His tongue met, and battled hers as she drew him against her.

"Annabel." The way he said her name sent shivers down her spine. It was both a promise and a warning.

"Cain."

His weight on top of her was thrilling, rather than oppressive. She wanted him to take her, but instead he began to kiss along her neck. He undressed her slowly, leaving hot trails down the length of her. His tongue slid along her stomach, and she gasped. Her skin felt hot as she clenched her fingers in the blankets. Even though she was exposed to him, she felt like his soul was calling out to hers.

Cain's lips explored her every surface as his tongue tasted her. His fingers teased her nipples, at times, he caressed her core between her legs. She felt he was worshiping her, and she was floating, levitated by his adoration.

"Please," her own voice sounded foreign as she begged. "Cain, please."

He pressed his lips to hers as he slowly thrust into her, deeper and deeper with each motion. Annabel heard herself gasp as she felt wild and liberated. Her hips moved with his, as their gazes fused together. She whimpered when he lifted her up to bury himself in her to the hilt—lost in a maze of all consuming passion. Her mind could only focus on the way he said her name— she felt his love resonate with pleasure into her very soul.

This is what the books had promised, this is everything she'd imagined, and more. She no longer felt like he was separate from her but melded with her very being. With each rocking movement, he was marking her as his; someplace only he'd be allowed to venture.

"I love you," she said with a gasp. He suddenly stopped before he let out a moan.

She fell back into the bed, but he didn't delay and started kissing her again. Smiling against his lips, she reached up to touch his face, knowing he'd reached completion. Before she could blink, he grabbed her wrist and turned her around. Gone was the shy man who had seemed hesitant the night before. He buried himself into her again, holding her up on her knees, one hand pressing against her stomach, as he drove into her.

He was merciless and she felt delirious with pleasure and exhaustion. Her body was shaking as she felt another eruption building slowly within her. His teeth bit softly into her shoulder, and she gasped at the sudden stimulation. The pressure that had been building within her exploded, and euphoria wrapped around her as she felt waves of utter bliss continue to crash over her. He helped her down slowly. His hands moved over her, touching her softly as she tried to focus.

"What is it?" Annabel asked, barely able to keep her eyes open.

Cain hesitated and she forced herself to look at him. In the moonlight he appeared thoughtful, but not in the way she liked. Her limbs protested as she sat up. Her fingers resting on his chest, enjoying the feel of him.

"I was too rough, I don't know…" he said, his tone almost panicked. "I don't know what came over me."

"You were unhinged," she whispered. "Like I was all that could sate your desires."

"Did I hurt you?" he asked, brushing a knuckle across her cheek.

"No," Annabel said with a laugh. "For all that is holy, you have ravaged me to the point that I love you more with each moment. I have never felt so happy or loved as I do in this moment."

Cain searched her face before kissing her. She breathed in, trying to hold onto the moment. When they parted, she was overcome, tears threatened to fall as she felt overwhelmed with emotions. How absurd that such happiness could elicit tears.

"You have to promise me," Annabel stared seriously into his eyes, "That you shall not hold back. I want you to do it again."

He chuckled. "I promise." He peppered her with kisses. "Now sleep, I'll be lucky not to get caught on the way back."

Annabel chuckled as she lay down and he tucked her under the blankets. "Be careful," she said as he moved towards her veranda. "Cain?" She called out to him.

"Yes?" He turned back, his hand on the glass door.

"I love you," she said, still basking in the aftermath of their lovemaking.

His entire face seemed to light up; she could barely make it out in the moonlight, but she heard him say as she fell asleep. "And I you."

Chapter 35

Annabel was slow to rise the next morning. Mostly because she was emotionally exhausted but also because she was going to have to send Cain away. She was going to have to reveal who she was and what she could do to convince him. She was terrified that he'd think she'd manipulated him in some way. That she'd concealed the information to deceive him. Though in a way she had—just not in the way he might imagine.

She didn't know what was worse. That she'd concealed her ability from him or that she was going to have to bend the truth about what she'd seen in her dreams to send him away. Annabel paced; her agitation real as she waited for the Van Brandt siblings. She was gripping a letter, hastily written to better portray the urgency of the situation.

When Cain entered, she took in how affectionately he gazed at her. She also recognized that, without saying anything, his face fell, likely sensing her distress. She's done nothing to hide the fear. Cierra closed the door as he rushed to Annabel's side and took her hand.

"What is it?" Cain asked, gripping her free hand in his warm one.

189

She took a deep breath and steeled her resolve. The fear was real enough, it gripped her like a snake round her throat. Squeezing the air from her. She struggled to shake it off so she could continue.

"I fear you shall think less of me," Annabel said, her voice quivered. "I've struggled on how to tell you the truth, but after what I saw, I can no longer keep quiet."

Surprise gave way to guarded concern. "What did you see?"

"The future." Annabel was nauseated over the exchange. "Everyone I care about dies at Lord Haywood's hand."

"I don't understand," Cain replied, his brows furrowed. "You've seen the future?"

Annabel averted her gaze. "Flashes of the future. Like what Lord Haywood was going to do to my family." Then she met his gaze. "But not you. Just matters affecting my family, like cousin Ver's proposal and wedding."

Lady Cierra gasped, "You really did see her wedding," Lady Cierra said, gasping. "In the carriage, you said you could see the future!"

"Yes," Annabel said and then saw the light dawn on Cain.

"That's why you asked if I was a Mystic. Because you are one." She could see he was reeling.

"I'm so sorry. It started right before you arrived. I thought the first one was just a bad dream. I wanted to believe I didn't have such a horrid ability." Annabel's voice broke as tears started sliding down her cheeks. "That's another reason why I wanted to help you. I felt alone and you made me feel like I wasn't."

His thumbs wiped at her tears. "I wish you would have told me sooner." He cupped her face in his hand. "I might have helped."

Annabel sniffled. "I need your help and I am afraid to ask."

"Ask me anything," Cain replied, and her heart broke at his unwavering devotion.

She pushed the letter against his chest, forcing herself to carry out her plan. "Lord Haywood is going to come for my brother for revenge. In just a few days, he's going to kill them. I can't leave the capital, father forbade it." At least that was true while she was a debutante. "I need you to warn Baltus and Dalus. They must return to the capital, if they don't, I shall die."

His head snapped up at her last words. "What do you mean...die?"

"I saw my death. Lord Haywood slits my throat in the throne room. I need my brothers," Annabel said, amending what was true so that Cain would be sent on an errand out of the city. "If they perish, so do I. Will you warn them for me?"

He simply shook his head as though baffled. She didn't begrudge his confusion. Instead, she patiently waited. Yet it wasn't Cain that spoke first.

"We shall go with haste. As your lady-in-waiting I am owed a royal escort," Cierra stated, surprisingly calm. "You have done so much for this family. It the least we can do." Then she looked at Cain. "Isn't that right, brother?"

"Yes, of course." Cain was nodding his head. His hands on her shoulders. "I will do whatever you wish."

Cierra stepped forward and held out a hand where Annabel placed the letter without pause. "I shall safeguard it until we can deliver it." Then she took a step back. "I will go and make arrangements to travel north. Brother, join me when you are able."

Then she left them alone. After a moment Cain said softly, "She really is a terrible chaperone."

Laughter burst out of Annabel; it was so unexpected. Tears in her lashes as she replied, "Or the best."

"Why were you afraid to tell me?" Cain asked, his knuckles grazing her cheeks. "It doesn't change how I feel."

"I haven't told anyone," Annabel admitted. "You and your sister are all that know."

He paused and seemed to contemplate her words. "Would you have told me? If you hadn't had the most recent dream?"

"I know this may change how you feel about me. If you can trust me after I've withheld this information, but know I only did what I thought was best." Annabel felt her stomach twist into knots as she fought for composure. She did not deserve forgiveness for what she was doing, nor did she plan to seek it. "I hoped they'd stop once Lord Haywood was captured. I wanted them to go away."

"And have they?"

"I am certain now that he is out there plotting again, that another will come. I simply fear it will be too late to prevent…the worst." Annabel suddenly felt so exhausted and laid her head against his chest.

They stood in each other's arms as Annabel took his in scent; soap and lavender. Despite the odds she very much wanted them to be happily married when Lord Haywood was no longer a threat. He was her person, the match and partner that she'd never imagined existed.

He kissed the top of her head before speaking. "I don't want to leave you."

Annabel held him tighter. "I have every faith you shall go to my brothers and return in time to save me by weeks end. I am sure that is what my next dream will show, but time is short, and we don't have enough to wait. I can only hope my wish comes true."

He kissed her, tenderly. "I see all of you and love you still."

Her breath caught in her throat. "And I you. With all that I am." The words barely made it out through quivering lips. "Be safe."

And then he was gone, and she was alone. How was it possible two moments could cause such pain? It incited another emotion; one she'd hadn't expected. Rage—she was going to find and crush Lord Haywood. By whatever means necessary.

Chapter 36

Annabel mobilized everything at her disposal. After two days with no dreams and even less sleep, Annabel was at her wits end. On the third evening since Cain's departure, she finally slept from sheer exhaustion. On the next morning, once she confirmed what little progress her brother had made, she'd decided to go to the information guild. All her life she'd heard rumors of the Phoenix Guild and its underhanded approaches. Even its connections to questionable deaths. It had been a thorn in her family's side for a long time because of how good they were, and her brother would have locked her up if he knew what she had planned.

"Password," the man at the door asked, eyeing her cloaked form.

She produced an amulet; one they'd taken from an informant years ago. Her brother kept it locked in a crate. She knew where he'd hidden the key. Used to take pocket change from it when she was younger. More for the fun than the money. She would then return it on her next allowance, her brother none the wiser. Apparently, old habits die hard.

"Forgive me, I didn't recognize you." He knocked and the door opened.

Annabel took a breath before stepping inside. There was a hallway that led to a room. A man sat at the chair, waiting with his fingers steepled. There was a scar on his cheek but regardless of that he was handsome; charming even. Lawrence had taught her looks were deceiving and she would not be fooled by the outward appearance of the man in front of her.

"Please take a seat." He waved at the chair across from him. She hesitated before taking the seat. "What is it that brings you here?" He asked.

"I need information," Annabel said bluntly.

He chuckled. "That is what we do. Any specifics' lady?"

"Lord Haywood."

The man stopped laughing. "He's gone. Likely with the wind. What do you want with him?"

"Mostly his head," Annabel said, trying to sound cold and tough. Perhaps that might mask her growing fear as someone shifted in the darkness at the edge of the room. "But I'll settle for where he might flee to or any recent sightings."

"That's all well and good, but that be an old medallion." He pointed to what she'd thought was an amulet around her neck. "So, I don't think we'll be helping you miss."

Taking the pouch from her pocket, she dropped it onto the table. "The medallion may be old, but this is new gold."

That stopped his condescending smirk, his eyes riveted on the bulging purse. The second thing she'd borrowed from her brother's chest. Perhaps he'd forgive her if she came clean and helped him hide the key better. The thought amused her and relaxed her some.

She leaned forward, her elbows on the table in a very unladylike fashion. "Are you interested or not?"

"You just want the information?" He asked, eyeing the size.

She opened the top of the purse and pulled a handful of coins out. Dropping them one at a time on the table she let them clink together. His entire attention was on the growing pile of glittering money.

"An advance," Annabel said before closing the drawstring on the pouch. "I want the information by tomorrow and the rest is yours."

"Tomorrow?" The man shook his head. "I'd need a week at least."

"For this much," she shook the massive pouch. "You can work faster. Two days and not an hour more."

"Come back in two days," the man said, swiping the coins off the table. "I'll have what I have." Not exactly the resounding promise she'd hoped for.

Annabel stood. "I've come to you this time. In two days, you'll come to me. The temple, I'll be seated in the back row."

He hesitated but acquiesced in the end. "At nine in the evening in two days."

Annabel was watching the hour hand tick down. It had been over a day since she'd gone to the guild. In a few hours she'd be meeting the contact at the temple. Part of her felt conflicted over what she'd done. Perhaps it was time to come clean to her brother. Perhaps Mayven would know what to do. Yet it wasn't Mayven she sought out.

She knocked at the door and waited. "Come in."

Annabel entered Yenni's room—a room that her sister had somehow turned into a small jungle with all its potted plants. Her sister was perched on an ornate, purple chair, sandwiched between two bushy plants with odd orange flowers. She had her knees up and a sketchbook against her legs. Her gaze was intense a moment before she returned to what she was doing. Despite her lack of invitation, Annabel entered and sat in one of the two large chairs that matched the sofa.

"I'm sorry for not telling you."

Annabel knew she was backed into a corner. A feeling she didn't like. The burden of the responsibility of their future was catching up with her. She'd tried to deny it, she'd gotten angry, and then she'd tried to outmaneuver it. She felt on the edge of a horrid cry, overwhelmed by feelings of being alone and without Dalus to turn to she went to the one person she trusted the most. Out of everyone in her family, Yenni had been equally fun and reliable. A winning combination.

"And?" Yenni asked. She was acting absorbed in her drawing as she made a show of turning to a blank page, but Annabel knew better.

"And..." Annabel hesitated. "For not being honest?"

"About?" She tipped her head the other way as though continuing with her sketch.

"My relationship with Lord Haywood?"

Yenni fixed her with a penetrating stare. "For keeping secrets that should never have been kept. I agree with Mayven, you did poorly." She turned back to her sketchbook. "Even if you did it with the best intentions."

"Yenni." Annabel's throat felt tight. "I'm sorry."

Her sister seemed unconcerned until she looked at her. "My goodness!" She was up out of her seat and wrapping her arms around Annabel. They rocked together as Annabel let all the emotions that overwhelmed her, out into the world. It was terribly cathartic.

"I've never seen you cry so terribly since father said you couldn't learn archery on horseback," Yenni said patting her back. "What happened?"

Annabel looked into her sister's eyes and knew she'd made the right decision. "I saw it. I didn't just guess what Lord Haywood was doing. I saw it. In my dreams."

"Your Mystic ability?" Yenni asked, her voice hushed as though the walls had ears. Annabel nodded. "Well why didn't you just tell that to father?"

"Yenni, the ability to see the future?" Annabel asked, upset by the idea of anyone finding out felt like a chokehold. "Do you remember what happened to our other grandmother?"

Yenni's face became grim. "Killed before she could reveal the truth about one of the noblemen." She sighed heavily. "I understand your hesitation. Nana always told us to keep the secret within the family, lest we suffer the same fate."

"Lord Haywood was already a threat to everyone; I couldn't add any other factors and have any hope of winning." Annabel felt her heart ease at sharing the weight. "He wasn't just going to kill me. He was going to kill everyone and become king."

"That's...impossible." Even as she said the words, Annabel could see Yenni wasn't so sure.

"He has an ability. He must. I just don't know what." Annabel inhaled deeply, taking in the soft floral scent that Yenni's room always had. "I know he will not stop."

"Why did you come to see me?" Yenni asked, her hand rubbing on Annabel's arm in an affectionate way.

"I needed someone to know. To understand why I'm doing what I am..." Annabel glanced at the clock. Time was ticking down.

"Annabel, what are you doing?"

Annabel looked at her sister and really saw her. She wasn't much older than Annabel, the youngest child of the first wife. A mother she didn't remember, another who died soon after childbirth, and a third crippled when she was a teenager. Yvette had married soon after the accident, so it was Yenni who had taken on a mothering role. A guide, and the person Annabel had sought out when she was lost.

"I'm sorry if I ever took you for granted." Annabel hugged her sister, holding her close as she felt nothing but gratitude for her. "Please tell Len I'm sorry. I hope she sees reason soon."

"Annabel don't make the same mistake," Yenni said, standing. "Let me help you."

"You don't have to worry, it isn't dangerous." Well not that dangerous. "I just need to get a new perspective." She waved a hand as she made her way towards the door. "Clear my head. Perhaps make a confession."

"Have you spoke to Lord Cain?" Yenni asked, following her.

Annabel paused at the door. "I saw something, and I sent him to help. Now I am conflicted over it and so many other things." She gripped the handle. "Promise you won't tell anyone."

"That is unfair," Yenni said, distressed.

"I know. If I'm not back by eleven, you can tell whoever you wish that I've done something rash." Then she slid through the door, intent on going to the temple well ahead of schedule.

The temple was lit mostly by a plethora of candles. There were so many it was as though they intended to compete with the stars in the sky. The scent of smoke and burned wax was heavy in the air. The high ceilings kept the smoke from gathering too heavily in one area, but she could still see it around the edges of the room. She's been there for hours, waiting near the back as she stayed in her cloak and watched the priests chant or sing.

Her guard was just outside, but so long as she was within, he would not join her assuming she needed time to commune with their God. Annabel was happy she'd thought of this place. In the chaos and heartbreak, this place was comforting. Perhaps she should have felt guilty, perhaps she should have made better choices, and perhaps she should have been more honest. It was the sum of all the decisions she'd made, and all the ones she hadn't, that had led her to this moment.

Annabel knew she should repent for what she'd done, but that felt like she would be admitting to a mistake, and she didn't feel that way. She hadn't made a blunder or error, she knew exactly what she was doing and didn't deserve forgiveness. She only hoped the everyone would survive, and her decision would offset this one morally questionable action. Instead of repentance, she'd settled on praying.

"You're early." The man from the Phoenix Guild said and Annabel jerked away from him. She's been so focused on her thoughts she hadn't even heard him sit down beside her.

"I thought to pray," Annabel commented, letting her clasped hands fall from where they had been tucked against her face while she prayed. "What do you have?"

"Lord Haywood was seen going north, towards the wall and even beyond it." The man set some folded paper on the bench between them.

"Beyond the wall?" Annabel asked, turning towards him before catching herself and facing straight ahead. She'd intended to give the appearance that they weren't conversing. Putting her hands back up by her face, she rested her mouth against her fingers in contemplation.

"That's what I found. And this, two privately owned properties." He tapped the file. "And one more thing."

"Which is?" Annabel asked, curious.

"Payment first." He demanded gruffly.

Rolling her eyes, she pushed the coin purse under the pew closer to him. "By your feet."

The man bent forward and retrieved it. It disappeared to the inside of his cloak. He did not seem amused by her attempt at discretion. She had a feeling he suspected who she was. That in a way he was humoring her, like one would a child. She didn't let it get to her. Her reputation of being unreliable was likely a factor. One of the many times it played in her favor.

"So?" Annabel said, as the silence stretched out between them.

"His father isn't sick by accident," the man explained, his voice hushed. "Quantities of medicine were purchased too often to not be a factor, if you understand." He cleared his throat and shifted in his seat. "Lord Haywood is also the second son, and his elder brother died under mysterious circumstances. Making him the sole heir."

Annabel knew he was a murderer, but to find out that he'd likely seen his own brother into an early grave and his father wasn't far behind, shocked her. She knew it shouldn't have, but it did. She swallowed heavily.

"Why would he go north of the wall?" Annabel asked, still unsure what his plan was.

"I gather information, I do not try to understand the mind of a madman." The informant abruptly stood and left.

Annabel continued to sit long after he'd left. She picked up the information he'd left behind and slipped it into the pocket of her cloak. She stayed long enough for the other man to leave entirely and for ten to drawn nearer. Once she was satisfied that he was gone, and no one would question her departure, she went towards the door. Not to mention she was worried Yenni might sound the alarm early.

"I'm ready to return," Annabel told the guard, who summoned the carriage.

Dozing inside, Annabel let the carriage lull her half to sleep. It was not long before she woke to a knock on the carriage door. Stepping out she was surprised to find an attendant waiting for her. Sighing, she shook her head.

"I'm too tired to see my brother." Annabel walked by him, intending on going straight to bed.

"The King wishes to speak to you," the attendant informed her.

Annabel stopped in her tracks, her fingers tightening their hold on her skirts as she paused on the steps. "My father?"

"Yes, Princess."

Could he already know what she'd done? Unlikely, but that didn't stop her heart from racing. Annabel glanced back at the carriage and considered how far she could make it. Deciding against raising suspicion, Annabel followed the attendant.

Her father was sitting at his massive desk in his office. It was littered with paper and books. He glanced up from where he was scratching his pen across parchment when she entered, unannounced. The frown seemed to crease every line upon his face, making him appear older and more severe. That did not bode well.

"Do you want to explain to me why your lady-in-waiting and your intended were spotted at a northern checkpoint?" He asked, setting the pen into the inkwell. "With guards I don't remember issuing?"

Annabel simply stared at him for a moment, she hadn't considered they'd be of any consequence to anyone until they arrived all the way north. The time she thought she had was substantially less than what she'd hoped for. It seemed she was going to have to come clean before she was ready.

"Lord Haywood's property is north. I wanted Dalus and Baltus to investigate. I asked Cain…Lord Cain to go and make the request." Annabel shifted her weight, but didn't sit down, instead facing her father head on.

"And here I thought I was king." Her father stood; anger etched in his features. "The hunting of Lord Haywood is your brother's responsibility. Not yours. You have done enough in that regard."

Annabel was suddenly exhausted. She hadn't asked to see the future, but that didn't change the fact that she did. "He hasn't found him." Annabel felt impatient at the lack of progress.

"Do not be so eager to undermine your brother. He has worked tirelessly to bring him to justice," her father said, scolding her.

200

"It isn't enough!" Her voice was raised slightly as her temper was getting the better of her. "I know what he is capable of! He must be stopped before—."

"That is quite enough!" Her father bellowed, his fist striking the desk. She drew back, shocked. He had been angry or disappointed more times than she could count, but he'd never yelled at her like that. "You are acting like an impatient child. Do you think your brother, or I do not understand the gravity of the situation?"

She stayed quiet, too stunned to respond. Bowing her head, she felt tears threaten.

"You are remanded to your room. I do not know what you used the money for that you took from your brother, but I hope it was worth it." Her father sat down. "I shall decide how you can repay him tomorrow. A punishment befitting the crime." He picked back up the quilled pen.

Annabel fisted her hand around the letter from the guild. "Lord Haywood was spotted crossing the wall into No-man's Land."

The king paused "Might I ask how you found this information."

"You might also wish to look in on the senior Lord Haywood," Annabel replied turning to leave the room. "It seems that Lord Haywood likes to use poison, just as he planned to use on all of us." She wrenched open the door.

"Annabel!"

She did as he'd commanded and went to her room. Stomping nearly the entire way there. When she reached her room, she undressed herself and curled under the covers. She emerged only once to get the sweets from her hidden drawer and take them back to bed. She cursed everyone and anything she could, using terms for each person as she ate her stress and anger until sleep took her.

Chapter 37

Dream

Annabel woke with a start at a roar that pierced the city's silence. Rushing from her bed she went to the terrace from her sitting room. She could see fire in the distance, but it was to her right and most was blocked by the rest of the palace.

Grabbing a simple robe she hurried towards her parents, certain they were under attack. Many were going out into the hall and guards were on high alert as they streamed around her and pushing her towards the chaos. She felt like a small fish swimming against a rushing river.

Finally, she was able to get free. Breathing heavily, she stuck close to the wall as soldiers and servants rushed through the halls. She stopped at the window to look out into the courtyard below. Annabel saw her brother, Mayven, shouting orders. Then she looked up at the skyline and saw the massive monster as it cut through the sky, slicing lines of fire into the buildings below.

Why was the dragon attacking them? They never traveled this far south!

Utterly shocked, Annabel couldn't move as she watched the horror play out. Someone bumped into her jolting her back into reality. Her feet carried her towards Mayven, her heart calling out to her brother. Despite having no proof, she was sure this was Lawrence's doing. She had to warn her brother this was no random attack.

When she turned down the hall that went down the stairs, Yenni appeared on the upper landing. "Annabel? Annabel! Where are you going?" Her hair was wild with ribbons tied in twisting knots.

Glancing at her sister, Annabel weighed her options as she continued down the stairs. "Go to the shelter!"

"Wait!"

Annabel didn't listen as she reached the bottom and hurried towards Mayven. In the chaos a few people took note of her as she hurried past them. Someone else called "Princess Annabel" but she ducked around the corner as she reached the massive entrance. One of the two doors was closed with only the smaller person size entrance being accessed. They were turning the cranks to close the other door as she rushed in the opposite direction the rest of the group was going.

They were fleeing into the safety of the castle, while she was trying to go out. As she turned the corner towards where she'd last seen her brother, someone screamed, followed by more shouts of fear. Annabel looked up as fire collided with the outer barrier. When it stopped, she glanced up and saw a man atop the dragon.

Lawrence Haywood.

Her heart was in her throat and her legs wobbled as she used the wall as support. Her fingertips trailed across the rough stone as she hurried towards her brother. He was yelling to Master Wil as dragon fire exploded in the sky again.

"Mayven!" Annabel yelled.

He whirled as she reached him. "Annabel? What in the world are you doing here?" He pointed at the guard. "Take my sister to safety." He took hold of her arm and tried to push her along.

"It's Lord Haywood!" Annabel yelled above the chaos.

That caused her brother to pause. "What?!" He yelled.

She pointed at the dragon. "Shoot Lord Haywood off the dragon! It's him!" As though on cue the dragon turned and there by its head was a man. "I don't know how but it's him. You have to shoot him down!"

The dragon attacked again, and Annabel curled away from the mass of flames. Suddenly, Master Wil shouted, "The barrier is weakening."

Mayven pointed. "Shoot at the man!" Then he dragged her behind him as he headed towards the door.

Annabel watched with horror as fire broke through the protective barrier. It licked the insides of the shimmering dome. Then the dragon pushed its head inside the men screamed as flames engulfed them.

"Open the door!" Mayven ordered as he approached. Annabel felt sick to her stomach as she reached for her brother. Was she going to die before she could fix her relationship with Len? Would she never see Cain's face again? Would Mayven forgive her?

The dragon turned in her direction, as though focusing on her specifically. Its mouth opened, as she was jerk around, she was pushed through the opening. She fell to the ground, her backside hitting first as she looked up at the face of her brother.

"Mayven!" She screamed, watching fire consume him as the door slammed shut. Her fists hit wood as she shouted his name and the ground split under her knees. Tears slid down her cheeks as she felt someone grab hold of her. She fought them. "Save my brother!" But in her heart, she knew he was already gone.

Present

Someone was shaking her awake. Her dream came back to her in a rush, and she covered her mouth, certain she was going to be sick. Then she saw Lady Ariah, her face flushed and fear in her eyes.

"He's coming. You must wake everyone and prepare. He is hours away," Lady Ariah's voice shook.

"I don't understand," Annabel replied, still feeling groggy.

"What you just saw is coming to pass in mere hours, he'll breach the outer wall and then come straight here," Lady Ariah explained, trying to help Annabel up.

"Why do you know my dream?" Annabel asked in disbelief.

Lady Ariah helped her into a cloak. "Because they are mine."

"It's...you?" The words came out slowly as she tried to put the pieces together.

Lady Ariah nodded. "I gave you the dreams. It was the whole reason I came here. To stop the war Lawrence Haywood would bring to all of Valor."

She'd just come to terms that she was a Mystic, only to find out it wasn't true. "So, you're a Mage?"

Lady Ariah shook her head. "A Magician. We need to go."

Annabel gasped. "But you're so young!" They went into the hall as Lady Ariah went towards the royal chambers—where her parents would be. Her questions felt silly considering the severity of what was coming, but her mind couldn't cope with what it saw. Instead of accepting it, she rejected it, and focused on what was right in front of her.

Lady Ariah face was somber. "It's a family trait." The sharpness in her eyes suggested that was the end of that line of questioning.

"Why didn't you tell me?" Annabel was caught between the coming threat and the shock of the truth. "Why trick me into thinking I'm a Mystic?"

"You had to believe them for yourself. You had to intervene yourself, it was the only way," Lady Ariah replied, glancing at an adjoining hall. "And you *are* a Mystic."

"That's what the orb said," her voice trailed off as she tried to put it together. "But if you are giving me the dreams, what can I do?"

"You...break things. Or break through them," Lady Ariah replied. "I can explain it more later, but right now you must wake your father and have him rally the guard and army."

"Break things? That sounds horrible." Lady Ariah gave her a scolding glance. "Right, Lawrence and his dragon. How did he get a dragon anyways?" Lady Ariah sighed. They reached the imperial guards in front of her father's door a moment later.

Their hands were immediately on their swords until they saw who it was. "Princess Annabel? Why are you here?" Sir Harl said as he stepped forward.

"I must speak with my father," Annabel commanded. "Now."

"Princess," Sir Harl started but Annabel cut in.

"*Raven's beak*," Annabel stated, the word to bypass all others. To be used only in the direst of circumstances.

His smile vanished and was replaced with solemn duty. "I shall rouse them."

Knocking on the door, he entered the antechamber. Their parlor entered into a secondary smaller drawing room with private dining area that was sandwiched between the king's and queen's private suites. Annabel waited patiently with the other knight; one she didn't recognize.

"How often have you interfered?" Annabel asked, suddenly wondering how much she'd been manipulated.

"Rarely if I could help it," Lady Ariah replied. "The picnic, Lady Zerwin's dress, and the masquerade ball."

Annabel gasped. "You ruined her dress?"

"Shush," Lady Ariah hushed her. "It was necessary. You could not arrive when you were originally set to. Otherwise, you would have danced with Lord Haywood, and he would have moved faster."

"Why didn't you warn me about Len?" Annabel was suddenly angry.

Lady Ariah frowned. "I tried to." She suddenly seemed exhausted. "Seeing the future doesn't always empower me to change it. I did what I could. A broken a heart will mend, a broken neck would not."

Annabel put a hand around her throat as she was left reeling. "Why didn't you warn me about Lawrence escaping? We could have prevented all this."

Lady Ariah side-eyed her. "You weren't asleep when I tried. You must have gone to sleep too late that night."

With warm cheeks she remembered exactly why she hadn't gotten much sleep that night and not until the wee hours of the morning. Cain. She was temporarily at a loss for words as new questions swirled around her.

Before she could ask more, Sir Harl returned. "They will see you now."

Annabel rushed around him and into the room. Her father appeared alert despite it being the middle of the night. To her surprise he didn't appear upset, only concerned creased his face. Even after their last encounter.

"Why have you invoked *Raven's Beak*?" King Alin demanded.

"Let me explain," Annabel started and then stopped. "No, we don't have time, let me summarize. I have seen into the future and Lord Haywood is bringing a dragon here. If we do not act now, he shall first take the city and then the palace." *And everyone will die,* she thought a lump in her throat.

Her father didn't appear convinced. "How do you know this?"

"When I say I have seen the future, I have seen it. Dreams have been coming to me for some time." Annabel didn't outright say they were her abilities, but her father was not likely to forget that his youngest had been marked with the possibility of a future ability.

"You are certain?" His tone implied there would be a punishment if this was unfounded.

Annabel nodded. "Positive or I would not have spoken the words." *Was it enough?*

Her father sprang into action, calling for Sir Harl as he stormed out of the room. Annabel stood in the middle of the room, stunned as she watched her father take charge. She'd never expected that he'd listen to her without her having to prove she wasn't being dramatic. Especially after their argument only hours before. She met Lady Ariah's gaze and saw the barest of smiles cross her face—as though she had known this would happen.

Her hand slipped into Annabel's and held fast. "It was the right choice."

Now that everything was moving there was one thing Annabel had to confirm. "Did you push me... towards Lord Cain?"

Lady Ariah's features softened. "There was nothing I could do to keep you apart. No matter what you changed, no matter what I showed you, you always fell in love. Your ability made you immune to his and your respective pasts connected you. I've seen it play out dozens of times." Annabel put the back of her hand to her eyes as tears streamed down her face. Lady Ariah's arms went around her. "He was the messenger that Lawrence killed in the first dream I shared and that was not the only time. You were not wrong to send him away to protect him."

"Annabel?" Her mother's voice startled her. She straightened as her mother sat in her wheelchair in the open doorway, appearing anxious.

"Mama," Annabel fell to her knees and threw her arms around her mother's waist as she cried.

"What is it?" Her mother asked, trying to pull her up. "What's wrong?"

"I loved him." Annabel sobbed in her mother's lap. "I still do, and I sent him away. I may never see him again."

The toll of keeping it all in was coming due. She knew that it would be better if he was alive in the world and safe, then by her side and dead, but it didn't change the hurt. The pain left her breathless and in agony.

"Oh hush, I am sure all will be well," her mother soothed her hair and whispered reassurances. "Lady Ariah, what has happened?"

"Princess, we must go. You are the only one who can break his hold on the dragon," Lady Ariah said, as though commenting on her need to arrange flowers for a centerpiece at a tea party. It wasn't a question; it was a matter of fact.

"Dragon?!" the queen asked, alarmed.

Annabel wiped her tears and stood slowly. She hugged her mother tightly before she kissed her on the crown of her head. "I love you very much."

Her mother grabbed her hand before she could take more than a step. "What does she mean a dragon? I need you to tell me what is going on."

"I'm sorry," Annabel replied. "I've always been sorry. I know it was my fault you are stuck in that chair. I tried to hide everything, protect myself and you from facing this fact."

Her mother was stunned. "You were a child."

"That does not change the facts that if I had listened to you, you could stop me now." Annabel pulled her arm free, before her mother could react. "I know now that my pity was stopping me from loving you as you are now, and for that I am even more sorry. I'll always love you." She hurried from the room, taking Lady Ariah's hand as she went.

"Annabel!" Her mother shrieked, calling for the guards, anyone to stop her, but they had all left with her father. Annabel's tears had dried on her cheeks, her sorrow replaced with determination.

"Where should we go?" Annabel asked, leading them towards the stable.

Lady Ariah pointed out the window. "The bell tower."

Chapter 38

Annabel was mounted on her horse, holding the reigns to Lady Ariah's mare when she realized how ridiculous it had felt to spend precious moments donning on a riding habit and retrieving her dagger. The only weapon she'd been taught to use in the event she was ever cornered. It was not lost on her that it would do little against a dragon.

A moment after this thought Lady Ariah appeared with a bow and a quiver of arrows in hand. She blinked at them as Lady Ariah mounted.

"Do you know how to use that?" Annabel asked.

"My mother is very proficient," Lady Ariah replied, with the first smile she'd ever shown full of pride. "A knight taught her, and she taught me."

Then she urged her horse into a canter as they made their way through the palace and out into the city beyond. The palace was busy with the sudden orders, already preparing, and far too busy to notice two women on horseback slip through. One guard tried to call out, but they simply avoided him and continued on their way. The city was quiet so early in the morning. In all her days she'd never seen it at that time. It did not take them long to arrive at the bell tower.

If her dream was right, the dragon would come soon after the first glow of morning broke. The starlit sky was already starting to brighten—the stars fading away with the tendrils of the sun. They were running out of time.

When the bell tower came into view, Annabel urged her horse up the wide steps and straight to the massive doors of the entrance. The heavy doors required them both to push open before they could slip inside. It was empty when they entered but she could hear the singing of the monks far away. If they were singing, that meant dawn was coming. Annabel led the way with Lady Ariah trailing behind.

The stairs felt daunting, but Annabel hurried up them with Lady Ariah keeping stride. They were winded when they exited at the top into the bell tower. The massive bell was above them, and now that she'd stopped moving Annabel realized, belatedly, she didn't know why they were there. In all the excitement she'd just followed Lady Ariah's directions.

"Why are we here?" Annabel asked, trying not to feel embarrassed at her own lack of awareness.

"Because you're going to stop a dragon," Lady Ariah said, going to the edge and squinting at the sky.

"Come again?" Annabel asked, walking up beside her. "I thought you were joking when you stated such to my mother."

Lady Ariah turned to her; her expression deadly serious. "You are going to stop Lord Haywood with your ability. It is part of the reason he wanted you so badly. He needed you to carry out his plans, because his ability to charm people and animals, doesn't work on you. Your ability breaks his. The only reason mine worked is I used it on you when you were asleep, and even then, I struggled at times. Especially if you went to sleep emotionally compromised."

"He's a Mystic?" Annabel was more surprised than she should have been.

"A Mage actually. He first charmed animals as a Mystic before moving onto us," Lady Ariah replied, nocking an arrow.

Annabel shook her head. "That's how he was able to talk my brother into inviting him. Mayven is not that forgetful. I knew something was strange. I should have questioned it more." Then she focused on Lady Ariah. "Wait, I don't know how to use my ability. Let alone stop a dragon."

211

"I know this is unfair. When Lord Haywood escaped, I never could have imagined this would happen." Lady Ariah said. "But every future I saw, every change I tried to make with others didn't work. You were the only one who could stop it because you were immune. There are no more fixes, not more chances, this is it."

"It can take years to make an ability work!" Annabel felt panic rising.

"You've been using it for years. You just didn't know it. Buttons popping off, cracks in the tile, and necklaces chains snapping. They were all you," Lady Ariah said. "In your dream, do you remember what happened right before it ended?"

"I screamed and then I died." Annabel was deadpan when she replied.

"Do you remember the ground?" Lady Ariah asked, putting a hand on her shoulder. "Think back."

Annabel shook her head but muttered, "It split open when the dragon attacked."

"That wasn't the dragon," Ariah said with no other explanation.

"The ground split open like a crevasse. I couldn't have done that." Annabel shook her head in denial. "It must have been the fire."

Ariah nodded. "It was you. Your power is tied to your emotions. If you were to apply them with intent, you could destroy Lord Haywood's hold on the dragon."

A roar cut through the air like lightning, quieting everything in the world but it's sound. Annabel's heart hammered in her chest as she saw the mysterious creature in the distance. Its wingspan sliced across the light of dawn like a shadow as it landed on a building. Annabel heard screams and felt her fear fade to resolve. She had to stop him and save her people. Save everyone she cared about.

"How am I going to do it?" Annabel whispered, still in awe of the sight.

"Use the arrow as a guide. I shall ensure it finds its mark, use it to focus your ability." Ariah lifted the bow as the dragon's imposing shape drew closer. "Use every emotion you have and unleash it. Every memory that meant something to you, use them and then direct them at the dragon."

Annabel focused on the monster but then closed her eyes. She let herself feel everything—the guilt about her mother, the heartbreak about Cain, and the anger at what Lord Haywood was trying to take from her. She let them swirl within her.

"Annabel!" Mayven's voice cut the air.

With a gasp her concentration broke. She glanced back at him as he made his way towards her. Her mind swirled with the images of his face from her dream. The one he'd made before he died. She waved him off, but her attention was diverted. She was going to fail!

"Focus!" Ariah cried as she let the arrow go.

Wildly she tried to focus on the arrow but couldn't feel it like she had before. Instead, it seemed to buzz around her like an angry bee. Unexpectedly, the bow string snapped, then Ariah screamed. Annabel fell back as the dragon landed against the bell tower.

Stone crumbled as Mayven helped them up. Ariah had blood running down her cheek as she stagged towards the stairs. Once Annabel was on her feet, she pushed her brother forward. Suddenly, something swept into the tower. She tried to duck but it caught her back and threw her to the ground.

Stunned, Annabel tried to find her bearings. Her ears were ringing as she saw the dragon's tail sweep above her. On her hands and knees, she made her way towards the stairs. Chunks of stone slammed into the ground around her, but she just focused on making her way to the stairs. Her brother was lying on his stomach a few steps from the top, Ariah was trying to rouse him.

"Mayven?" Annabel asked, tears running down her cheeks as she tried to see him through the blur.

With a groan he rolled to his side. Annabel hugged him, clinging to him as debris rained down on them. Her stomach twisted in knots at the thought of losing him; she felt paralyzed by it.

"We have to go!" Ariah called, blood staining her dress down the front.

The girls helped Mayven to his feet as they escaped. The dragon roared again, and fire filled the air above them. The heat seemed to singe her hair as they hurried towards safety. Annabel was wild with fear and the certainty that at any moment she would die. They reached the bottom and helped Mayven into one of the pews.

Dazed, Mayven lulled to the side, and he seemed to be struggling to stay conscious. "Brother? Mayven, look at me."

His heal lulled around. "Annabel?" He sounded so confused.

"He may be concussed," Ariah said, suddenly slumping into the pew's seat. She brought her hand up to press against her scalp and hissed in pain. She then produced a handkerchief and pressed it to the wound above her forehead.

The temple shook again. "Can you make it to the horses?"

Ariah nodded. "Barely."

Annabel slapped Mayven's face who seemed to sit up straighter. "Stand up!" She yelled and then put his arm over her shoulder and helped him up. She would not let her dream repeat—he was going to live.

In spite of how he appeared he was able to stumble alongside her towards the temple door. The heavy doors were opened as they approached, as others also escaped through the door. Outside the horses were yanking wildly on their reins, eyes wide and mouths foaming in fear.

When the ground shook, Annabel nearly fell. To her surprise, Ariah took hold of the hilt of Mayven's sword and cut through the reigns. The moment they were free the horses fled.

Before she could yell at her for letting their ride escape, Ariah yelled, "This way!" She pushed him in the opposite direction, close to the wall.

As the horses fled, fire rained down and consumed them. Their screams chilled Annabel's blood as they escaped around the side. Ariah pulled them across the shorter square and led them down an alleyway. Annabel glanced back at the temple's tower, where Lord Haywood stood on the shoulder of the dragon.

Mayven seemed to come around, standing on his own as they stood between two buildings to catch their breath. "What is happening?"

"Lord Haywood is controlling the dragon," Annabel replied, gasping for breath.

Despite the blood, Ariah didn't seem as tired. It made Annabel wonder what kind of life she'd led until then. "We need to return to the castle." Ariah informed them. "What is the fastest route?"

Mayven glanced at Annabel in surprise, as though looking for an answer to the sudden change in her lady-in-waiting. Annabel shrugged by way of answer. After squinting at her, he turned back to Ariah.

"Why?"

"That is where Lord Haywood will go." Ariah straightening, glancing out of the alleyway.

"How do you know that?" Annabel asked.

Ariah appraised her for a moment. "Because that is where he'll expect to you go."

Annabel swallowed heavily at her answer. It should have been obvious that she was Lawrence's target. She likely was his entire focus, even in the dream from earlier he'd likely been after her. It made her blood run cold.

"Why Annabel?" Mayven asked as they joined her in inspecting the abandoned street.

Ariah's eyebrow rose as she appraised Mayven. "You ask a lot of questions." Then slid around the corner and made her way along the building.

"Was she always like that?" Mayven asked, astonished.

Annabel shook her head. "She had everyone fooled."

Mayven had an odd lopsided grin she hadn't seen him use before. It replaced her serious brother with one possessing impish charm. It caught her off-guard about as much as his next statement.

"I like her better this way." Then he hurried to catch up, leaving Annabel to follow along. It had been a traumatic experience for them all, and it was far from over, but Annabel felt herself smiling despite the situation. Mayven had just shown his first interest in a woman. What odd timing her brother had.

Chapter 39

Her amusement was soon lost due to the terror-filled race through the city. Each corner and open area filled her with dread. A roar would sound, sometimes the flapping of massive wings as the dragon flew overhead. The most chilling was when she heard Lawrence call for her by name. She knew she should send her companions away and draw the dragon to her, but she was unable to bring herself to do so. It felt like hours had passed when it had not even been one.

The closer they drew to the palace, the quieter it became. They saw less and less of the dragon until they were nearly to the capital's heart. Then she saw part of the castle's towers beyond the safety of the barrier had been melted by fire.

They paused at the edge of the rows of buildings. The wall that surrounded the castle was just ahead. Mayven had expertly navigated them to the main entrance. There were soldiers, guards, and masters from the magic tower. It was chaos, except for King Alin at its center giving orders.

"Let's go." Mayven moved forward but Annabel caught his arm before he could go far.

"Wait." Annabel remembered the dream and feared for her brother's life. "The moment Lord Haywood knows I'm at the palace, he'll attack it."

He put his hands against her arms, as though to comfort her. "Do not worry, sister. The barrier will protect us."

"It never holds for long," Lady Ariah replied, her voice resigned. "It was made for arrows and trebuchet attacks. Not dragon fire."

"You can't know that for sure," Mayven insisted, glancing at Annabel for help.

"I saw it myself; it'll fail and quickly." Her voice hitched at the end.

"What do you mean you saw it?" Mayven asked.

Annabel waved a hand, to ward away the topic. "It doesn't matter how, only that it's true."

"Then what do you want to do?" Mayven asked, glancing again at the guards just within the barrier. "They need to know what they are up against."

"You saw it, Lord Haywood is controlling the dragon. I need to sever that connection." Annabel felt sick to her stomach even as she was saying the words. "I'm the only one who can."

"You aren't ready," Lady Ariah cut in. "I am sorry that I tried to force you when you don't have full control of your abilities. It is too great of a risk. If we work with the Magic Tower, there may be a way."

"The only way anything works, is if I draw him out." Annabel wanted to end this and stop Lawrence's reign of terror. "You and Lady Ariah need to come up with a way."

"We'll find a different way," Mayven said and then unceremoniously picked her up over his shoulder.

"Mayven!" She yelled but he was already jogging across the square. "Put me down!" Although she was firm, her voice wasn't as loud for fear it would draw attention.

"Not on your life," Mayven replied, unmoved.

Her ribs screamed out against his shoulder, and she tried to push herself loose. He wouldn't budge, holding tight to her legs. When the dragon roared, he didn't turn, just ran harder. Annabel looked up at the dragon bearing down on them.

"Faster!" Annabel screamed. Fire filled the street behind them.

She felt the heat as Mayven yanked Lady Ariah to the side. They fell to the left before they sprawled across the street. Annabel hit the street hard, the momentum of the fall causing her to roll a few feet away from them. There were guards rushing towards them, someone yelled and pointed as Annabel tried to catch her breath. The dragon was returning.

Annabel lifted her arms as thought they would stop her impending death. Before she could scream, she felt something grab onto her, and a dark hand lifted to the sky. A massive spike soared through the air and connected with the dragon as it reared its head back to spew fire. It was as though someone had thrown a spear. The mighty beast was thrown to the side, propelled by the force of the strike. The ground shook as it crashed to the ground.

Annabel glanced up and saw Cain's face. His entire attention was focused on the monster. The creature turned around and snarled but then stopped short. It thrashed around, losing ground, as though fighting an invisible monster. It seemed confused and scared.

It hastily took to the sky, turning its tail and running. Once it did, Cain slumped, breathing heavily as tears bubbled down her cheeks like liquid over the side of a boiling pot. Her fingers blindly searched for his face as she knelt in front of him from where he was half crouched. He lifted his head and she put one hand on each of his cheeks.

"Cain," Annabel whispered, her voice wobbled with each word. "You came back."

"I told you; I'd be back," Cain replied, still breathing heavily but he pulled her into a crushing hug. "I almost lost you."

It that moment Annabel realized part of her hadn't believed him. She thought once there was distance between them, his affection for her would fade. That her troublesome personality, one she didn't intend to change, would not be worth the effort. Part of her had doubted him and doubted his love for her was genuine and not driven by her immunity to his curse.

Yet his actions, coming to her aid at the risk of his own life, had driven that all away. She knew as she clung to him, that he truly did love her as much as she loved him. Ariah was right—no matter the story, they were two souls bound together by fate. He was always meant to be her future, no matter what she dreamt of.

Annabel opened her eyes and saw a faint glow around Cain. Blinking she eased back and could see the dark red with tips of swirling black. It didn't seem to be hurting him as Annabel wondered if she was going insane.

"What is it?" Cain asked, touching her cheek in concern.

"Are you injured?" Master Wil asked, interrupting them.

"No, I—" Annabel stopped mid thought when she saw a glow of white coming from the center of Master Wil's chest. Unlike Cain's, which seemed wild, his seemed controlled. It was at that moment Annabel knew what she was looking at.

"I can see your magic," Annabel said in awe as she pointed at his chest.

Master Wil's eyebrows arched. "My magic?"

"Yes," Annabel said as she reached out to touch Cain's. In an instant, the black smoke that had been like a second shadow vanished.

Cain straightened and touched a hand to his chest. "What was that?"

"I don't know," Annabel said, wrapping her arms around his chest. "But I look forward finding out together."

Dalus came up to them with sweat on his brow. "Where is Haywood?"

Mayven was right behind him and pointed. "There."

Following where he was indicating, Annabel tried to find where Lawrence was. It was only then that Annabel saw the crumpled body on the ground. Lord Haywood's limbs were at odd angles, like a discarded doll. Annabel covered her mouth in shock. Despite how horrible it was, she couldn't help but think it was a fitting end to a terrible man.

Chapter 40

Annabel sat on her private veranda. The summer breeze brushed against her cheeks as she rested her eyes. She felt something on her shoulders and glanced up. Cain smiled down at her as he tucked her shawl around her.

"Thank you," Annabel said, clasping his hand.

Cain sat beside her, running his fingers down her hair and to her cheek. "Are you feeling better?"

It had been a few days since Haywood's reign of terror. The dragon had not returned and for the first time, Annabel felt relaxed. There was no horror on the horizon or promise of a dream. Only a newfound ability to break not only things but apparently break abilities, albeit temporarily.

"Much, now that you are here."

"I brought someone with me," Cain said, glancing back.

Annabel shifted, expecting to see Cierra, but found Ariah instead. "Princess," Ariah said as she curtsied.

"Ariah. Please," Annabel said, feeling nothing but companionship for her lady-in-waiting. "You needn't worry about formalities here."

220

Ariah smiled and took a seat. Cain moved behind Annabel, putting a hand on her shoulder protectively. She had told Cain everything, everything but the origin of the dreams. Those she'd said were not her secret. He'd asked no more about it.

When the silence stretched on, Annabel patted his hand. "We need a moment."

"As you wish," Cain said, kissing the top of her head. She watched him go, basking in contentment.

"I didn't tell him," Annabel said before meeting Ariah's gaze. "I haven't told anyone. Though I believe Mayven suspects."

"He is...perceptive."

Annabel couldn't help herself. "Do you see a future with him?"

"Even if I did, that is my burden to bear," Ariah replied. She really did appear to be so much older than she was. Once more Annable was thankful she did not have such a dreadful ability. "I've come to bid you farewell."

Annabel sat up straighter. "You're leaving? Why?"

"I did what I came here to do," Ariah replied with a sad smile. "It is time I returned home."

"I am guessing you are not a daughter of Baron Dymus." Annabel had done her homework since the whole dragon incident.

Ariah smiled knowingly. "I wanted to thank you. Without you, none of this would have been possible."

Annabel sighed heavily as she slumped back, as unladylike as possible. "I can't even be angry that you used me, because everyone I love would be dead if it wasn't for you. Which is why I have something to give you."

Standing slowly, Annabel moved carefully towards her dresser. Picking up the box she moved to set it in front of Ariah. Patting the top, she stiffly sat back down. During the mad dash trying to escape the dragon, specifically when she'd tumbled off Mayven, her side and ribs had suffered the most.

"What is it?" Ariah asked, eyeing it.

"Shouldn't you know?" Annabel asked, coyly.

Ariah pursed her lips. "I usually only see major events. Weddings, battles, and death." She put her hand on the box. "I try not to see every day, but instead live it. Especially now that I don't see war coming to Mayrid."

Annabel laughed aloud. "Just open it. I promise it won't bite."

Slowly she undid the ribbon and opened the box. Inside she picked up a pendant, a crown with a sword through it. For a moment she frowned at it, before understanding seemed to light up her eyes. They snapped to Annabel in question.

"Yes. It is the symbol of our house; you are now an ambassador to our great city. Every door will open, and every citizen will recognize what you have done for Itreia." Annabel was quite pleased with herself. "It comes with a nice residence in town and a title. I had thought you were a Baron's daughter when I did it, but now I am certain you come from a more titled family."

Ariah set it back into the box. "How did you do this? No one knows what I did and yet this happens?"

"Mayven told father you were there. Explained what you did to protect our lives. It was easy for us to persuade him." Annabel folded her hands in her lap. "You are granted full citizenship of this country in addition to your own. More than that, I hope when you return, we can become better acquainted. I find this Ariah is far more interesting than the one you were pretending to be."

"That is how I am normally," Ariah replied with a frown.

Annabel paused, her mouth ajar. Then Ariah laughed and after a moment Annabel joined in. She was finding this Ariah far and away better than the emotionless one she'd known for months. It was a pity she was leaving so abruptly.

"I think I shall return," Ariah replied with a smile. "Though I miss my family."

"I understand," Annabel glanced along the wall, knowing just beyond her sight around the bend were Yenni and Len's rooms. "Family is everything to me."

"On that we agree," Ariah replied, her gaze direct. "How is Princess Lenora?"

"Recovering," Annabel replied, feeling pain in her chest. "Or so I am told. She will not see me but after Lawrence died, she returned to her sensibilities."

"I have a sister of my own," Ariah replied with a soft smile. "I hope you are able to mend the rift."

"Older or younger?" Annabel asked, eyeing her. "And do you have any brothers?"

Ariah's green eyes danced with amusement. "I do. One. Plus, enough cousins spread across our lands, and in other lands, to mount a small army." Ariah stood before picking the box up, signaling the end of that topic. "Thank you for all that you have done. Though no one will ever know the true magnitude of it, you are the person who saved countless lives."

"You and I know. That is enough." Annabel touched her arm as she went by. "Plus, I could not have done it without you and your dreams."

"No, the future could not have been rewritten without you. I tried." Lady Ariah gazed off into the distance. "You will never know the extent that I endeavored before I came here." Ariah pinned her with her gaze. "Before I shared my dreams with you."

"Why me?" Annabel whispered, something that she had wondered for some time.

"I finally saw what caused the start of the war. Your supposed assassination," Ariah replied, her voice barely audible. "After that I knew, I had to come to the source."

"Because I was the start," Annabel said, astonished. "I don't know how to thank you. You've saved my life." Her hand swept towards the city. "Our future."

Lady Ariah shook her head. "You don't understand. I only had the dreams; you changed the course of history. I made little changes, but nothing worked. Not until I sent the dreams to you. I saw myself trying with others, but you were the only one that I saw reshaping the future." Lady Ariah put a hand on her shoulder. "You changed the future I saw."

Annabel felt her words lodge in her throat. "I hope to see you again soon." Her voice cracked at the end.

Ariah nodded. "Soon, if we are lucky."

When she left, it wasn't long until Cain rejoined her. He sat down silently. After a while he took her hand in his, his fingers playing with hers in a gentle caress, before he asked, "Is everything well?"

"Perfectly. Ariah is going to return to her family. As Lady Pheobe has already done." Annabel glanced at him. "There is an important matter I've been meaning to discuss."

"Which is?" Cain's brows furrowed.

Annabel captured his fingers firmly in her own. "What do you think about eloping?"

Chapter 41

"I'll be fine," Annabel said again, as she stood in her brother's study.

Mayven hugged her again with one arm. "You aren't even married. What is father thinking?"

"That we all almost died." Annabel shrugged. "It puts things into perspective." It had been over a month since Lord Haywood and the dragon. "Plus, I shall be married shortly." Since Cain had come up with a better idea than eloping.

"Apparently it put everything in perspective for everyone but you." Mayven shook his head. "You'll write?"

Annabel laughed as she patted his back. "If I have time."

He kissed the top of her head. "I never thought you'd leave so soon. I thought we'd have more time."

Annabel glanced through the window at the destruction left by the dragon. "You'll have your hands full here. Lady Ariah has agreed to act as an ambassador." She hoped Lady Ariah would return soon—they'd exchanged letters constantly since she'd left. Finally revealing she was the daughter of

Marquis Chadwick. It made her wonder what sort of powers her Magician parents had. All in due time.

Annabel watched Cierra and Cain down by the carriages. She knew he was waiting for her. "Do take good care of her." Annabel sent him a knowing smile.

Mayven's eyes narrowed. "She is a representative, nothing more."

"I'll be sure to tell that to mother." Annabel laughed.

She eyed her brother, who was still nursing a dislocated collarbone from when he'd fallen. He'd taken the brunt of the fall and Lady Ariah's added weight had popped it out of place. Annabel hoped to never personally find out how painful such an injury could be. Watching her brother suffer a lengthy recovery was horrible enough—the temple had already helped it as far along as they could. Though at least after they'd healed him, he'd managed to make it into the study from his bed.

"I shall visit when we travel through." Annabel kissed his cheek. "Take care of mother and father. I shall miss you."

"Try to stay out of trouble," Mayven called after her.

"Never!" She called as the door closed behind her. But not before she heard his laughter.

With a pep in her step, she nearly ran face first into Yenni. She was also dressed, preparing to leave in the opposite direction. Her father had not only permitted them to marry but allowed them to shorten their engagement. Annabel planned to return in the fall, just in time for the event.

Laughing they hugged. "I shall miss you."

"You shall always be with me," Yenni insisted, putting a hand on her chest. "In here."

"You have been a constant comfort. We shall return in time for your wedding." Annabel was overjoyed for her sister.

"Promise?" Yenni asked, tears in her eyes.

"You couldn't keep me away." They hugged again as Lord Euros appeared.

"We're going to be late for the fitting," Lord Euros said. Then turned to Annabel to explain. "Your sister is going to need heavier clothing to survive in the harsh north." He was grinning ear to ear. "I want to make sure I can take her home immediately after we marry."

"Take good care of my sister," Annabel said, holding Yenni's hand, swinging it back and forth like they had as children.

Lord Euros bowed his head. "I shall do more than simply care for her."

Yenni's cheeks warmed as she gazed lovingly at Lord Euros. Annabel knew it was time and hugged her sister, whispering to her, "I love you and I shall see you before you know it."

"You had better." Yenni kissed her cheek before going with Lord Euros.

Annabel sighed and then hurried towards the courtyard. She saw her father there with her mother. They were speaking with Lady Cierra and Cain. Her mother was holding Cain's hand as he took a knee next to her. He was nodding his head, his face split by a great grin. She paused at the doors, waving for the servant to not open the door. He was agreeing to something her mother was saying—such easy affection between them since the moment her mother had met her betrothed.

Annabel knew she loved him beyond words. This truly kind and wonderful man would soon be her husband. A term she had once feared, she now reveled in. Her husband. She was going to be his wife. Could there be anything more intimate and wonderful than the joining of two souls?

"I'm ready," Annabel said softly. The servant bowed and opened the door.

She hurried down the steps and to her family. The sun was warm and the day beautiful. Her father was there first, she hugged him, having mended all fences and repaired all bridges. She'd never felt closer to her father than she had in the last few weeks. They were more alike than she had first realized.

"Be safe." Her father kissed the side of her head, a rare public show of affection. "Come visit soon."

"I shall," Annabel confirmed. Cain was still standing next to her mother; he was beaming at her as Annabel bent down to give her mother a hug.

"I never blamed you," her mother said, hugging her close. "So, stop blaming yourself and live the life you want." Her mother put her hand under Annabel's chin. "That is the best thing you can do for me."

"I promise." Tears formed in her eyes. "I will."

"Good, now where is Heddie?" Her mother asked.

Annabel stood, looking back towards the palace private entrance. They'd decided to avoid all fanfare. Instead sign their name to mark their marriage and go off on a grand adventure. It had been Cain's idea and Annabel had decided, why not the next day? So, they'd packed their things and prepared to leave posthaste.

"Is that her?" Annabel shielded her eyes from the sun but then stopped.

Her brothers, Dalus and Baltus, came down the stairs. Annabel rushed over to hug them. They spun her around as she laughed.

"I shall miss you," Dalus said, clapping her on the back.

Winded she coughed. "Thank you for rescuing me." Annabel held fast to him. "And for understanding me." Her newfound Mage ability could cut off a person's magic, though temporarily. Her brother had been her biggest supporter besides Cain.

"You are the one who saved us first," Baltus reminded her, always the logical one.

"Father said you'd be visiting us on the Southern Islands," Annabel said, excited that Baltus would be visiting her sooner rather than later.

He nodded. "As representative of the temple. I insisted."

"Then I shall see you soon." Annabel laughed heartily as Dalus clapped her brother on the back.

"I have it!" Heddie cried, interrupting them.

Annabel laughed, her arm around Dalus's waist as Heddie came rushing down the stairs. She held open the book and jostled a quill and inkwell. Lady Cierra held the inkwell as Heddie held the book. Cain signed his name, and then Annabel placed hers beside it.

"There." Annabel smiled at her family and friends. "All done."

Her mother burst out crying. "Oh dear, I thought this day would never come." Her father was quick to comfort her.

Annabel had wondered why her father had agreed so quickly and now suspected that her mother had made it all happen. Likely suspecting that Annabel would elope if forced into anything public. Her mother did know her so well. Annabel hugged everyone one last time, including Heddie, as Cain stood beside the carriage.

She took Cierra's hands in her own. "Thank you for your encouragement."

"Thank you for what you have done for my brother. I am pleased to call you sister." Cierra kissed her cheek, and they giggled in shared joy.

"Shall we go, wife?" Cain called, holding out his hand as Annabel turned towards him and the waiting carriage.

"I believe we shall, husband," Annabel took his hand.

"Be well, brother," Lady Cierra said, tears of joy streaming down her face.

"I shall see you soon." Then Cain helped Annabel into the carriage.

The footman cracked the whip, and they lurched forward. She waved at her family, calling how much she loved and would miss them. They threw petals and wished her luck.

"Wait!" A voice called and they instantly slowed.

Lenora rushed towards the carriage. Annabel threw open the door and wrapped her arms around her sister. Len had a bundle of white roses as they clasped each other.

"You came." Annabel held her close. She'd feared that Len would never speak to her again.

"Yes. To say goodbye," Len said, her face crumpling. "And to say I'm sorry."

Petting her hair, Len cried as Annabel comforted her. She knew Lawrence's hold had been because of his ability. Knew that after the months that he'd been courting her, it was a hard bond to break. That it only broke at death, but even then, Len hadn't wanted to see her. Annabel had to blink back tears.

"It is I who am sorry," Annabel said, her throat choked with emotion. "I never wanted to hurt you."

"I know. I am sorry I kept turning you away, I was so ashamed." Lenora was sobbing now. "I said all those hurtful things, I didn't mean any of them. You are the best sister."

"You shall always be my sister." Annabel stood nose to nose with Len. "That is something not even a dragon could take away."

Len nodded. "I shall miss you every day." They hugged again and then Annabel wished her goodbye. Cain was waiting for her, and he helped her into the carriage. Once more it started down the road, but this time, Annabel waved only once before clinging to Cain.

"I am happy Princess Lenora came," Cain said, his arms wrapped around her. "I know how much it means to you."

Annabel lifted her head and gazed into his eyes. This man knew her and loved her. She would spend every moment making sure he felt the same.

"Even though I won't have any more dreams, I don't need them. I know my future." Annabel kissed him. "It's you."

Cain kissed her back. "Then I shall endeavor to make your dreams come true."

K.T. Munson is a life-long author. First published at 5 years old in the young writer's conference, she has pursued writing ever since. She was born and raised in the last frontier, the great state of Alaska. She maintains a blog creatingworldswithwords.wordpress.com that is about writing and her many fantasy, romance, and sci-fi novels.